C000176636

WELCOME

John Melmoth

Copyright © John Melmoth 2012

First printed in this edition 2012

Perigord Press, part of GunBoss Books,
3rd Floor, 207 Regent Street,
London, W1B 3HH, England
www.perigordpress.com

The right of John Melmoth to be identified as the author of this work has
been asserted by him in accordance with the Copyright, Designs and Patents
Act, 1988

All rights reserved. No part of this publication may be reproduced, stored in
a retrieval system, or transmitted, in any form, or by any means, electronic,
mechanical, photocopying, recording or otherwise, without the prior
permission of the publishers.

This book is sold subject to the condition that it shall not, by way of trade or
otherwise, be lent, resold, hired out, or otherwise circulated without the
author's prior consent in any form of binding or cover other than that in
which it is published and without a similar condition being imposed on the
subsequent purchaser.

This novel is a work of fiction. Names and characters are the product of the
author's imagination or are used fictitiously. Any resemblance to actual
persons, living or dead, is entirely coincidental.

Requests to publish work from this book must be sent to John Melmoth,
care of Perigord Press.

ISBN 978-0-9573977-3-6

Cover photo: © Mike Pope 2012

Front cover design: © Gordon Butler 2012

Interior design and back cover: Dean Fetzer

For Barbara, Edmund and Alex
who were there at the beginning.

And for Phil.

Shouted at in a whisper

I mean, just look at her. Marks out of ten for scariness? A straight ten. Marks out of ten for weirdness? Ten again. Marks out of ten for the welcome provided? Nought point one. (She does at least seem to be expecting me.) Marks out of ten for my chances of having a good time? None. Niente. Nul point. Nada. Less than zero.

And it's all Mum and Dad's fault. Their fault that I'm standing here being met by an aunt I've never seen before. An aunt who looks like no one I've ever seen before.

Mum and Dad who for years have been trying to get me to call them Liz and Jim. But I won't. Their fault for going to the United States for a whole summer. Their fault for not taking me with them. Their fault for putting themselves first as usual and putting me nowhere.

Well, not so much nowhere as just about anywhere, really.

Because that's where they want me to be. Anywhere except with them.

That's why they are always farming me out.

They send me to Gran's whenever they go off on one of their weekends.

I like going to Gran's of course, but I always feel when I get there that I'm not wanted at home. And that spoils things a bit.

Or they send me to stay with my uncle (Mum's brother) and his wife and their three kids during school holidays. They're really nice – I think they feel sorry for me – but their kids are little and there's nothing for me to do there.

But at least I get some sense of what normal families are like.

Or I get sent to a childminder. Someone they pay to look after

1

me. Mrs Figes with the lumps on her face. Or Mrs Lillian who makes me watch daytime TV with her. How sad is that? Or Mrs Lionel who looks after five or six kids at once and who has converted her basement into a kind of games arcade.

I get on well with other kids I meet in these places. But their situation isn't like mine. They're there because they come from single-parent families or because their parents are working late.

I'm the only kid I've ever heard of whose parents are so obsessed with each other that they don't have room in their lives for him.

Who love each other so much that they don't seem to have much love left over for their only son.

Who just seem to want to be with each other. Who don't seem to need anyone else. Not even me.

I'm sure that when they got the chance to spend six weeks in California – Dad writes scripts for TV – they never thought for a moment of taking me with them.

I'm sure that while they were arranging it, all they were thinking about was their chance to rent a house *together*; to have breakfast on the terrace every morning *together*; to go out to dinner every evening *together*; to visit museums and art galleries *together*.

I'm sure they just took it for granted that I'd be staying in England. They were just so pleased at the chance to spend a couple of months together that they never thought of including me.

In fact, I guess they were so pleased about spending time together *because* they both knew that I wouldn't be there. Wouldn't be getting in the way. Wouldn't be getting in between them.

The first I heard of it, they'd already booked their flights (just the two) and found a place to stay.

The first I heard of it, they assumed that I'd be staying with Gran for the whole summer.

Of course, when they told me this, I threw a major strop. Shouted and screamed and carried on. And just as of course, it made absolutely no difference at all.

They just looked sad and hurt.

What do they have to be sad and hurt about?

And they went on looking all disappointed for a couple of days. Like they always do when I make a fuss about anything.

But there was never a chance that they would change their minds.

I knew that, of course; they never have.

It wasn't like I was expecting them to say, "OK. We know how you feel. We'd love to have you with us. We'll book a third ticket tomorrow."

I knew they wouldn't. But I just wanted to make myself felt. To get them to recognise that I exist. To be noticed.

But this just makes them switch off even more.

As far as they were concerned, it was all settled. They were going to America and I was going to Gran's.

The trouble was that they hadn't bothered to ask Gran and when they did get around to mentioning it, she told them that much though she'd love to have me, she and two of her mates had planned a trip to the Italian lakes. They had their schedule all worked out – cathedrals, art galleries and operas – and it would not, in her opinion, be appropriate for a boy of nearly 15 to "traipse through Italy" with "three old bags."

She told me afterwards that she also suggested to them that the way to solve the problem was to take me with them. But they clearly never gave this idea any consideration.

Instead, they asked Uncle Phil, but he couldn't have me either. They're having a loft extension done and the whole top floor of their house is uninhabitable. All five of them are sleeping in the downstairs bedroom. In fact, Uncle Phil suggested that *he* ought to go to America with them in order to get some sleep.

I guess by this point they must have been getting pretty worried.

Even they realise that they can't send me to any of the Mrs Figes, Lillians or Lionels for the whole summer.

They must have begun to worry that their dream of all those weeks alone together was not going to come true after all.

But then Dad had his brainwave: I could go and stay with his sister.

The fact that he hardly knows her — she's only his half-sister really and 12 years younger than him — didn't seem to enter his calculations. Nor did the fact that he hadn't seen her for years and I had never met her.

Dad says that's not true, that I did meet her when I was two or three, but I don't remember. And besides, even if I did, that doesn't change anything.

She's an ecologist. She teaches something called Earth Sciences at a university and was working abroad for years in Africa, in India and South America. She only came back to England about a year ago, when they made her a professor.

The fact that she might not want to do Dad such a huge favour or that she might not want me cluttering up her life for weeks on end probably never occurred to him.

He has this way of just assuming that people will do what he wants them to.

He certainly expects me to, which is why he looks so disappointed if I step out of line.

Never *says* or *does* anything, just *looks*.

And what's even more annoying is that everyone usually *does* do what he wants. They seem to want to please him, to make his life easier and more comfortable.

He has what people call charm and it works like magic. He seems to get everything he wants just by asking in his gentle way. All he has to do is switch on this charm and people start dancing around him like slaves.

It's pathetic.

He's the pushiest, most selfish person I've ever met, but you'd never know it.

When he gets to work on you, it's like being shouted at in a whisper, beaten up with a feather or blown head over heels by the slightest breeze. It's like he takes you over completely, without you really noticing it. He invades you.

He makes you think you're the most interesting, and amusing person in the world; and all the time he's thinking about himself, about what *he* wants.

And what's worse is that you feel good about yourself at the same time as putting yourself out for him.

Oh, I don't know, it's impossible to explain.

And I'm just the same as everyone else. I can fall for his charm, just like everyone else.

I keep finding myself thinking about things to do for him, ways to make things easier and nicer for him.

And I have to fight really hard against these feelings. Refuse to give in to them.

I was in the room when he rang her up. And that's just like him as well.

He never thought that it might be better if he made the call in private. That she might say no and that my feelings might be hurt. He just went ahead.

"Hello, Dina, it's me... Jim... your brother Jim... I've been meaning to ring you for ages to find out how the new job's going... is it really 18 months? Seems like just a few weeks since you were in India... I mean South America, of course. Anyway,

5

how's things in the crazy world of zoology?... all right Earth Sciences, then."

At this point, Dad did something amazing: he appeared to listen to what the person at the other end of the line was saying. But only for about ten seconds, and maybe I imagined it after all.

"Well, that's great... Listen Dina, I've got to go to the States for a few weeks... Yeh, I'm working on the pilot for a series about six gay lawyers in New York who give up highly paid jobs to open a vegetarian restaurant... No, I don't suppose it does sound like your sort of thing... Anyway, Liz is coming with me. We've rented a house in the Valley. Sandra Bullock used to live a few blocks away... Sandra Bullock, the movie actress... Oh, never mind... So the thing is, Nick's going to be at a bit of a loose end this summer and we were wondering if he could come to stay with you for a bit. It would be a good chance for him to get to know his favourite aunt... Of course he knows who you are... I've told him lots of things about you... About how clever you are and how you spent your childhood wrapped up in books... No, I know I wasn't actually there very much, but I still took an interest... Besides, it would be great for him to spend some time in the country. You could teach him so much about biology... Sorry again, I meant Earth Sciences... Of course, he wants to come... he really wants to spend some time with you... Well, that's great and thanks but we were thinking about a bit longer than a week... Well, more like four or five weeks really, if that's not asking too much... He could go to Mum for the last couple of weeks of the school holidays and then Liz and I will be back... No, my Mum not your Mum... No, of course he won't be bored... Not a problem, he doesn't really like TV anyway and he's very quiet so you'll be able to get on with your work... No, he understands that there's not much to do, but he's very good at making his own entertainment... And, naturally we'd be willing to pay. You know, help out with his keep... No, sorry, of course I understand that you wouldn't accept any money. Silly me. I do seem to keep saying the wrong thing don't I?... No, there really isn't anyone else I can ask... No, of course he wouldn't rather come with us. He'd be bored. He'd be so much better off in the countryside with you... You will, that's fantastic. Thanks, Sis... Sorry, sorry, thanks Dina...Yeh, I'm talking about the second week in July until the third week in August... I'll be in touch in the next week or so to finalise arrangements... No, no, of course I won't spring things on you at the last moment... Thanks, again. You really must come and have dinner when Liz and I get back... No, I don't suppose you do get to London that much but we could invite some entertaining friends for you to meet. Maybe, find a man for you... OK, I know it isn't any of my business and I didn't mean anything by it... I think I'd better go before I say the wrong thing again... Bye now. Love you."

He looked so pleased when he came off the phone that I felt sick.

He'd done it again. Got his own way.

"Well," he said, "she's really looking forward to spending some time with you."

He must think I'm stupid.

And then he pretended to get all enthusiastic about a summer in the country. About how I'd have a marvellous time and learn loads of stuff about the countryside. About how it was a great opportunity for me. About how Dina would be great fun to be with.

Do me a favour.

And I knew that all the time what he was really thinking was: "Sorted."

I really hate him sometimes.

And so here I am at some horrible little station in the middle of nowhere (Norfolk) watching this woman who I've never seen before watching me (who she's never seen before) as if I'm something that an Earth Scientist is used to seeing through a microscope.

They put me on the train in London, of course. And gave me a packed lunch and some magazines, but all the time I felt that they couldn't wait for me to be gone. As though their life together wouldn't begin properly until my train pulled out of the platform.

How's that for a send off?

I move towards her my hand out to shake hers. My heart is thumping in my chest like it's going to explode and I feel incredibly miserable, but I'm well trained.

"Hello," I say, "I'm Nick."

"I thought you might be," she says so loudly that it makes me jump. "But I wasn't sure with all these people."

We both look round. Of course, the platform's empty apart from some old bloke who looks like he's been waiting for a train since the First World War.

This is obviously a joke. I try to smile but it comes out all mangled.

And then she screeches, "And you've probably worked out already that I'm Dina."

She's very tall – over six feet, I guess. She's very thin and she's very brown. In fact, she looks as though she's been baked in the sun for years.

Her hair is brushed straight back from her face like a man's.

She's wearing wellies and an old set of bib-and-brace overalls, underneath which she's wearing a red checked shirt with the sleeves cut off.

Her arms are as thin and brown as the rest of her and there are tattoos on both of them. On her right forearm there's a rose, and on her left upper arm there's some kind of bird.

Her fingers are very long and very dirty and stained with nicotine.

She's got a fag in her mouth. A roll-up.

But what you really notice about her are her eyes. Even when they are scrunched up against the sun and the smoke from her fag. They are the palest blue. Just like Dad's. And they look even more dramatic than Dad's because her face is so brown.

But they're not easy to read. She seems friendly enough but it's hard to tell what's going on behind those eyes.

And then there's her voice: very upper class and much louder than necessary. As though she's talking to a group of people, rather than just me. A group of people who've all gone a bit deaf at the same time.

And then she says (shouts is more like it), "Listen Nick, I don't suppose it was part of your plan to spend five weeks here. I'm sure you'd rather be in London or California with your Mum and Dad. But if we work at it, maybe we can both enjoy ourselves."

I don't know what to say, but I do know what to think: "You must be completely out of your mind. Out of your tree. Utterly barking. Bonkers."

It's about as likely as a one-legged man winning an arse kicking contest.

She probably thinks it's best to start things off by being honest, to admit that we neither of us really chose this situation. We both know that I'm here because I have to be and she's here because she's doing a favour to a brother who had very little time for her before he wanted something from her.

But maybe it didn't need saying.

"Come on, then," she hollers and heads off down the platform towards an exit sign.

The sun's really warm as I pick up my bag and take off after her. She's so tall that I have trouble keeping up.

9

The exit sign leads us to a tunnel under the tracks. A tunnel without graffiti and without those mysterious stains on the walls and the floor that you always seem to get in tunnels and underpasses in London and that make you want to close your eyes and not think about what caused them.

It's very cool and dim in the tunnel, so when we emerge onto the gravelled area at the end, the light seems blinding.

"Welcome," booms Dina, throwing out her arms, "to one of the stranger parts of the UK."

I have no idea what this is supposed to mean.

"Take this gravel, for instance," she says. "It came from a local cemetery. For some reason, they chose to put this cemetery on the largest ice-borne gravel bed in the area. Seems a pretty odd decision given how many bogs we've got around here. Every time they dig a new grave, they end up with a new heap of gravel. The cemetery has been selling it to local people for garden paths for generations, and now the council's buying it up."

I don't know what to say about this, but I'm pretty sure the Norfolk Tourist Board doesn't include this particular piece of information in its guides to the area.

Two vehicles are parked on the gravel. One of them is a battered old wreck of a thing that looks as though it's got about a million miles on the clock. The other is a large, shiny, black and chrome pick-up truck.

No prizes for guessing which is Dina's.

But I'm wrong. She walks right past the old wreck and opens the door of the pick-up.

"Chuck your bag in the back and jump in."

I do as I'm told and as I climb up into the cab an old sheep dog squirms and cowers away from me in terror.

"This is Harry," says Dina. "He's very friendly once he gets to know you but a right old scaredy cat at first. He's been with me about a year. I got him from a rescue centre and I think he must have had a pretty hard life. Haven't you, boy?"

Harry is as thin as Dina, but whereas she seems completely at ease and self-confident, he's nervous and doubtful and twitchy.

I hold out my hand for him to sniff. I can see in his eyes that he wants to make friends, but he just squirms further away from me, rolling his eyes in fright.

"Don't worry," says Dina, "he'll soon get used to you. Right, let's go."

And with that, she puts the truck in gear, releases the handbrake and zooms out of the car park, spraying gravel all over the battered wreck.

Through the open window. I can hear the gravel from the graveyard pinging against its windows and windscreen.

... ...
... ...
...
There's a...
... pain...
...behind...
... my...
... eyes.
There...I've said it...
... or thought it...
... I'm not sure... ...
And perhaps it doesn't matter...
... I am lying on my back...
... but I don't know where my arms and legs are...
... I suppose they're where they should be...
... but I can't seem to feel them...

... ...
... My eyes are...
... closed tight... stuck... glued together...
My eyelids are so...
... heavy.
I want to open my eyes...
... see where I am. But it's so hard.
... It's... like they've... been... nailed... shut.
I can't turn my head...
... either to the right or the left.

....
... ...
I'm...
... I'm afraid...
... In the end though... I know I have to open them.
I feel the light like a pain...
... It's like staring straight into the sun...

Welcome to my humble chapeau

The moon is really pissing me off. It's too bright. It's stifling in here. I'm so hot that the sweat is running off me. The sheets are soaking. I can't sleep, so I get up to look out of the window. And the moon seems to fill the whole sky, making everything look bright and spooky.

Next door Dina and Gerry are shagging.

I can hear them through the wall – grunting and muttering, talking and laughing. They've been at it for ages.

Every once in a while I can hear a match being struck so that they can light their terrible roll-ups. I can smell the smoke in here.

It's disgusting. And it can't be good for them at their age (the shagging or the fags). They'll probably both have heart attacks.

Serve them right.

But then, on second thoughts, I'd have to be the person to discover their bodies. Locked in rigor mortis.

And that would be even more disgusting.

I just wish they'd stop.

And I just wish that moon would disappear behind a cloud, or set or wane or whatever it is that it's supposed to do.

I just wish I could sleep. That way a few hours of this terrible so-called holiday would pass quickly, instead of dragging on and on.

I have to admit, though, that the journey here from the station was interesting.

Dina drives like a lunatic. It's ten miles from the station to her cottage, but it only took us about ten minutes.

The land is flat, but the hedges are so plump and full and round that they look like they've been blown up by a huge bicycle pump. Every once in a while we pass a thatched cottage painted pink or lilac with a neat garden in front. There are a couple of pubs and a tea room. Fields of sweetcorn and a windmill.

But I don't get much chance to take any of it in because the whole time Dina is hurling the pick-up round corners or barrelling down the middle of the road at 80 mph with only one hand on the steering wheel.

And the whole time she's talking, without seeming to look at the road.

Talking about the trees in the hedges (hawthorn, elder, wild cherry, birch and oak, as if I could care less), about how the thatching material is once again being grown locally, about why the bends in the road happen when they do (because the road follows the line of an old drover track, where animals used to be herded).

It's not really like a normal conversation. She's just yelling out a load of thoughts and opinions and bits of information. I suppose this is what it's like when she gives one of her lectures.

Her driving is kind of exciting, but kind of scary too. Dad never drives like this. He's always so calm, so in control of himself. (And so in control of everyone else.)

After a bit, Harry climbs nervously onto my lap and sticks his head out of the window. His ears blow back from his face like he's in the slipstream of a jet.

At first I wonder if he's going to be sick, but then I realise that he thinks it is hilarious and is loving every minute of it. The wind rushing past his face makes him look years younger. His eyes are shining and his body is tense. He's actually laughing.

So, I decide that if it's all right by him it's got to be all right by me. I sit back in my seat and start to relax a bit.

After a couple of minutes, we pass through a village which

seems to consist of a single row of houses on either side of the road. And a minute later, Dina changes down and swings off the road (much too fast) onto a narrow path with hedges on either side, the truck's tyres spitting gravel through the hedge and onto the fields to either side.

I guess they'll need to dig a few new graves to keep Dina in gravel if she always drives like this.

The path runs for about 100 yards and then quite suddenly opens into a clearing, to one side of which is a tiny cottage built of red brick, with a grey slate roof.

Dina cuts the engine.

"Welcome," she practically roars, "to my humble chapeau."

I don't know what this means, but she seems to think that it's funny.

We get out of the truck, walk across a small patch of lawn and into the cottage.

The door opens onto a small kitchen with a scrubbed table and four chairs in the middle. There's a multicoloured rag rug on the floor and a vase of orange flowers on the table.

On the other side of the kitchen is a door leading into a sitting room. Here there are a couple of battered armchairs and a pretty expensive looking sound system.

One wall is completely covered with shelves which are filled with books, many of them old-looking. There's a picture on the wall of an enormous sheep jumping over the moon, with a tiny cottage in the corner. It looks exactly like this one. Come to think of it, maybe it is this one.

Dina tells me that she bought this place about 18 months ago and spends as much time here as she can. She has a small flat in Cambridge, where she lives during term time. "But," she says, "this is where I now think of as home."

I think it's nice, but pretty small. The ceilings are so low that

15

she has to stoop as she's showing me round. And there is a musty, damp smell, even though all the windows are wide open.

Upstairs, there are two bedrooms. Hers on the left, with a double bed, mine on the right.

It's really plain, but I do quite like it. The floorboards are stained black and there are faded flowery curtains at the window. There's an old chest of drawers, a very narrow single bed with a quilt on it, and a bedside table with a small reading lamp and a single white candle in a brass holder shaped like a shell. There are some wild flowers in a small vase on the window-ledge.

"I hope you'll be comfortable here," yodels Dina. "The candle's there because the electricity supply is so unreliable. There's a shower in the lean-to at the back of the house and also a loo. But don't use it unless you absolutely have to – it costs a fortune to get the septic tank emptied. And don't flush it more than once a day whatever you do. The great outdoors has been good enough for the generations of people who've lived here before me. And I have to admit to really enjoying an al fresco bowel movement myself, but I guess that's not very ladylike of me."

I dump my bag on the floor because Dina wants to show me the garden.

We go back out of the door we came in by and walk round to the other side of the cottage.

"I've only been working on it for a year," says Dina. "But I'm getting it into shape."

Of course, I don't know anything about gardening, but even I can tell that it's beautiful.

It's not very big, but it's bursting with flowers. All of them brightly coloured – reds, oranges, purples and pinks. And the flowers seem to grow everywhere, not in neat rows. There's a tiny bit of lawn with a faded old deckchair in the middle and a hammock between two flowering trees.

In one corner there's a metal statue of one of those things that's half man and half horse. He's carrying off a woman who doesn't seem to be protesting too much and whose clothes have started to fall off for some reason.

And there's a murmuring, rustling noise in the garden, caused by the thousands of bees working on the flowers and by the dozens of dragonflies – red, green and electric blue – darting between the sunlight and the shade.

"It's very nice," I say.

I'm sure that if this so-called holiday goes on long enough, I may even think of something interesting to say to this hideous mad woman. She must think I'm the stupidest person she's ever met.

But, oddly enough, she seems pleased. "Glad you like it."

And just then, an enormous bird flies slowly over the house, across the garden and on towards the trees in the distance.

At first I think it must be a heron – I've seen those in our local park. But then I'm sure it has to be an eagle.

I point at it.

"Ah yes," yells Dina, "it's the six o'clock marsh harrier – flap, flap, glide. That means that the bar is now open."

So we head back into the house and Dina pours herself a huge gin and tonic (more gin than tonic) and lets me have the tiniest bottle of beer I've ever seen. It looks like something that belongs on the end of a key ring.

"Sorry," she says, "but I forgot to check with your Dad what the drinking arrangements should be. Still, nobody could object to such a small bottle."

I want to say that at least one person *could* object to such a small bottle.

Dina suggests that I might like to take my beer into the garden while she makes supper. As she says this, I notice that she's topping up her glass.

The bees are still muttering and the dragonflies are still crackling around. And then the six o'clock marsh harrier comes over in the opposite direction, not taking any notice of me.

As I sit here trying to make this thimbleful of beer last, London seems a long way away. And California seems completely impossible. And I'm surprised to discover that I don't feel quite so angry.

Supper, which Dina brings into the garden, is lamb, potatoes and mushrooms. The lamb is delicious. (Dina tells the neighbourhood that that's just as well as she has half a sheep in her freezer.) The potatoes taste of wax and mud and I'm not as surprised as I should be when Dina tells me she grew them herself. The mushrooms, which she picked in the fields this morning, taste of wood and fibre and damp earth.

Dina washes it all down with about a gallon of red wine. I get fruit juice.

Then we sit and talk about nothing for ages, while she smokes 200 roll-ups and the sky turns yellow and the sun slides down behind the trees.

And just when I think that we're probably going to be here forever, she comes up with another surprise.

"Right," she says, "pub time. Just give me five minutes to get tarted up."

After a few minutes she comes back looking exactly the same except for the lipstick on her teeth and the smell of toothpaste.

And if I thought her driving from the station was a bit different, then her driving to the pub is a bit different many times over. But Harry has his head out of the window and is still laughing.

The pub, which is called something like The Strangled Ferret, would be Mum and Dad's idea of hell. They like cool, bare looking places with expensive food and the odd glass of expensive white wine. This place is packed, thick with cigarette smoke and loud conversations, and boiling hot.

I whisper to Dina, "I didn't think smoking was allowed in pubs anymore." But she just grins.

An old hippie is playing the guitar in the corner and singing some mournful song.

Three seconds later, I'm introduced to Gerry, who kisses Dina and grabs Harry's ears, much to Harry's obvious pleasure.

Gerry is a warden on the local nature reserve at Revenant Broad and nearly as thin and brown as Dina and even taller. He wears the same clothes and has the same haircut as she does. They could be twins.

He's also completely bladdered.

His words come out in a rush and he seems to have trouble standing up straight. That doesn't seem to have any impact on Dina and Harry both of whom are staring at him with these stupid grins on their faces.

Gerry buys pints for him and Dina, coke and crisps for me. We squeeze in at a table with about six other assorted loonies of both sexes. All of them are smoking roll-ups and all look as though the live and work outdoors. They shout hello.

Harry curls up on the floor and continues to stare longingly at Gerry.

And that's how the evening goes.

Them all smoking and drinking and shouting at each other. And laughing all the time.

Harry dreaming of moving in with Gerry and being patted by him throughout the whole of eternity.

Me completely surplus to requirements.

Gerry is telling a story about a rare butterfly that showed up at his nature reserve, swiftly followed by eleven middle-aged men with big binoculars and even bigger cameras.

He calls them "twitchers" and wants to know what they get out of it.

I notice that his hand is on Dina's leg.

How, he demands, can anyone enjoy a rare insect in the company of ten other blokes, all of whom are getting in each others' way?

One of the other loonies (denim jacket, hairy jumper, pierced eyebrows) thinks it's the same kind of thing as train spotting. That the important thing is to tick it off in the book. Been there. Done that. Got the T-shirt.

A lady loony (long black velvet dress, massive cleavage, wellies) agrees and says that these poor twitchers get so hung up about seeing rare things that they forget about enjoying them. She says that a famous writer, whose name she can't remember, said that giving a plant a name is like putting a dirty pane of glass between you and it. A couple of others (purple hair, AC/DC T-shirt; corn-rows, floor-length grey overcoat – possibly naked underneath) say that they think they remember reading this somewhere as well, but they can't remember who the writer was either.

And then Gerry says, "But they're such little insects and such big cameras," and everything goes quiet for a moment. And then they all fall about laughing and buy more drinks and roll more ciggies.

I start to wonder if there are any worse ways of spending an evening and then I find out.

The guitarist in the corner stops singing and everyone starts a kind of folky karaoke.

First, he accompanies a girl in a shawl who is sitting by the fireplace. She has a nice little voice.

And then, to my horror, Dina and Gerry stand up and start singing about whether or not they're going to Scarborough Fair.

They've even got their fingers in their ears.

And when they get to the bit about *"She once was a true love of mine"*, this soppy expression appears on their faces and they look into each others' eyes while everyone else around the table cheers and whistles and shouts encouragement. (As if they needed any.)

For a moment I think about joining Harry on the floor, but he's still looking longingly at Gerry.

Then it's a few million more beers and a few million more fags.

And then it's last orders and time to go.

When we all spill out into the car-park, the sky is alight with trillions of stars.

Gerry wants us to admire Orion's Belt but seems a bit vague about exactly where it is.

Then he and Dina have a discussion about who's going to drive home, which he wins.

I think I'm glad about this.

And then we drive back to Dina's cottage incredibly slowly, with me and Harry wedged between Dina and Gerry, the windows down and the pick-up full of the smell of beer and cigarettes and dog and warm vegetation.

... ...
...
At first, I can't see anything...
... I'm dazzled... blinded.
Maybe it's the tears in my eyes, but the sky... ... ...
... wobbles...like water... like the sea.
It's like looking at the world through the bottom of a bottle.
It's... confusing, frightening...
but it's better than the darkness.
... Shapes... move from one side to the other.
... I think they must be birds.
... I think that sound like singing must be the wind.
I'm so cold... I'm trembling all over.
My lips won't stay still... ...
There's a burning, fiery feeling... where I think my feet must be.
... ...
My jaw aches with the cold....
... My tongue feels swollen.
... My head feels like it's been crushed.
... I want to... ...
... I want to cry out... but when I try to nothing comes out.
... ...
... I don't seem to have a voice.
... ... All I can hear is...
the wind in the trees...
... and the sound of my breathing and my heart settling.
...THUD... THUD... THUD... ThuD ...ThuD ... thuD ...
thud... thud.

... ...
I'm going to have to move...
I don't want to, but I know that I can if I try hard enough...
I can't stay here... freezing and listening to the wind and to my
heart...
... thud... thud... thud.

So much sea and so much sky

It's morning and the room is cool at last and I seem to have slept well all things considered. The light is dazzling.

I can hear Dina singing in the kitchen downstairs, but fortunately I can't hear the words. She's probably still on about Scarborough Fair and her true love.

I look out of the window. The bees are back and so are the dragonflies. Dew is sparkling on the lawn and Harry is fast asleep on the faded deckchair.

There's not a cloud in the sky and I know it's going to be a scorcher.

There's no sign of the marsh harrier, but a pair of swallows are flying in and out through the open door of a large, tiled shed at the far end of the garden.

I love the way they seem to be putting no effort into it. Swooping up and down and turning corners simply by dipping their wings and not changing speed. In fact, their flying's a bit like Dina's driving, only more elegant.

When I get downstairs, Dina's looking very pleased with herself. There's no sign of Gerry.

"Morning Nick, sleep well?"

I don't like to say that I didn't – at least for the first half of the night – or why.

So I say, "Yes, thanks." (I told you I was well trained.)

Over breakfast – cereal, toast and honey for me, black coffee and another roll-up for her – she talks about Gerry.

"I suppose I'd have to call him my boyfriend, although I don't like the expression. Of course, he's years younger than me; just 30. He was one of the first people I met when I bought this place."

She seems to want me to like him.

"He's very intelligent and very funny. He could be doing a job that challenged him more. But he says that this is the only way that he can get to work with animals and, even more important, it's the only way he can support himself living here. He says he couldn't imagine living anywhere else. And I have to say I can't imagine it either. He's been to stay with me in Cambridge a couple of times, but he's never seemed really comfortable there. He claims he's never been to London, but I don't know whether or not to believe him."

This is more information that I really need, especially the stuff about him staying with her in Cambridge.

Dina says she has to work this morning – she's preparing these lectures she has to give in the autumn – and asks me if I can entertain myself for a few hours.

"Why not have good look round?" she says. "You can walk anywhere you want as long as you're careful. Take Harry with you, if you like, he could do with a proper walk. But take a lead and keep him away from any sheep you come across. He sometimes forgets he's not a working dog anymore."

Harry agrees to come for a walk, but he groans as he clambers off the deckchair and I don't think he's too pleased about it. But, like me, he doesn't want to seem rude.

As we reach the gate at the end of the garden, classical music starts blasting out of the windows of the cottage behind me.

Harry winces and looks at me as if to say, "I agree, but what can I do about it?"

As soon as we pass through the gate, the land opens up in front of us.

Here's the marsh. Reed beds and ditches stretch for at least a mile to a stand of trees directly in front of us.

It's very still.

I can see a few groups of sheep grazing, but apart from them and a couple of pigeons nothing much seems to be happening.

And there's still a slight mist hanging over everything.

I can also see three church towers from where I'm standing and the walls of a ruined monastery or manor house.

There's a track large enough for a small tractor running down the right hand side of the marsh towards the trees.

So, Harry and I take it. He's keeping an eye on those groups of sheep, and I'm keeping an eye on him.

The air is already hot although the grass is still wet. There's almost no breeze.

The water in the ditches is about two feet deep and completely clear. There are yellow flowers growing out of the water in some of the ditches. There are dragonflies everywhere.

When we get to the wood, the trees aren't very tall and they are covered in moss and grey and yellow splodges, which may be a plant or could be a disease for all I know.

It's very cool and green in here but also a bit airless.

The ground squelches underfoot.

From the far side of the wood, we can see sand dunes. I guess the sea must be just the other side, but all I can see is a grey smudge of haze at the bottom of the sky.

Harry and I poke around the place for a bit, watching the geese flying over and listening to the sheep pulling at the grass.

A couple of times a jet tears the sky open directly over our heads.

On one of the ditches we find a pair of swans and six chicks that are just beginning to turn white. Harry looks angry when he spots them, but not nearly as angry as they look when they spot him.

I put his lead on and drag him away quickly, just in case he gets too stroppy.

And after a bit, we head back down the track and we can hear classical music long before we can see the cottage. Dina must still be working.

It's really hot now and I'm sweating and Harry's tongue is almost dragging along the grass.

Once we're back in the garden, I decide to check out the shed while Harry climbs wearily onto the deckchair and looks like he's determined never to move again.

It's even hotter in here. Even though the door is wide open. There's a pile of logs, a few suspicious looking containers of chemicals, some ancient fishing tackle and a couple of old bikes.

Out of the corner of my eye, I see a swallow fly in through the open door.

I look up, and there stuck to the side of one of the rafters is a nest made of pale reddish mud. I can't see the swallow chicks but I can hear them screeching and pleading for food.

The adult bird perches on the rafter for a moment, its beak full of insects — at least I assume that they are insects, what I can see is mostly cobwebby wings. But then it disappears into the nest for a second or two, reappearing with its beak empty.

Then it's off out of the door. A couple of minutes later it or its mate appears with more food before setting off again.

In the 15 minutes I stand here, the chicks are fed eight times.

And speaking of being fed, I guess it must be time for lunch.

After lunch (lamb casserole), Dina suggests a trip to the beach.

About ten seconds later, the pick-up crunches to a halt in a cloud of dust by one of the churches I could see from the gate in her garden.

Close up, I can see that it's ruined. The windows have been boarded up, there's ivy most of the way up the flint tower, there's a padlocked gate across the porch and the graveyard is completely overgrown.

26

We walk through a gap in the dunes and we're on the beach.

There's so much sky and so much sea it's hard to know what to look at first. It's all so enormous.

The beach is wonderful – sand stretching in both directions, and almost no one around. The sea is flat and milky.

Standing here is like standing at the very edge of the world, like there's nothing beyond the horizon.

Dina booms that the beach used to be pebbles but that they've built new sea defences up the coast and that has completely changed it. The sand appeared almost overnight. She's a bit concerned about the impact all this will have on the local wildlife. But I think it's great anyway.

Dina suggests a swim and starts to peel off her overalls. For one horrible moment I think she might have skinny dipping in mind. I wouldn't put that past her and Gerry and the pub loonies.

I can just imagine them all butt naked doing a synchronised swimming routine still dragging on their roll-ups. Still talking and laughing.

But then I'm relieved to see that's she's wearing a one-piece, blue costume underneath.

Of course, my trunks are in a bag, so I have to wrap a towel around my waist and do that ridiculous thing of getting out of my pants and into my trunks while balancing on one leg and nearly falling over.

I can feel Dina smirking, but I'm not going to make eye contact with her.

The sea is horribly cold but brilliant. We splash about for a bit trying not to gasp. And then Dina dives under the water, emerges and starts swimming away from the beach. She's a great swimmer, really stylish.

And she just keeps going and going.

After about five minutes I'm starting to watch her carefully

And a few minutes after that I'm getting really worried.

Harry is inspecting a particularly interesting pile of sand a bit further up the beach and is taking no notice at all.

Then she stops swimming, and all I can see is a tiny head bobbing up and down in the water.

Behind her, just this side of the horizon, gulls are folding themselves up in mid air and diving into the sea like paper darts.

My heart is pounding. And I feel really angry with her.

But then, to my relief, she starts swimming lazily back towards me. A few minutes later, she is stretched out on the sand reading a paperback.

I lie on my towel, wipe the salt out of my eyes and immediately fall asleep. After a couple of quick, mad dreams about Harry buying me pints at The Strangled Ferret, I wake up sweating and dribbling gently into my towel.

It's really hot. Dina, meanwhile, hasn't moved a muscle and is continuing to roast herself.

My skin feels warm and a bit dry and prickly so I know I shouldn't lie in the sun any longer. I cover myself with my towel and turn on my side, facing the sea, nestling down into the sand.

As I lie there dozing, a flock of tiny black and white birds flies urgently by. Aeroplanes are unravelling perfect vapour trails across the sky. A tanker is creeping ever so slowly along the line of the horizon, taking all afternoon to move from right to left. The sea laps and rustles gently. Dina turns the pages of her book.

For the moment, I'm happy to be here.

There's just time during the drive back for me to tell Dina about the swallow's nest in the shed.

She says that they nested there last year not long after she moved in, but that all the chicks died suddenly after about ten days. Gerry's theory was that they were fine while they were really small but that as soon as they were able to lift their heads above the edge of the nest, they were exposed to a north easterly wind blowing between the roof tiles.

"So, they died of cold?"

"I guess so. They weren't fledged so they didn't have much protection."

"But that's horrible. Could it happen again?"

"Yes, if the wind changes. Let's hope for the sake of the chicks that this warm weather lasts."

"But supposing it doesn't?"

"Well, then I guess they're in trouble. I know it sounds awful Nick, but nature's like that. And you have to assume that if the chicks couldn't survive the wind then they probably wouldn't have been much use as adult birds."

"But there must be something we can do."

"Well, Gerry said that short of putting a new roof on the shed, which would cost a fortune, the only thing we could do was block up the cracks between the tiles. He thought newspaper might do the trick."

"Well, can't we try that?"

"Sure, why not?"

One of the things I'm quickly learning about old Dina is that she means what she says.

Having performed an entirely unnecessary emergency stop outside the cottage, she's off in search of old newspapers.

She can't find many because they get recycled every week.

But she does find a stack of ecology magazines. She subscribes to this magazine but says it's far too boring for anyone to actually read.

The ladder is in the shed.

We lean it up against the shed wall and Dina says, "Up you go."

I climb the ladder while Dina stands on the bottom rung to stop it from slipping.

The sun has been shining on the roof all day and the tiles are really hot. You could fry an egg on them. They're also old and cracked and mossy and don't fit well.

Looking through one crack, I'm looking straight down into the nest. There are four little chicks with clumps of feathers and huge gaping beaks rolling about in the bottom of the nest. They look like four mini-dinosaurs.

And then a parent bird flies in and drops more cobwebby food into a couple of gobs before taking its leave. As far as it's concerned, I simply don't exist.

So, I roll up one of Dina's ecology magazines as tightly as I can, and stuff it into one of the largest cracks.

And then I work my way down the roof, sometimes using a whole mag, sometimes just a few pages.

Then we move the ladder to the other side of the shed and I do the same there.

After I've finished, the shed roof looks a bit odd, with bits of paper sticking out at all angles, but I feel confident that less wind will get in.

"Well," I say, once I'm on the ground again, "at least we tried."

"Good job," says Dina. "And now I think it's opening time."

We're sitting in the garden in the dark after supper (lamb kebabs) when the phone rings and Dina runs into the house. I guess it must be Gerry, but then after a couple of minutes Dina comes out again and says, "It's for you Nick. It's Liz… your Mum."

"Hello," I say.

"*Hello, darling,*" she says. "*How was your journey? How are things at Dina's? Is she nice? Do you like her? What's her house like? Have you been doing lots of interesting things?*"

I start to tell her about the beach and about the swallows, but I suddenly realise that she's not really listening.

"Well, that's marvellous," she says.

What is? I've just been telling her about last year's swallow chicks dying of cold. What is she talking about?

"Jim and I are having a wonderful time, although I'm still a bit tired from the flight... The house is lovely with a beautiful garden... Jim had his first meeting with the TV people today. He's really positive about it. He says that everyone seemed delighted he was working on the project... He sends his love by the way... He's having a rest at the moment... Tomorrow, we're being taken out to a really posh restaurant for lunch... I'll let you know if we spot anyone famous."

By now, I'm not really listening either.

"Well," she says, *"I've got to go now. I need to check that Jim's OK. Lovely talking to you... I'm glad everything's going so well... Thank Dina again for us, won't you? I'll ring again in a couple of days."*

And it's only after she hangs up that I realise that she hasn't asked me how I am.

"Mum says thank you," I say, when I'm back in the garden.

"Did she?" says Dina.

For a moment I think she's going to say something else but she doesn't.

... ...

... It's nearly dark, but on the horizon the sky is alight...
It's making my eyes water.
They're NOT tears.

... ...

The air is like... honey. It slips through my chest like butter.
I'm not so cold now that I'm moving again.
My legs are stiff and I can feel the stones under my feet.
But I keep going... and going
... I remember...
teaching little Arthur to walk... they're NOT tears.

... ...

He was just about a year old. He'd been shuffling around on his
arse (I'm not supposed to say that) for a few weeks. He kept
trying to stand. He would arch his back and push himself upright
with his little fists. But then he would collapse...

... ...
... ...

Sometimes he fell back into a sitting position, with a surprised
look on his face and no harm was done.
Sometimes he would fall forward and bang his nose or his
forehead on the floor. And then he would howl...
... We were in the garden and I'd just seen him fall face forward.
... He had a mouth full of earth. I held out my hand to him and
he took it...

... ...

... and pulled himself upright... ...
... and I walked him around in a long, slow circle.
His eyes were shining... ... ...

... ...

... They're not tears...
... I keep going.

What the sea says

And that's how the next few days go. Not the phone call from Mum bit – those are obviously going to be few and far between. But the rest of it.

I wake up every morning in dazzling sunlight and start my little routine.

First, I look out of the window to see if the swallows are about. And they always are. Zooming in and out of the shed, round and round the garden, without a moment to waste.

Then I go downstairs and say good morning to Dina who's always in the kitchen with a cup of coffee and a fag.

Then I head down the track about 20 yards and have a pee in the hedge. I usually pick a target – a wild flower or a dock leaf.

Then I go to the shed to check on the swallow chicks. So far, so good. I can hear them all yelling for food. It won't be long before they're strong enough to hold themselves upright and I should be able to see them from down here.

Then it's breakfast – about the only meal in the day that's guaranteed not to have lamb in it. And it's the only meal we eat indoors. All the kitchen windows are open and the sunshine is splashing on the stripped wood table.

I don't talk much over breakfast, but Dina more than makes up for it. She always seems to have something to shout about – the news on the radio, something in her book, something she's been doing in the garden.

She doesn't seem to mind that I don't say much in return.

Maybe she doesn't even notice.

But she always asks me about the swallow chicks. How they seemed this morning. Whether or not everything is going well.

33

And this is odd because it's her garden and her shed and they're her swallows.

But she talks about them as if they're mine. As if I'm responsible for them. She could easily go into the shed and see for herself, but she never does. She always waits for me to report back on them.

A couple of times I notice that the magazines have slipped out from between the cracks. So, I get the ladder out and force them back in again.

Every morning Dina works. She's very disciplined. But she says three hours a day are plenty.

So, for those three hours, Harry and I hang out together.

And then it's lunch and no escaping the lamb.

Every afternoon, we go to the beach. And every afternoon, Dina swims miles out and I get worried. But so far she's always come back safely.

Then she reads and turns even browner, while I lie in the sand and watch the sea. I'm hypnotised by the way the water swirls in and slips away again over the sand.

Dina's found me a novel about the Normandy Landings. But I don't seem able to concentrate on it. I must have read one sentence – "Captain Watkins's first impression of France was the dead animals in the fields; sheep, cows and even donkeys, all lying on their backs with their legs in the air"– about 30 times.

But all the time I'm really listening to the sea's murmuring. And my eyes keep drifting off the page and towards the water's edge.

It's a bit like being in a trance.

I've never really done nothing before. It's odd.

Then it's back to the cottage in time for the six o'clock marsh harrier, who signals opening time.

And while Dina's getting the drinks ready – she's stuck to the just one tiny bottle of beer rule for me and the just one tiny gallon of red wine rule for her – I nip into the shed for a final check on the chicks.

Then Dina and I sit in the garden until it's dark and the moon is up. And we talk a bit and listen to the leaves moving in the trees.

And then, when I get to bed, I get my mobile out and text Billy and Jack, my best friends from school.

Billy's on safari in Kenya with his family and he sends me messages about the animals he's seen. I text him about the swallows, but I don't suppose he's very interested when he's seeing things like cheetahs and flamingos every day.

Jack is still in London. His parents are divorced and he lives with his Mum. She can't afford to go away for a summer holiday, but Jack doesn't mind because he fancies this girl in our class called Emily. He's dedicated his summer to getting off with her. He hasn't had much luck so far, but they have been to the cinema together. Trouble was, he says, there were some older boys from school there, and he felt really embarrassed. He texts me about the clothes that Emily is wearing and the things she says. But I can't get very excited about it. Emily's all right, I suppose, but I can't see what's special about her. Maybe that's because I've known her since I was five. But so has Jack.

It's strange, but in some ways, Jack feels further away than Billy, even though he's only a hundred miles away.

I keep texting them because I want to feel that I'm still in touch while I'm stuck here. But it doesn't seem to be working.

The longer I'm here, the more distant my life in London feels. It's almost like it happened to someone else. It's as if, if I stayed here long enough, I would forget about it altogether and turn into someone else.

And I don't know what I feel about that.

One morning, Dina suggests that I might like to go into the

local village to get, "A few things that we need. Here's a list. Why not take Harry? He'd really enjoy the walk."

I ask her if I can use one of the old bikes in the shed. She says sure but she doesn't know if either of them work. All that stuff was left behind when she bought the place. So, I spend about half an hour sorting out the huge, old-fashioned, black sit-up-and-beg with only three gears and a basket fixed to the handlebars by three leather straps. But once the tyres are pumped up and I've given it a bit of a wipe down with a wet cloth, it seems OK.

So, we set off. Me on the bike which rattles and vibrates, and Harry trotting along beside me on a lead looped round the handlebars. You can tell he used to be a working dog, he's so brilliantly trained and does what you want him to. He seems to be enjoying himself.

At least, to begin with he does. But after we've gone a mile or so, Harry is puffing and panting and his tongue's about a foot long.

He looks into my eyes and suddenly he seems desperate. He's an old dog after all, and at this moment he looks completely knackered.

I get off the bike, undo the lead from Harry's collar and both of us sit in the shade at the side of the road.

We sit there for about 20 minutes while Harry gets his breath back.

In that time, just two cars pass us – one in each direction. Both drivers are women and both wave as they go past.

To begin with, Harry lies flat out on his side a bit away from me. But then he gets up, ambles over to me, tells me that he forgives me and, to prove it, lies with his head on my lap while I stroke his ears.

Then we head off again, me pushing the bike this time and both of us walking slowly.

We soon get to the outskirts of the village that we passed through when Dina picked me up from the station. On both sides of the road there are gardens full of flowers.

Some of the houses have little home-made stalls at the side of the road with tomatoes, raspberries, strawberries and bunches of flowers for sale. Most of them have a small blackboard with the prices on it and an honesty box in which you are supposed to put any money.

There's an old-fashioned school house on the right hand side, with a small playground in front and a cottage that must be for the teacher. The school building has a short tower with a bell in it, and there's plaque on the side which says "1884."

The school house has two entrances. Over one, the word "BOYS" is carved on a block of stone. The other says "GIRLS."

There's a brightly-coloured metal climbing frame in the garden and a couple of swings made of tractor tyres. There's a newish sign which says "St Mary's Church of England Primary School."

There are obviously enough little kids around here for it to be worth keeping the school open.

A bit further on, we pass the church, which is set back about 100 yards from the road, but you can see the tower above the cottages.

It's not built of flint like the one near where we go swimming, but of some orangey-coloured stone.

It's also much bigger than the church near the beach. There are monster heads in each corner of the tower to spit out rainwater. There's also a flagpole on the top, but no flags are flying today.

In the centre of the village is a large wooden sign that says something about winning third prize in "Norfolk in Bloom."

And there's just one shop with an enormous tractor parked directly outside it.

Harry knows that he's not allowed in and just slumps down by one of the tractor wheels. He seems relieved to get the weight off his feet.

When I open the door, a bell rings. A lady of about 60 with grey curls is standing behind the counter serving an old man who must be the tractor driver. He is wearing very old clothes, has a very brown face and not many teeth. He has a greasy, flat tweed cap on his head and there are deep grooves in the back of his neck.

"I'll be with you in a minute, my lovely," she says, "when I've finished serving this gentleman."

The tractor driver is obviously here for his lunch. He buys a packet of sausage rolls, a large iced cake in a box and a bottle of cherryade. I thought tractor drivers were supposed to eat ploughman's lunches of bread, cheese and apples washed down with a glass of ale under a spreading chestnut tree. But obviously no one has told this bloke, who's buying children's party food.

No wonder he hasn't got many teeth.

I look around. The shop doesn't seem to be an enormous success. There's a large block of bright yellow cheese and a huge pink ham behind the counter with one of those old fashioned slicing machines. There are tins of soup and cans of vegetables and boxes of cereal on the wooden shelves, and lots of spaces. There are some very scruffy tomatoes and apples in a box on the floor, nothing like as nice as the things in front of the houses. I can't believe that anyone's going to get rich running a place like this.

The old man nods to me and says, "Mornin'," as he leaves, with his terrible food and fizzy pop.

I get Dina's list out of my pocket and the "few things that we need" turn out to be a newspaper and some cigarette papers and a couple of ounces of tobacco. How come I'm not surprised?

I should think that they are the last things that either of us need.

And, of course, I know what's going to happen.

"Sorry, love," says the lady, "but I can't sell you tobacco, even though I'm sure it's not for a sensible lad like you."

"No, it isn't," I say. "It's for my aunt."

"Who's your aunt then?"

"Dina. Dina Lumsden. She lives in a cottage a couple of miles away."

"Of course, I should have twigged, what with you asking for her favourite tobacco. I'd heard that you were coming. What's your name, she did tell me but I've forgotten."

"It's Nick," I say.

"Well, I'm Mrs Maddox, Brenda Maddox. And I live here with my completely useless husband Charley. He's around somewhere, but I haven't a clue where."

I say. "Are you open this afternoon? Maybe Dina can come in on our way to the beach."

"Listen, love," says Mrs Maddox, looking at me very hard, "can you be trusted? Will you keep a secret?"

"Yes," I say, not having the faintest idea what she's on about.

She reaches into the shelf behind her and hands me a packet of tobacco. "Now put that in your pocket quick and don't let anyone see you. And tell Dina to pay me next time she comes in. If I don't take any money from you now, nobody can say I've sold it to you."

I stuff the tobacco in my pocket, feeling a bit like a smuggler.

"Come back any time," says Mrs Maddox winking at me. "That senile old whatsit of a husband of mine would enjoy meeting you. He's always moaning about how boring life is around here."

"Thanks," I say and scuttle out.

Harry is still lying in the dust and doesn't look much like a dog who's looking forward to a long run home.

So, I pick him up – he's really skinny and lighter than I expected. I can feel his ribs. But he doesn't seem to mind being

39

picked up. I try to put him into the basket but, skinny as he is, he's too big.

In the end, I sit on the saddle and grab Harry under one arm and lift him until his back paws are in the basket and his front paws are on my shoulders and his head next to mine.

And that's how we get back. Me cycling slowly, clattering and wobbling about, and Harry standing upright in the basket looking back the way we've come. His ears keep tickling my face. It's not as much fun as sticking his head out of the pick-up window but he does seem to be enjoying it.

On the way back we stop to buy Dina a bunch of flowers from the front of one of the cottages but I can't put them in the basket because Harry will tread on them and I need both hands to steer with. So, Harry agrees to hold them gently in his mouth.

I can't imagine what we look like, but fortunately we don't pass a single car on the way back and Dina seems really pleased with the flowers. I can't imagine why; they only cost 50p and she has a whole garden full anyway.

. . . .
Remembering is the best way to keep going.
It makes me feel more cheerful.
Stronger.

. . . . . .
. . . I remember the six of us sitting by the fire while the wind rattled the windows. It would sometimes roar straight down the chimney and make the coals in the grate glow and spit.
. . . While we listened to the booming of the wind, the room seemed to grow lighter for a moment.

. . . .
I remember the smell of the wheat when it was being harvested and how the hares were always the last animals to leave the field — waiting until there were only a few square yards of uncut wheat in the middle of the field before they bolted. If you were quick enough you could break their backs with a stick.

. . . .
. . .
I remember the taste of the milk straight from the dairy at Manor Farm — warm and thick and buttery.
When I drank it, I couldn't tell whether I felt more pleased or more disgusted.

. . .
I remember the feel of the earth in the garden — thick and clinging,
Mother's touch,
how the stars moved from month to month and season to season, the whine of mosquitoes in those endless summer nights, how beautiful the snow looked on the churchyard, the scratch of my blankets, ice on the broad.

. . . .
. . . . . .
I remember being happy.

. . . . . .
I remember everything.

Waiting for something to happen

The next morning, Harry and I go fishing. I've never tried it before but how hard can it be?

The first job is to sort out the fishing tackle in the shed. When he hears me fiddling about with it, Harry is interested enough to get off his deckchair to come over and find out what I'm doing.

He sits happily in the dust looking sleepy, glancing up occasionally as the parent swallows fly in and out.

There's an old rod made out of cane. It looks about 100 years old but the two sections fit perfectly together and the brass fitting is like new.

It's very thin and whippy and I think it must be a fly fishing rod.

I can't find a reel but there is a tangled ball of line. After about ten minutes, I've untangled about 15 feet of it, which should be enough.

There's also a matchwood box with three compartments. In the box are: one battered float, some rusty hooks and about ten scruffy flies pinned to a card.

I know the flies won't be any use – there don't seem to be any streams around here only ditches – but I rub the smallest of hooks on the brick floor to clean it. Then I tie it to the length of line and tie the other end to the eye at the tip of the rod.

I thought I was going to have to dig for worms, but Dina has given me a tin of sweetcorn which, she yells, the fish are going to love. "They'll be biting your hand off."

There's still a mist out on the marsh and it's absolutely still.

Harry and I walk along the tractor path, but before we get to the woods, we turn off and follow one of the ditches that meet the path at right angles.

I've no idea whether or not there are any fish in it, but it seems worth a go.

We walk a couple of hundred yards along the ditch, which has lots of yellow water lilies in it. The surface is being stirred into thousands of tiny ripples by thousands of tiny beetles, making it look as if it's raining. Green, red and blue dragonflies clatter up and down.

Harry and I sit down by a large fence post which is streaked with bird shit. In the dust at the bottom of the post are all these balls of fur and tiny animal bones.

I put a piece of sweet corn onto the hook and swing it into the middle of the ditch, which is only about six feet wide.

There's water weed growing in patches but the float lands in clear water. It lies flat on the surface for a moment and slowly starts to straighten up. But before it can do so it suddenly disappears.

I've got a bite, and with my very first cast.

I pull the rod sideways and can feel a fish wriggling on the hook.

Because I haven't got a reel, I have to hold the rod above my head and lift the line out of the water.

And there on the end is a beautiful golden fish with scarlet fins. It's five or six inches long and still has the yellow lump of sweetcorn in its mouth.

I swing the line towards me and my hand closes around the little fish. I can feel its strength as it arches its body in my fist.

Now the urgent job is to get the hook out of its mouth. I don't want to hurt it – it's so pretty.

I hold the hook firmly between two fingers and turn it back on itself, and it immediately comes out of my fish's mouth.

And now it's lying in my hand. Its mouth is gasping and its gills are working and it's giving off a muddy smell. Its tiny black eyes are staring at the sky.

I call Harry over to show him. He sniffs it once, but then goes back to whatever he was doing before.

I feel incredibly happy.

Then I kneel down by the water's edge and put my hand under the water, which is colder than I was expecting, and open my fingers and my little fish swims away.

The whole episode probably took less than a minute. And now it's like it never happened.

But I know that it did.

And although everything seems the same as before, it isn't.

I think about trying to catch another one but decide against it.

That's enough fishing for one day. It really couldn't get any better than that.

So, Harry and I sit in the grass for ages watching the water and the patterns made by the beetles. Pigeons fly overhead and we see the marsh harrier cruising over the woods at the edge of the marsh. The mist clears and the church towers come into focus. It gets hotter. The trees barely move. I can hear Harry breathing. I can feel the blood travelling through my veins. It's almost as if I can feel time passing. Incredibly slowly.

On our way back, we notice that something is different. Instead of classical music, rock's blaring from the cottage.

Harry starts to make these squealing noises and obviously wants to run on ahead without me. But I guess he's feeling responsible for me because he stays.

When we get back to the cottage there's an old motorbike on a stand next to Dina's truck.

By now, Harry is beside himself with excitement. And with one last look back – a look that says, "I'm really sorry but I just can't help myself, you're going to have to excuse me," – he goes tearing into the house.

It's Gerry, of course.

When I get into the kitchen, he and Dina are drinking beer and smoking. So, no surprises there. And Harry is trying to clamber onto Gerry's knee, but Gerry is gently pushing him away.

"Hello, matey," he says as I come into the room. And I'm surprised to find that I'm pleased to see him.

Dina, of course, is looking as if she's just won the lottery. She's smiling so hard that it looks as if her face might come apart. She's smiling so hard her teeth could crack.

In spite of their tans, both Dina and Gerry are looking a bit red and sweaty. Something tells me that Dina probably hasn't done her full three hours' work this morning.

What is it about this bloke that can turn the other two occupants of this house into gibbering idiots just by being here?

I'm still so excited about my fish that I tell them all about it. Gerry says it sounds like a rudd and if there's one in that ditch then there must be loads of them.

Then he says that he's seen what I've done to the shed roof.

I ask him if he thinks it will work and he and Dina look at each other before he says that he hopes it won't be necessary. He says that the chicks may be at a disadvantage because the parent birds were so late to start nesting. That the chicks should be more or less full-grown by this time of year.

Dina says that Gerry is working on Revenant Broad this afternoon and called in because he wondered if I'd like to go with him.

She says that if I want to go she'll just have to be brave about going to the beach on her own. I know she's joking and will be perfectly happy alone, but I like the fact that she's pretending. And I know that if I said I wanted to go with her, she'd be cool about that as well. Pleased even. Mum and Dad would be pushing me towards Gerry by this stage, already planning what they were going to do together while I was gone. But Dina seems to think it's up to me.

And part of me is drawn to the idea of another afternoon on the beach watching and listening to the sea, but a bigger part of me is drawn to Gerry's motorbike.

Besides, it'll be nice to spend some time with a bloke after these days with just Dina.

So, I say that I'd love to go, if she really doesn't mind.

She just smiles.

Gerry's got a crash helmet for me in a wooden box at the back of his bike. I climb onto the saddle behind him and suddenly feel really shy about being so close to him. There's a leather strap at the back of the seat which I can hold behind my back. But Gerry says I'll be safer if I put my arms around his waist.

I'm expecting him to take things slowly; after all he drove Dina's truck at about three miles an hour. But he lets out the clutch and roars down the track onto the road.

We're flying. I can smell his leather jacket in front of my face and if I turn to the side, the hedges are just a blur.

We whizz through the village and turn left down a small side road with open fields on either side. There are a few cottages scattered along the roadside. Then we make another left, and stop in a tiny car park at the edge of a large lake.

All this time, Gerry has been shouting over his shoulder about how the nature reserve has a boat that is used to take tourists out onto the broad and that everyone who works at the reserve does a couple of shifts a week on the boat. He shouts that you'd go bonkers if you had to say the same things six times a day, six days a week.

When I climb off his motorbike I discover that my legs are trembling a bit.

There's a small, wooden jetty and moored to it is the boat. Its name – *Piranha* – has been painted by hand on the side.

Anything less like a piranha is hard to imagine. It's flat-

46

bottomed, made of fibreglass, has wooden benches for about ten people and a canvas roof that fits over a metal frame. A small outboard motor is mounted at the back. It clearly isn't built for speed. A predator that was designed like this wouldn't last five minutes. It's more like some stupid, slow flat fish. I think there's something called a flounder, which would be a better name for this boat.

Gerry is wearing his uniform – a khaki shirt with the reserve's emblem on it and khaki trousers. But he then spoils it by putting on a leather cowboy hat, which he gets out of the box at the back of the motorbike. I wish he hadn't. He obviously thinks it looks cool. It doesn't.

We sit in the boat and wait for the first customers who turn up about ten minutes later.

There are six of them, three men and three women, all middle-aged and all wearing sensible clothes and sensible shoes. They all have expensive-looking binoculars or cameras hung round their necks. Maybe they're some of Gerry's twitchers.

Gerry checks their tickets and then he starts the engine, unties the rope holding *Piranha* to the jetty and we're off.

It's really hot once we're in open water, but everyone seems to be having a good time. The grown-ups are looking at different kinds of ducks through their binoculars and seem surprisingly excited by it all. They ask Gerry all kinds of questions.

In between answering their questions, Gerry goes into what I soon learn is almost a set speech.

He tells us about the sail-driven wind pump on the far bank, which was working until well into the twentieth century. He tells us about how the broads were nearly destroyed forty or fifty years ago because of the agricultural run-off from the nearby fields. The fertilisers the farmers were using leaked into the water and encouraged algae to grow, which made the water murky and nearly choked everything. But things are getting better now and the water is clearer than it's been for years.

He tells us what the different dragonflies are. And he tells us how swallowtail butterflies will only lay their eggs on the leaves of the milk parsley plant (the only food their caterpillars will eat), which is just beginning to make a bit of a comeback in Norfolk.

(I realise that it must have been a swallowtail that the loonies were on about in The Strangled Ferret the other night.)

Gerry breaks off to tell the driver of a motor launch to slow down because the wash from his boat might damage the banks.

Then he tell us about the huge pikes that some people believe live in Revenant Broad; pikes that weigh more than 30 pounds. There are reports of them taking ducklings and even, according to some people, full-grown ducks.

He says he's not sure about these rumours but he has found a dead pike – probably hit by a boat – that weighed nearly 20 pounds.

He tells us a story about a yachting party here about 60 years ago.

It was a hot day like this and everyone was swimming from this luxury yacht, including a small dog. As they were all splashing around and laughing, suddenly the small dog – Gerry says he likes to think of it as a poodle – disappeared without a sound beneath the surface and was never seen again. The broken-hearted owners always believed it had been taken by a pike.

Everybody shivers at this and pretends to be spooked. One of the ladies makes a big performance of pulling her hand out of the water where she has been trailing it. I remember what Dina said about the fish biting my hand off.

We can see a large, white weather-boarded house on stilts built at the water's edge. Gerry tells us that it used to be a hunting lodge. That one hundred years ago they used to have enormous

48

shoots on this broad. Really important people used to come up from London in the winter and kill hundreds of birds. All the local people used to get involved as well. For them, it was a chance to earn some money in hard times.

There's nothing much happening in the middle of the broad, just a few swans admiring their reflections.

We can see two yachts with brilliant white sails. But there's almost no wind and no one on board them seems that bothered.

Normal service is suspended and no one seems to care. It's very hot and still and I think everyone must be feeling as sleepy as I am.

The water is like glass. It's like the whole world is pausing for breath. Waiting for something to happen.

It's just as well that Gerry swings the boat into the shore when he does, otherwise we might all really have fallen asleep. Like the people in fairy stories who have spells cast on them and sleep for a hundred years.

I can imagine *Piranha* going slowly round in endless circles year after year, with everyone on board dozing their lives away.

Gerry takes us for a short walk through a stand of trees. The ground is moist and spongy under our feet. It's like walking on rubber.

In a clearing there's a large oak tree with a kind of rough ladder fixed to the trunk. The ladder disappears into the branches above.

Gerry asks the grown-ups if they think they can make the climb. It's not easy, and as we go up hand over hand, I'm surprised that the others are making it. I look down and the ground seems a long way away. My stomach turns over.

As we climb up past the branches we reach a wooden platform right at the top of the tree with a rickety wooden handrail around it.

Some of the grown-ups are puffing a bit and looking nervous.

From up here you can see the whole world. Well, not the whole world, maybe, but a fair bit of it. Well, a few square miles of Norfolk anyway.

But the land is so flat and the horizon so low and the sky so huge that it seems like more.

Over there is the sea. And over there, behind those trees, is the marsh and Dina's cottage. There are church towers everywhere. And Revenant Broad is like a mirror of the sky.

And here as well everything is still. It's like the whole world has breathed in but not yet breathed out again.

When we get back onto the spongy ground, we're all sweaty and the mosquitoes start to notice us. I get bitten three times on my arm before we get back to boat, which we do a bit quicker than we got here.

Once we get safely back onto the water, leaving the mozzies behind, Gerry starts to talk about oak trees. He says that enormous numbers of oaks used to be needed for shipbuilding and that people used to grow them like a crop. They needed to be coppiced, which means that they were cut down a few feet above the ground and that new branches would grow from the stump. And after about 20 or 30 years these branches were big enough for shipbuilding.

Gerry says that people used to disagree about whether it was better to grow them in woods or in hedgerows. The difference is that in a wood, the branches of a coppiced oak will grow straight up to the sky, like capital I's – I I I. But if you grow them in hedges, as they used to in Norfolk, then the branches grow outwards and upwards at the same time. This gives them a natural curve, like brackets – (((– that made them perfect for a ship's ribs, but wasn't so good for the roofs of barns.

I can see that the adults find this interesting, but I'm so hot that

I'm not really sure that I can bring myself to care.

And after about another 20 minutes we drop this party off at the little jetty. They say goodbye and make jokes and one of the men hangs back a bit and gives Gerry a fiver as a tip. Gerry thanks him, waves goodbye to them and then whispers to me that it'll be good beer money.

Then we get a break of about 20 minutes before the next lot arrive. Gerry lies on his back in the boat and covers his face with his stupid hat. I also curl up in a patch of shade on a plastic covered cushion. The water is so still that the boat is barely moving and I still have this feeling like I'm caught in some kind of spell.

The next bunch of people are pretty much like the first lot, all adults and all jolly. They even seem to have the same cameras and the same binoculars. So Gerry gives them more or less the same speech, but adds some new details and stories. When we tie up *Piranha* the flounder near the large oak tree, I decide not to go with them. I can't be bothered to climb the ladder again and besides the mozzies will be waiting for me. So I stay in the boat. The sun on the water is so bright that I have to close my eyes. I realise that I can't now remember whether certain people – the lady in the red T-shirt for instance – were in the first group or are here now.

I think I may have fallen asleep because I'm startled when everyone comes hurrying back to the boat swatting at mosquitoes on their arms and legs. (The lady with the red T-shirt isn't with them, so either they've tied her to the top of the tree where the marsh harrier can peck out her eyes or she was with the first group of people after all.)

While we're waiting back at the jetty for the third party of people, Gerry takes the chance to smoke a couple of roll-ups.

I have a fantasy about throwing his hat into the water where it is immediately swallowed by a giant pike.

He asks me if I'm having a good time staying with Dina and I say that I am. He tells me how much he admires her and how clever she is. He says that she makes him feel really stupid sometimes. But then he seems to be taken over by the spell that's had me in its grip all afternoon. And he just sort of goes quiet as though all the air has gone out of him.

Of course, I'm not working or anything, but I enjoy these breaks between trips, sitting here with Gerry with the water underneath us and the sky above us.

By the time the third lot of customers arrive, it has begun to get a bit cooler and the sky is hazy. But there's still no breeze.

In fact, we hear them before we see them. Kids shouting and arguing. It's two families: four adults and five children. The youngest of the kids is about four and the oldest is a girl of about 15. She's not particularly pretty but she has this wonderful shiny chestnut-coloured hair. Gerry looks at me and smiles when he sees me looking at her. I immediately look away. I don't want him to think that I fancy her or anything.

The younger kids are really badly behaved. They refuse to put on the life jackets that Gerry says they have to wear. The parents ask Gerry if they really have to and he says yes and that the trip can't begin until they do.

Eventually the little kids are bribed with sweets to put the jackets on and we set off. But they won't sit still and keep talking over Gerry when he tries to get through his set speech.

He's telling the adults about the wind pumps when one of these kids starts shouting for a drink. The parents tell him to shush, but immediately stop listening to what Gerry is saying and start fumbling around in a picnic bag. They find a carton of Ribena and give it to the kid. Which sets off two of the others who say it isn't fair and they want a drink as well. At which point, the other parents join the search for drinks.

All this time, Gerry has been trying to tell them about Revenant Broad, but they're so flustered by their children's behaviour that they don't really seem to be taking it in.

Gerry remains very calm and friendly but I reckon he's pretty fed up.

I sneak a look at the girl with the hair. She's sitting on her own, not taking any part in any of this. She looks as if she wishes that she wasn't here. When she sees me looking she looks away.

One of the children nearly falls overboard. Gerry tries to frighten them into behaving better by telling them about the pikes. He says that if they don't sit still and fall in the pike might get them.

The children's parents don't look very pleased about this but they don't say anything.

But the children do. One says that he doesn't believe Gerry. The others start to chant, "Liar, liar, pants on fire." Everything goes quiet for a moment and then the parents tell the children not to be rude. But with no real force and the kids don't take any notice and one throws his Ribena carton into the water.

The girl with the hair still says nothing but she looks completely embarrassed. And so do the parents, but they just don't seem to be able to control the little ones.

Gerry has obviously had enough by now, because he cuts out the visit to the oak tree. Probably doesn't fancy the kids' protests when he tells them that they can't go up the ladder. I expect he'd quite like to feed them to the mosquitoes if he had a chance.

As we head back to the jetty, the kids are squabbling and rolling about in the bottom of the boat. Their voices carry across the water like the squawks of some annoying animal.

But at least they've broken the spell that's kept everyone paralysed all afternoon.

They barely bother to thank Gerry, but walk away from the

jetty, with the kids still arguing, and the parents still looking harassed and the girl still hanging behind and having as little to do with them as possible.

I feel sorry for her.

"Jesus," says Gerry, "I sure earned my money with that lot."

We sit there for a while to recover. Then Gerry unhooks the motor from the back of *Piranha* and locks it away in a small tin shed, not much bigger than a cupboard. The sun is right down below the trees and the sky is orange and yellow and pink.

Gerry asks me if I want to come to the pub with him, but I say that I think Dina will be expecting me for dinner. "Lamb, by any chance?" he asks. I say that I wouldn't be surprised. He looks at me sympathetically.

When we get back to the bend in the road by the cottage, Gerry stops the bike and lets me off. I ask him if he's going to come in but he says he's off to the pub, and that anyway he's had enough sheep meat to last him some time.

As I set off down the track, Harry comes running out of the gloom to meet me. It is my imagination of does he look a bit disappointed that Gerry isn't with me? Dina certainly does, though she does her best to hide it.

I tell her Gerry has gone to the pub, and she says, "Well, he might have asked us."

I don't tell her that he did ask me.

"What did you think of the hat?" she adds.

I don't really know what to say.

We're sitting in the garden and the stars are out before she remembers that Mum phoned earlier while I was out. "She said she'll call back in a couple of days."

"But why didn't she call me on my mobile? She knows I've nearly always got it with me."

There's silence for a moment and then Dina says, "Look, I

didn't ask for her number in California but maybe 1471 works internationally. Shall we try it? Maybe you could call her back."

"No thanks. It doesn't matter."

"Are you sure, Nick? It won't cost much, so don't worry about that."

"No, I'm sure. It's fine. I'll speak to her in a couple of days. Thanks."

I don't feel much like talking this evening and after a bit I tell Dina that I'm going to get an early night.

She asks me if I'm OK and I say that I am.

So I leave her in the garden with her twenty-seventh glass of red wine.

I get a text from Billy in Kenya. He says that they saw elephants today. I decide not to text him about my rudd. It probably wouldn't have that much impact all those miles away in Africa. And I don't suppose Jack would care much either. In his mind, a rudd's probably not much competition for Emily.

As I'm lying in bed, Dina's still in the garden. I can smell the smoke from her cigarette.

After a bit, I get up and creep to the window. I can't see anything except the glowing tip of her fag. When she drags on it, the end lights up and I can just make out her face in the darkness. She looks very thoughtful. And a bit sad, although I may be imagining it.

. . . .
Mother... . . .
. . . . is very proud of her hands, even though
they are red and cracked.
Sometimes the skin peels off them in tiny white flakes.
. . .
In the winter, when it's cold, cracks appear round her knuckles.
Which open and bleed.
But mother doesn't seem to notice.
She says that her hands are very elegant and that she has the
fingers of a duchess, only dirtier.
. . . . . . That they are perfect for wearing diamond rings.
And she flexes them out in front of her as if she is playing the piano.
I know she is joking. But I still think she is proud of them.

. . . .
She doesn't touch us very often.
Maybe because her hands are painful... . . .

. . . .
She is a private person.
She keeps herself to herself.
It's as if she's keeping something closed up inside...
But sometimes...
when we are sitting at the table...
she will rest her hand on the back of mine − just for a moment.
. . .
It's her way of making sure I understand or keeping my
attention...

. . . .
. . . . . .
I want to say that her touch is softer than any duchess.
But I don't.

. . . . . .
. . .
We don't say things like that in our family.

. . . .
. . .

Such a loser

As soon as I wake up I know that things are different. For a start, I'm freezing. The quilt has slipped off the bed and I'm shivering.

The light's gloomy and there's a terrific noise outside like a train roaring through the garden.

I get out of bed, wrap the quilt round my shoulders, and stumble to the window. I can hardly believe what I'm seeing. The sky is purple and the rain is lashing down in huge drops. There are pink and white petals scattered across the lawn like confetti. And worst of all, the wind is howling in from the sea, screaming past the corner of the cottage, rattling the windows and bending the trees and shrubs in the garden almost to the ground.

There's no Harry, although I can see that his old deck-chair has been blown over.

What about the swallow chicks?

All at once, I feel like I'm right on the edge of panicking.

Of course, there's no sign of the parent birds. How could there be? Even they couldn't cope with this wind. Maybe the babies are dead already.

I pull on some clothes and run downstairs. My heart feels like it's going to burst through my chest.

There's no sign of Dina, but I haven't got time to wonder why as I run into the garden.

It's like a nightmare. I'm wet through the moment I step out of the door. The noise of the wind is even louder out here and the rain is blowing straight into my face and stinging my eyes. The ground is soaking and squelchy and every step I take towards the shed, it's as though the ground is trying to suck me down.

It's like being in one of those dreams in which you are in a hurry to get somewhere but the more you run, the further away you seem to be. But at least in a dream you can force yourself to wake up.

It's pitch dark in the shed, but even while I'm shaking the water out of my hair and wiping my eyes, I can hear the rain dripping through the roof and onto the concrete floor. As my eyes get used to the dark, I can make out the parent birds huddled together on one of the beams, wet and shivering and looking miserable.

I want to shout at them. To scream at the top of my voice, "How can you be so bloody stupid? How can you sit there while your babies are in the nest and need you? What's wrong with you? You're supposed to be looking after them. You're not supposed to sit there feeling sorry for yourselves."

I grab the ladder and go outside again. As I climb it, the wind threatens to blow me off sideways.

Some of the paper I stuffed in between the cracks has just gone, vanished. It could be a hundred miles away by now. The rest of it is soaking and beginning to come apart. I know I shouldn't, but I can't help myself, and lift one of the tiles directly above the nest. The babies are lying in the bottom of the nest, their stumpy feathers are wet, and they're not really moving, just trembling slightly. As I lift the tile and even more rain sloshes down on them, one of the chicks lifts its head a little as if it's trying to see why the sky has suddenly got lighter. But it hasn't got the strength.

I know that they are all going to die, but I don't have the first idea what I can do about it.

I want to scoop them up and put them inside my shirt to keep them warm. But I know that's no good, because the parent birds would almost certainly abandon them once they've been in contact with humans.

For a minute I even think about picking up the whole nest and running with it back into the cottage where at least I could keep the chicks warm. But I know that if I did that, the nest would fall to bits and that would be the end of everything.

It's no good. The chicks have to stay where they are and if the parents aren't able to feed them in this weather, then all I can do is keep them as warm and dry as possible. I jam the tile back into place and squeeze some sodden magazine pages into the gaps around it. Part of me notices that wet paper is actually better at filling cracks than dry paper. But that isn't really much consolation.

I come down the ladder, hardly noticing the wind anymore and run back into the cottage for more magazines. I'm forcing pages as hard as I can into some of the smaller cracks that I hadn't bothered with when the weather was hot, when Dina's voice startles me so much I nearly fall off the ladder.

"What can I do to help?" she shouts.

I look down and she's standing at the bottom of the ladder with Harry. She's wearing some kind of old jacket which is wet through and her hair is plastered to her face. Harry looks like one bundle of misery. It would be funny if it wasn't so terrible.

"I don't know," I scream down at her. "They're soaked and freezing and I don't know what do."

Upset as I am, I notice that Dina hasn't asked me what I'm doing or told me not to be so silly and get in out of the rain. She hasn't said that they're only birds. Just asked if she can help. I feel a tightness in my chest.

"Do you suppose cotton wool might help?" she yells into the gale.

I don't know. But it might.

She goes back to the cottage and fetches a box of cotton wool pads. Then she climbs up the first few rungs of the ladder and passes it up to me. As she hands them to me, I touch her fingers which are freezing.

I lift the tile again, and reach my arm through and push the cotton wool pads around the edge of the nest. Surely the parents won't abandon their babies because of this. When I'm finished, you can hardly see the chicks for the mass of cotton wool. Then I push the tile back into place for what seems like the fiftieth time this morning and pack the edges with fresh pages, which are already soaking.

Then I work my way round the roof again, forcing in a few extra sheets of paper here and there. Dina and Harry continue to stand at the bottom of the ladder looking up. Dina doesn't say anything. I guess she knows there's nothing she can do, but she wants to be supportive. And just having her standing there does help in some weird way.

After about half an hour, I reach a point where I can't get any more paper into any more cracks. There's nothing else I can do.

When I get to the bottom of the ladder, Dina puts her arm around my shoulder and says – pretty quietly by her standards – "Come on, let's get some breakfast." Harry also looks as if he feels sorry for me and sniffs my hand and then licks it.

We head back to the cottage. Dina's arm is still on my shoulder and Harry is walking on the other side, so close that his body keeps touching my leg.

Dina suggests that I go and have a hot shower, while she goes to change her clothes.

At breakfast, she tells me that she and Harry have been to open a couple of the sluice gates to let some of the water out of the ditches to make sure that the marsh doesn't flood. The owner is somewhere in North Africa on holiday and she's looking after it for him.

She says that when she and Harry came back and saw me on

the shed roof with the wind howling round me, it was a bit like a book by some bloke called Thomas Hardy. She says that I'm a proper little Gabriel Oak.

I don't know what this means but I can tell that she's trying to cheer me up. I try to smile but it doesn't come out right.

"Dina, I'm just so worried they're going to die. It's so unfair. They were fine yesterday when the weather was good. And the stupid parent birds don't seem to be doing anything for them."

I can tell she's thinking about how to react to this. In the end, she says, "Well, you've done what you can. More than most people would have done. We'll just have to wait and see. I think you've been brilliant." Which seems a bit weak really.

I'm sure I can smell whisky in her coffee.

Dina says she's not going to work this morning, she has to go into town for the usual "few bits that we need" (presumably tobacco bits and alcohol bits). She asks if I want to go with her, but I say no. I know there's nothing I can do, but I want to stay here with the birds.

I sit at the table and watch the rain coming down and the wind making a mess of the garden and the sky seems to get even darker.

I hear the pick-up truck screech down the lane.

Harry comes wandering back into the room. He looks as fed up as I feel. He sits by my feet and puts his head on my lap so I can stroke his ears. But he doesn't say anything. Just sighs.

I keep thinking that the weather must get better, but it doesn't. The rain is just as heavy, but instead of blowing in gusts, the wind is just about continuous. A few ragged birds, crows or pigeons, are blown across the sky.

I'm not sure who I feel sorrier for, me or the swallows.

After about an hour, I hear a truck on the path. But it isn't Dina, it's the postman. He's wearing shorts and obviously wants to chat, but after a couple of minutes he gives up on me and heads off. There's quite a lot of post for Dina, some of which has a Cambridge University postmark on it. And there's a postcard for me.

It's from Gran.

> "Darling Nick, the three old bags are having a marvellous time in Italy. Every restaurant we go to, the waiters fall in love with us and beg us to marry them and stay in Italy forever. In the morning we get our fix of culture – churches and art galleries – before it gets too hot. In the afternoon, we toast our wrinkles by the hotel pool. I can't tell you what we get up to in the evenings. I know how easily shocked you are. I hope you are having a good time and I'm really looking forward to your coming to stay when I get back. Please give my best wishes to Dina.
> Hugest Love, Gran XXX (if you're not too big)."

I don't know what to feel. This postcard doesn't seem to have anything to do with me at the moment. It's like a message from another galaxy. Greetings, Earthlings.

On the front of the postcard is a picture of the cathedral at Siena. A bright, white building bathed in sunshine, with a clear blue sky behind it.

I hold the postcard up to the window, where it makes a tiny, pathetic oblong of blue and white against the black sky.

It's like some horrible joke. Like it's taunting me. Taking the piss.

If the weather was like that here, there would be no problem. If the birds were in Italy, rather than this terrible place, there'd be no problem. The parents would be skimming around the cathedral's tower, enjoying the sunshine, collecting food for their chicks. If I was in California with Mum and Dad, I would never have known about these birds in the first place.

I'm really angry. I rip the postcard into pieces and then screw the pieces into a ball in my fist. I jump up from the table – nearly knocking Harry over – and stuff the torn bits of card into the rubbish bin in the kitchen.

Immediately, I feel worse. It wasn't Gran's fault; she was trying to be nice and funny. She couldn't have known what would be happening here. I feel as though I've let her down. I also feel that I've let myself down. I've behaved stupidly; like a baby. Tearing up that card was just as babyish as stamping my feet or banging my head against the wall. I hate myself for it, but I also feel as though I've let Mum and Dad down. If they'd seen me tear up the card, they probably wouldn't have said anything. Just done their disappointed bit. It would be another reason for them to be together on their own.

This time it is Dina. In the back of the pick-up is an old paraffin stove that she's borrowed from someone she knows in town and she's even managed to buy a large tin of paraffin.

We unload it and carry it into the shed. Dina fills it with paraffin and then lights it with a "whoomph" sound. It smells terrible but Dina says that doesn't matter because there's plenty of ventilation and that the place will soon start to warm up.

I can hardly believe that a grown-up would go to so much trouble for some baby birds in a shed. I have this ridiculous urge to hug her. But, of course, I don't give in to it.

The parent birds are still huddled together on the rafter and they can hardly be bothered to look at us while all this is going on. Stupid. Stupid.

After lunch, the rain eases off but it's still windy and cold. Dina says we should go for a walk on the beach. I say that I'd rather stay here but she kind of insists. She says that she doesn't think there's any point in hanging around all day. That a walk would be good for us (I think she means me). And that we won't be gone long.

So we go to the beach, but when we get there it's awful.

The sky is still the colour of slate and the sea is only a little lighter. Huge waves are running up the beach and there are dirty, oily-looking piles of seaweed and plastic bottles and bits of rubbish everywhere. A few miserable gulls are cluttering up the beach. The sand is whipping up and blowing into our faces. You have to screw your eyes up to be able to see at all.

The place where we've spent all these peaceful dreamy afternoons, is being ripped to shreds by the weather. And the sea that has been whispering to me so gently, is now rampaging all over the place and has nothing at all to say to me.

I hate it.

Harry, on the other hand, seems to love it. He races up and down the beach as fast as his old legs will carry him, with his ears tucked back and his eyes shining. He grabs a plastic bottle with his teeth and wrestles with it, ramming it into the sand and then tossing it into the air over his shoulder.

He even runs into the waves – the first time I've seen him do this. But he soon comes out when one knocks him flying. He dashes up the beach and shakes himself angrily and then he's off chasing plastic bottles again.

When we get back, I check the shed, but nothing's changed.

Before supper, Dina makes an announcement. "Today is officially a two drinks day. You can either have two beers or a beer and a glass of wine."

This is the first time we've had supper indoors and for some reason I feel shy with Dina in a way that I don't when we're eating in the dark garden, but the two tiny beers help a bit.

Dina asks me about yesterday and whether I had a good time with Gerry.

I tell her about the family with the out of control kids and what Gerry said about earning his money.

And then we start to talk about families.

Sometimes, it's really easy to see what's going on in people's heads. When Dina asks me if I'd like to ring Mum and Dad this evening, I can tell that she must be feeling sorry for me.

I say that it's OK and that Mum will probably call in the next couple of days.

But Dina doesn't want to leave it at that. She's got a cigarette in one hand and a glass of wine in the other and she's all set for what grown-ups like to think of as "a good talk."

Which, in my experience, are usually anything but good. And this evening's no exception.

"Are you missing your parents, Nick?"

"Not really. I'm used to them being away. I go and stay with Gran a lot."

"It's not really my business, but would you like to spend more time with them?"

I can't think what to say. Part of me wants to tell her about what it's like not to exist. About being the one who's always left behind. The other half of me – this is how stupid I am – wants to make excuses for my parents, explain why it's necessary for them to do so many things on their own, without me. The pressure of Dad's work and all that rubbish.

There are so many things that I want to say that I can't say anything.

And then suddenly, without any warning, before I know it, I start to cry.

These huge tears are rolling down my cheeks.

It happens so suddenly, that I don't even have time to pretend I need to go outside for a shit or that my shoe-lace needs tying. I can't seem to move. Just sit here blubbing. Not even covering my face.

It must be the double ration of beer.

Poor Dina. Here she is sitting opposite this kid she's had landed on her. She has to feed and entertain him. And how does he repay her? Sits at supper crying his heart out. At this moment, she must be particularly glad that she agreed to me coming to stay. Not.

In fact, she looks really worried.

"Nick, I'm so sorry, I didn't mean to upset you."

I'm so busy trying to get the tears under control that I can't trust myself to say anything. I'm such a loser.

In the end, Dina drags her chair round to my side of the table and puts both her arms round me.

Part of me wants to make a run for it. But the other part wins and I put my head on her shoulder.

She's wearing an old, checked work shirt made of some rough material, which scrapes my face. She smells of fags and booze and sweat. And I can feel her bones through her shirt. We sit here, not saying anything, for a bit. Even when I stop crying I stay where I am, caught in Dina's bony embrace. It's not as bad as I would have imagined – if I had ever imagined such a thing. Which I didn't.

After a while, we have to make a decision: stay here with her arms around me forever, or move.

"Pub time," says Dina in a voice that must be making the slates rattle on the roof.

I think we're both relieved to get away from the table. But it wasn't that bad, even if a bit strange.

Just for a change, Gerry is pissed. And he's got his hat on.

I'm all for pretending we've never seen him before in our lives, but Dina marches straight over to sit with him and the loonies. We've arrived just in time to hear Gerry tell one of his stories. (In fact, I reckon that whatever time you arrived tonight it would be just in time to hear Gerry tell one of his stories.)

In the time it takes him to down another pint, Gerry tells us the story of the Brazilian three banded armadillo.

When he was in Brazil, he says, he stayed in a cheap hotel in Sao Paolo. The hotel had a veranda right the way round it, and in the evenings he and the other back-packers used to sit out talking and drinking. So, no change there. The place was lit by candles in large glass lanterns.

Every night just before midnight, this armadillo used to trot onto the veranda, slapping its back legs on the boards. Gerry says that it looked like an animated football and that this was odd behaviour for such a solitary animal.

Anyway, the reason that it came was for the insects. Every time a particularly large insect – a cricket, a beetle or a cockroach – crashed into one the lanterns and fell stunned onto the ground, the armadillo would amble over to it on tippy-toes and swallow it. After two or three hours and several hundred insects, it was twice the size it was when it arrived.

But the best bit, says Gerry, was that it was so stuffed with food that it would allow itself to be picked up. It would sit on Gerry's knee, making no attempt to escape, as if it wanted to join in the conversation. If you put your ear close to it – and he swears that this is true – you could hear the doomed insects fluttering inside it. That its shell was acting as a kind of echo chamber.

He says that when he put it back down on the ground, it was so stuffed that it could hardly walk, and rolled its way back into the shadows. The loonies love this story and express their appreciation by offering to buy him more pints and making roll-ups for him.

He just sits there looking pleased with himself.

It occurs to me that he's so full of beer that he's a bit like the Brazilian three banded armadillo. But if you put your ear close to him (and that probably wouldn't be a good idea), it's not fluttering you'd hear but sloshing and gurglings.

Dina, on the other hand, isn't looking very happy. I think I know why.

"When were you in Brazil?" she asks him.

"Oh, four or five years ago," he says carelessly.

"Funny that you've never mentioned it before."

I can see where this conversation is going, but I don't think it's a good idea.

"And how did you get there?"

The loonies are a bit subdued now. Even they've noticed that something is up.

But not Gerry.

"By plane, it was too far to cycle."

Not a good answer.

I'm hoping that Dina will drop it but she doesn't.

"And where did you fly from?"

This is beginning to sound like an interrogation. And it doesn't seem to me like Gerry's in the mood to be interrogated.

"From Heathrow."

By now, everyone round the table has gone quiet. You can feel the tension.

"But you said you'd never been to London."

"Well, says Gerry with this nasty smile on his face, "I must have been speaking metaphorically, don't you think. A clever person like you with all those degrees must know about speaking metaphorically."

I can't understand why he's being like this.

He looks straight at Dina as if challenging her to make something of it.

No one else knows where to look. Even Harry, curled up at Gerry's feet, seems embarrassed.

I'm really hoping that Dina won't make a fuss, I get the feeling that Gerry would enjoy that.

In the end, she tries to smooth things over. She forces a smile and says, "It's just that I'm surprised you never mentioned Brazil before. You know that I've been there and yet you haven't talked to me about it."

"That's me," says Gerry stupidly, "international man of mystery."

This gives us all the chance to laugh, which we do, gratefully. But the mood round the table is still uneasy.

I have to go through the other bar to get to the toilet. And there are the awful families from yesterday – minus the youngest ones, thank God. The girl of about my age is with them, looking a bit fed up. She sees me looking at her and looks straight into my eyes. I smile and she smiles back. I wouldn't have expected to see them in The Strangled Ferret, but then there aren't many pubs to choose from around here. And no wine bars at all.

I'm only back in my seat a few minutes when Dina says, "Right everybody, we're off. Are you coming, Gerry."

Maybe she doesn't know it but there's a challenging sound in her voice. I know, even if she doesn't, that Gerry won't be coming with us.

"No thanks, Dina. I've got an early start tomorrow. See you in a few days."

I guess Dina doesn't really want to leave, but she doesn't have any choice.

In the pick-up on the way back, she doesn't have much to say for herself. I'm trying to think of things to talk about but can't come up with much.

Dina comes with me to check the shed. Although the wind is dropping, it's still cold outside. But the shed is warm and moist and stinks of paraffin. Droplets of moisture run down the broken panes of the window.

There's no sign of the parent birds, but in the torchlight we can see bits of cotton wool scattered all over the floor, where they've been chucked out of the nest.

Dina thinks this may be a good sign and that the adult birds are back on the nest. I'm not so sure. Maybe they're just refusing to be helped.

I'm in bed with an extra blanket (which I'm definitely not going to throw out of my nest) and the wind is still gusting against the window. I can't stop thinking about the birds. And I can't stop thinking about Dina who is still sitting at the kitchen table and has just lit another fag.

When Revenant Broad freezes, the crust of ice is
the same colour as the sky.
If you walk on it,
it seems to vibrate like a violin string.
If you throw a stone onto the ice, it strikes with a high ringing note,
which travels outwards towards the edge, getting lower as it travels.
By the time it reaches the dead reeds at the edge of the broad, the
sound is nothing more than a low hum...

...

Father breaks the ice with a long wooden pole with a metal spike
on the end.
He's creating open water for the ducks and geese.
As he hits it, the ice rings like a bell.
As soon as he carves out a few yards of open water, the ducks and
geese waddle across the ice and jam themselves in.
They look like they are lined up on a butcher's slab.
It's as though they are huddling together for warmth...
Sometimes father throws them a few handfuls of grain.

... ...

Grandfather says that when he was a boy, it was so cold and all
the birds were so hungry that they lost their fear of people.
Owls and harriers sat on people's roofs in miserable rows,
waiting to pounce on any scraps...

... ...

Some even tried to get into houses and shops...
Grandfather says that he was fishing one morning when he felt a
tap on his back.

...

He turned round
and a skinny bittern was trying to get its beak into his pocket
where he was keeping the bread that he was using for bait...

Charley

I don't sleep well and the noise of the wind seems to get into my dreams. I keep thinking that Mum and Dad are coming to get me in an aeroplane and that they are trying to land in Dina's garden. As the wind roars, the plane just circles round and round.

This morning, the rain has stopped, but the wind is, if anything, even stronger than yesterday. It's still cold. The garden's a mess and, of course, there's no sign of the swallows.

Dina's at the kitchen table as usual, fag on as usual. But she's quieter than usual. I know I ought to be more sympathetic but I'm just so worried about the chicks.

I'm shivering as I walk across the wet grass to the shed. The parents are still huddled together on the rafter, but they don't look quite as wet and bedraggled as they did yesterday.

I can hear the chicks peeping frantically, so they're still alive. But no thanks to their stupid parents. When did they last eat? How long can they go without food?

I fill the stove with paraffin and re-light it – but there doesn't seem to be much else I can do to help.

On my way to breakfast I check the roof but, as far as I can tell, the newspaper is doing its job and holding together. This feels like the first good news I've had in ages.

Other than that, it's a shit morning.

Dina is obviously unhappy and doesn't say much. Just sucks on her ciggie and looks out of the window. Then she says she'd better get on with some work but she doesn't sound as if she's looking forward to it very much.

For the first time since I got here, I don't know what to do with myself.

I think of taking Harry for a walk but he's lying on the rug carefully avoiding eye contact. He's making it as clear as possible without being rude that he has no interest in leaving the house.

I suppose I'll have to read a book to make the time pass. But I'm sick to death of old Captain Watkins and his dead cows. I need something else.

I ask Dina if I can get something from her shelves and she tells me to help myself.

Most of the books seem to be about the landscape or about animals and plants. She's got David Attenborough's *Life of Birds*, which I remember seeing on TV and something called *Meetings with Remarkable Trees*, whatever that means. There are pamphlets about local nature reserves and churches and loads of Ordnance Survey maps. But no novels.

I suppose it's asking a lot to think that Dina might have the latest Chris Ryan or Minette Walters.

Right at the end of one of the shelves I find a beaten up looking red hardbacked exercise book. It's the wrong shape – wider than it is tall, like a sketch book. On the front cover is a yellowing label with *A Year At Revenant Broad (1896)* written in faded black curly handwriting.

Inside, I see it's a diary with the months and days marked off in tiny, perfect writing. There are also lots of little ink drawings of birds. I don't know how accurate they are, but it's like – I don't know how to say it – whoever drew these pictures was looking at real birds in real situations, not just remembering them or copying them out of a book.

I ask Dina about it and she says that Gerry found it at a local jumble sale and gave it to her as a present. "It seems to have been written by the man who was the chief gamekeeper on Revenant Broad at the end of the nineteenth century. Back then, the whole Revenant estate was owned by Lord Osley who used to come here for the shooting a couple of times a year. The man who kept this diary must have worked for him. Gerry thinks it's interesting because he's working on the broad now and says they sort of have the same job. A lot of the book is lists of the birds they shot, but our man seems also to have been interested in birds for their own sake. Why not see what you make of it? But be careful, some of the pages are loose."

I open the book carefully on the kitchen table. There are dozens of drawings, a few of which are coloured in with watercolour paint. Each picture is labelled. A grey and yellow bird on a branch is a siskin: *"a winter visitor to Revenant Broad."* There's a green sandpiper standing on the sand. There are Bewick's swans and yellowhammers, snipe and a black-necked grebe, *"a visitor from Europe."*

There's an entry for most days of the year. On 1 January 1896, the wind was blowing from the north west and there were squalls of hail. Almost a year later, on Christmas day, the wind was from the west and there was heavy rain all day.

In fact, the weather seems to have been awful for the first few months of 1896. There are lots of references to frosts and freezing rain and thick mists and snow falls.

On 21 February, he reports that Revenant Broad has been frozen solid for ten days and that the ice is now several inches thick.

A lot of the diary seems to be about running the estate. The writer's job seems to have been to encourage migrating birds to visit Revenant Broad to provide winter shooting for someone he describes as *"Lord O"* – presumably Lord Osley. He also was responsible for rearing partridges.

And Lord O and his mates seem to have shot pretty much anything that flew, and probably pretty much anything that didn't as well. Lots of the entries are about how many guns there were on that day and the different bags of pochard ducks, mute swans, mallards and even moorhens (although it's not made clear why anyone would want to shoot a moorhen).

They also used to shoot coots. The writer of the diary reports thousands of coots arriving one night when the moon was full. He says that when he went to bed there were only a few on the broad, but when he woke up, there were so many that he could hardly see the water.

Apparently this was the signal for anyone posh enough to get taken out on a boat and blast enormous numbers of them. There's a drawing of a man sitting down in some kind of boat with his gun to his shoulder. I hope he fell in, but I don't suppose he did and I guess that was why he was sitting down and not standing.

Apart from this, the rest of the diary seems to be about birds that weren't being shot. I think the writer must have been an early form of twitcher. Most of the entries are pretty dull (unless, I suppose, you happen to be a twitcher yourself). On 17 March, the entry is, *"Saw a bittern near the house."* On 21 June he saw an adult black tern on Revenant Broad. And so on.

But some are a bit more dramatic. On 18 August he watched a marsh harrier eating a coot and on 15 November was startled to see a grey shrike grab a blue tit.

He seems to have been an odd mix this bloke: sometimes enticing birds to the broad so that they could be blown to bits by chinless wonders from London, but at other times coming over all sensitive and caring about small brown birds that only he could identify.

I spend a couple of hours looking through the diary, hoping to find something that might help me look after the swallow chicks. But, of course, there's nothing.

At lunch Dina's still sad. I want to cheer her up but I don't really know what to say. What with me crying last night and Dina

75

looking as though she might burst into tears now and the swallow chicks dying of hypothermia, this really is turning out to be some kind of holiday.

We talk about this and that, and we don't mention Gerry's name.

Then Dina tells me that we've been invited to tea with Brenda the lady in the shop but that I "don't have to go if you don't want to." Well, of course I don't want to. There's almost nothing that I can think of that I'd like to do less – apart from more karaoke in the Ferret. But I can't bring myself to say any of this.

I may only score about one out of ten on the cheerfulness scale but if I go then at least Dina won't have to go alone. I could be wrong, but I feel that she would prefer it if I went.

This is not a situation I find myself in very often with Mum and Dad, so how am I expected to deal with it? "Yes," I say, "I'd love to come." Even I can tell that I need to work on the sincerity a bit, but Dina seems pleased. "Great, you'll be able to meet Charley Maddox, which can be an interesting experience."

Dina takes the pick-up but I decide to take the bike. We leave Harry at home. This is the first time he's been left behind since I arrived, but he doesn't seem to mind. Maybe he sees this as a chance to catch up on his sleep.

Now, Norfolk is supposed to be one of the least populated counties in UK but today it seems I can't step out of doors without running into someone.

I've only got a couple of hundred yards down the road towards the village, battling against the wind, when I see the girl with red hair coming towards me on a bike.

This is embarrassing, but I can't really just cycle past and pretend I haven't seen her. I can't just say good afternoon and go on my way.

So we stop and say hello but I can't think what to say next.

Fortunately, she doesn't seem to have the same problem. "I'm cycling to the beach," she says, "is it far?"

"No," I say wittily, "it's about a mile up this road."

She has a really nice voice – soft and confident – and her eyes are nearly as blue as Dina's. Is this unusual with red hair?

She says that she loves cycling in a gale and then she says, "Sorry about the other day."

Me: "Eh?"

"I mean about the way my brothers and cousins behaved on the boat the other day. Not that my parents were much better."

"Oh, that's OK. I didn't mind, although Gerry was a bit fed up."

"They're always like that. Always fighting and arguing. Never listen to what anyone is saying. And my parents and my uncle and aunt don't seem to be able to control them. Do you work on that boat every day?"

"What? No, I don't work on it at all. Gerry, the bloke I was with – my aunt's boyfriend – works on the nature reserve. I was just there for the ride."

"Sometimes I get so fed up with my family, can't get a moment's peace, that I feel I just have to get away for a bit. That's why I'm here now, escaping from my family. Even though the weather's so terrible."

"It's the opposite in our house; my family are always trying to escape from me." I wish I hadn't said this. It just slipped out before I knew it. But she just laughs and doesn't ask me to explain.

There's a bit of a pause.

Then she says, "What's the beach like then?"

"It's really nice when the weather's OK." Sometimes my way with words amazes me.

It looks like this conversation might be over.

In a final attempt to make myself interesting, I tell her that I'm staying at my aunt's cottage. "You'll pass it on the right in a minute or so, but you won't be able to see it because it's tucked back off the road."

So why am I telling her about it? There are plenty of things that she won't be able to see on her right. The Taj Mahal for instance, and the Empire State Building. The pyramids at Giza. The maze at Hampton Court.

"Its garden backs onto about 60 acres of marsh. We've got a marsh harrier and rudd in the ditches." God, this sounds lame. I sound like the bloke who kept the diary. I wouldn't want to get stuck in a lift with me.

"It sounds lovely."

"Would you like to come and see it?" Why did I say this? Of course, she's going to say no.

"Yes, please. I'd like that."

"Well, what about tomorrow afternoon?"

"That would be great. We're going on some trip in the morning – more opportunities for the kids to misbehave – but I could get here around 4 o'clock. Where should I come to?"

"A bit further along, you'll find a gravel path going off to the right, that's if my aunt hasn't squirted all the gravel into the field by then. Turn down there and the cottage is on your left. We'll hear you coming."

"Great, see you tomorrow then. And now I'm going to find that beach."

We set off in our separate directions.

"By the way," she calls over her shoulder, "I'm Rachel."

"I'm Nick," I yell back in a voice that Dina would be proud of.

As I pass the old school on my way to the shop, I see a kid in the playground.

He's all on this own. Not playing football or anything, just seems to be hanging around.

He looks about ten years old and his hair has been cut so short that he's almost bald. He's wearing old clothes and looks pretty dirty from where I am. He's probably the kid of some hippy family or other, there seem to be plenty of them judging by The Strangled Ferret's customers. They probably think it's encouraging self-expression never to wash his clothes. Certainly, the way he looks shows how little they must care about appearances.

He must have heard the bike because he walks to the fence and lifts his head up to look straight at me. His face is as dirty as the rest of him. As he looks at me this slow smile spreads across his face and he lifts his right arm to wave at me.

I wave back and shout "hiya" but I've got no intention of stopping. The conversation with Rachel was intense enough for one afternoon and I'm already beginning to regret having asked her.

Poor kid, he's probably got no one to play with. I can feel his eyes still fixed on me as I cycle past.

Dina's right, meeting Mr Maddox – Charley – is a bit of an experience. A pretty strange experience.

When I get to the shop, Mrs Maddox is selling a bottle of lemonade to an old lady. What is it with these people? Life here seems like one long children's tea party, but without the peanut butter sandwiches.

"Hello, my lovely," she says, "just hang on while I deal with Mrs Owen."

It only takes Mrs Owen about an hour and a half to extract a pound coin from her purse, discover to her amazement that it's not enough, rummage around in her bag again, pull out her keys, some old tissues, some battered photographs, a couple of envelopes, a tube of Polo's, a biro, a small mirror, a plastic flower (I swear this is true), some more keys, a length of string, a lipstick (what can she want a lipstick for?) and a battered fiver, pay Mrs Maddox, witter on about the weather, put her change down on the counter and then pick it up again, take her purse out of her bag, put the change in it and then put it back in her bag (all in slow motion) say goodbye to Mrs Maddox and then to me, put her bag down on the counter and pick it up again, look confused and then allow herself to be escorted to the door by Mrs Maddox who has come round from behind the counter to hold her arm, say goodbye to Mrs Maddox and to me again and finally, slowly, hesitatingly, reluctantly, infuriatingly to leave.

Mrs Maddox closes the door behind her and locks it, smiles at me and flips round the sign in the window so that it displays CLOSED to any other ancient locals with a sweet tooth.

I think she's going to pull a face or make some joke about the old lady who's just left. But she doesn't.

"There," she says, "all set?"

I'm not really clear about what she's asking me, so I just smile.

"Come on and meet the most useless old geezer you've ever clapped eyes on."

We go through the door behind the counter, through a room with two old armchairs and hundreds of boxes marked "Beans" and "Weetabix" and "Pot Noodles" and "Garden Peas", through another door and into the garden.

The garden is long and narrow, with stepping stones laid out on a lawn. At the end of the garden is a summer-house which, for some reason, has been painted bright purple.

There are beds either side of the path, but instead of flowers, they are full of fruit and vegetables – sweetcorn, runner beans, raspberries and a tall lacy plant which looks a bit like the cannabis leaves you see on people's T-shirts. It occurs to me that the Maddoxes probably don't eat much of the stuff they sell in the shop.

Brenda takes me into the summer-house. Dina is talking to a very old man. It's hardly worth mentioning that he's very thin and very brown with very blue eyes and looks very tall – his knees are almost under his chin and the faded armchair he's sitting in looks too small for him. It's beginning to seem like Dina only knows people who look like her.

He's got very long white hair, tied in a pony tail, three or four gold hoops in each ear and he's wearing some kind of faded blue smock.

He and Dina have already started on their tea, which appears to come in a bottle with the words "Sauvignon Blanc" on the label.

Brenda says, "Darling, this is Nick. Nick this is Charley Maddox, my beloved husband and help-mate. We've been married for almost 40 years and I'm still trying to find out what he's good for. See what you can make of him."

I notice that as she's saying this, her eyes are fixed on his face and that she's smiling in that daft way that Dina and Harry look at Gerry. It's a hideous thought, but she's obviously in love with this wizened old bloke. It must be something in the water around here.

For some reason, Charley Maddox decides to stand up to shake hands with me. This is a more complicated operation than it sounds. For a start, it takes him about half an hour. First he shuffles back in his seat, then he grips the arms of the chair with both hands, and then slowly, ever so slowly, he starts to move, part pushing himself up with his arms, part lifting out of his seat by using his knees. Up and up he goes. First, his head is level with my chest, then with my head and still he keeps going.

For a minute, I think he's going to keep straightening up until his head passes through the roof of the summerhouse. But eventually he stops, with his head a foot above mine. He must be at least six foot six in his bare feet – and he does have bare feet with long crooked toes.

"Pleased to meet you, Nick," he says in a deep voice that sounds as though it's coming from the bottom of a well. And when he smiles, he has the kindest face I've ever seen.

Then he starts to head slowly back into his chair by putting his getting up moves into reverse, although he speeds up the final stages of the process by falling the last couple of feet.

He and Dina go back to the conversation they were having before I arrived. They seem to have been talking about some people who have recently moved in to the village and it's clear that neither Dina nor Charley thinks much of them. In fact, Charley is being incredibly rude about them, and Dina is laughing for the first time since her row with Gerry. "Bloody woman," says Charley, "she couldn't find her bum with both hands."

"That's not very nice," says Brenda as she takes the tin foil off some sandwiches, but I can see that her eyes are laughing.

Charley and Dina don't seem all that bothered about the sandwiches, but Charley does produce another bottle from under his chair and opens it with a silver corkscrew. Brenda says she'll join them in a small glass, "Just to be sociable", a fact which they decide to celebrate with large glasses of their own.

And here we sit, for a couple of hours, chatting about this and that.

At one point, Charley asks me what I think about Norfolk and the Revenant area. Trust me to come up with something original, so I say that I think it's very nice.

"Do you really? I'm not sure that's how I'd put it. I'm not from around these parts, you know. I'm originally from London just like you. I first came here more than 50 years ago and now that I'm stuck with old Brenda here I don't suppose I'll ever get away."

This seems to be Brenda's cue to smile adoringly at him.

"But 'nice' is not how I'd describe it. Interesting, yes. Weird, certainly. Bleak. Scary. Strange. You probably think I'm a silly old bastard ('scuse my French), but things happen here that I don't think happen anywhere else. It's almost like living at a funny angle to life in the rest of the UK. Like another dimension. Because so much of the land used to be under water and has been reclaimed, you can't even trust the ground under your feet. I sometimes think that life on Mars couldn't be any weirder, and this summer seems weirder than any other I can remember but maybe that's just because I've drunk too much and I'm so old that there's hardly anything left of my brain."

And as if to prove the point, he pours himself and Dina another drink. I don't know what he's talking about or what to say. But I'm good at keeping quiet.

Eventually, Dina says we must be off.

She bends down and kisses Charley on both cheeks. He puts his arms round her and I notice that he puts his hand on her bottom on the other side from Brenda so that she won't see. Dina doesn't seem surprised, in fact she doesn't react at all.

"I'd see you to the door," he says, "but by the time we got there, it would be time for you to come and visit again."

We shake hands again, and for someone so old his hand is surprisingly warm and his handshake is as firm as a much younger man's.

"Come back any time." And he smiles.

One the way out, Brenda says to Dina, "Sorry about the hand on the bum bit, but you know what he's like."

They both laugh.

To my surprise, Brenda gives me a hug. This is the second time in two days that I've been hugged by strange women. But whereas Dina is all bony and scratchy, Brenda is soft and plump like a pillow and smells of perfume. Whatever else I'm discovering on this holiday, I'm certainly learning that women come in different shapes and sizes.

It's getting dark as we leave through the front of the shop with the CLOSED sign swinging behind us. The weather has changed. The wind has dropped and it's got warmer.

We load my bike into the back of the pick-up and I climb into the front with Dina. It seems odd to be sitting here without Harry. Dina rolls down the windows, lets out the clutch and we're off, though more slowly than usual.

As we drive through the village, she tells me that Charley Maddox is 92, much older than Brenda who is in her early sixties. He was in his fifties when they married, although she was only just out of her teens. Apparently, he wrote a successful novel in the 1950s and has written a lot of unsuccessful ones since. Before he retired, he taught at a boy's private school near Norwich. He and Brenda bought the shop with his pension money. She runs the shop and he does a bit of gardening, and sits in the summer-house and writes a weekly column called "Country Matters" for the local paper. He gets £20 for a column and he spends the money in the off licence.

As we pass the school, I'm amazed to see that the kid is still in the playground. Hasn't he got anyone to play with? He obviously doesn't hear us though, because he's standing with his back to us, looking out towards the marsh. As we pass, he doesn't turn round.

I think of calling out to him, but decide against it.

There's a strange girl in the village called Betty.
She's about the same age as me and I think she is pretty,
Although she never brushes her hair, which is all tangled...

... ...

She has huge green eyes.
She often walks through the village singing in a clear, thin voice.
Her father is dead and she lives with her mother in the cottage
near the large elm tree....
When I meet her on the lane, she usually turns away and looks at
her feet and passes me without saying a word.
Once, though, she stopped me and asked me...
... she asked me the strangest question:
"Are you alive or dead?"

... ...

"Why do you ask?"
"Because, I've just seen a boy who looks like you in St Mary's
churchyard. He was wearing a blue shirt just like yours."

... ...
..

I know she can't help the things she says,
There's something not quite right in her head.
But it made me shiver.

Common cranes

I can feel the warmth even before I wake up properly. The sun's shining again and, for what seems like the first time in ages, I can't hear the wind.

I go to the window and I see one of the adult swallows dashing around the garden.

It's stupid how happy this makes me. I can almost imagine how the bird feels as it flies in and out of the shadows with the sun on its back. It must seem like it's been dead for two days and now it's come back to life.

I feel so much more cheerful at breakfast that it comes as a bit of a shock to see that Dina is still miserable.

I remember to tell her about Rachel coming round this afternoon and she says we must ask her to tea. I say that will be nice but secretly hope that it won't have anything to do with Sauvignon Blanc.

When I go outside, it's like the terrible weather of the last couple of days never happened. The air is soft and warm and although the garden's a bit of a mess and some of the plants have blown over, it's still full of colour and snoring bees and crackling dragonflies.

I feel like I'm coming back to a place I haven't visited for ages.

More good news in the shed. The air in here is warm and dry and I can hear the chicks squeaking. Somehow they've survived. And then, one of the parents comes in with a mouthful of bugs and swoops down on the nest, pauses for a second and then it's off again, out of the shed door like an arrow. It's wonderful.

Dina is working on her lecture notes, but you can feel her sadness filling the whole cottage. Gerry obviously hasn't called.

I want to do something to cheer her up but I can't think what. She's so private. So self-sufficient.

The sight of Harry rolling on his back in the leaves on the lawn gives me an idea. Maybe I could clear the garden up a bit, Dina would like that.

I head back to the shed for the rake and the wheelbarrow.

I've never really done this sort of stuff before – we only have a small garden in London and Mum and Dad use a company who come in once a month to tidy it up.

I wheel the barrow into the centre of the lawn and then stretch the rake out in from of me as far as it will reach and then pull it back towards me. Its teeth trap all the leaves in its path and as it travels towards me it exposes a strip of perfect grass underneath. It's almost like I'm painting the garden green.

Harry looks a bit surprised, but then he strolls over to the path, flops down on his belly and starts watching me carefully like he can't believe what he's seeing.

I repeat the process – rake out in front of me as far as it will go, pull it slowly back in and reveal another strip of lawn. After a few minutes I've made a kind of star shape with me and a pile of dead leaves at its centre.

All the while, I'm aware of the huge clear sky over my head and the swallows dipping up and down around me.

The next job is to get the leaves into the barrow. As I bend down to grab an armful, a thin golden snake about a foot long shoots out of the pile of leaves.

I jump back in fright, but even so have time to notice that it's exactly the same colour as my rudd.

It wriggles frantically towards the flower beds a couple of yards away. Harry has spotted it. He's also jumped in fright and is now looking anxiously at it.

But by now I've had time to realise what it is. I've seen them on TV. It's a slow worm – there aren't any yellow snakes in Norfolk. It's not even a snake; it's a lizard. It must have been catching some rays on the lawn and then got raked into the pile without me even noticing.

I say most of this to Harry, which proves how nervous I was for those first few seconds.

I've never seen one before. Harry and I watch it disappear into the flowerbed. You can almost feel its sense of relief as it hides itself away.

Then I wheel the barrow over to one of the compost heaps and tip the leaves out. Harry follows along to supervise.

Then we repeat the process a few times until the lawn is pretty well clear.

I'm a bit nervous about doing anything to the flowerbeds, not because of the slow worm but because I don't really know anything about flowers and might do some damage.

In the end, I decide to stake up some of the larger plants that have been blown down.

As I go into the shed to look for some canes, one of the swallows flies right over my shoulder, almost touching me before it disappears into the nest.

Staking up the plants is not as easy as it sounds. I may not know anything about gardening but even I realise that Dina is not the sort of gardener who likes everything in straight, neat rows. The trouble with tying flowers up is that they stand up like soldiers and look completely unnatural.

In the end, I tie slip knots in the thick green string I found with the canes so that I first pull the plants upright and then slowly loosen the loop letting the plant droop down a bit until it looks natural.

The best way to tell if I've got it right is to try to look at the bed as a whole at the same time as letting my eyes slip out of focus. What I see then are patterns and shapes and colours rather than plants. And then if something doesn't look out of place, I leave it as it is.

Dina is really chuffed when she sees what I've done. And, after a couple of awkward movements with her arms, gives me another hug. It's different from the hug she gave me last night. Then she was feeling sorry for me. But today, she's just saying thanks. It's like the kind of hug you'd give a mate... except, of course, that you wouldn't hug a mate, at least I wouldn't.

Dad said that I'd learn a lot in the country, but I don't suppose he meant that I'd learn what different kinds of women feel like and that there are different kinds of hugs for different occasions. Actually, come to think of it, I don't suppose he meant anything at all.

We have lunch (need I say more?) in the garden. It's really hot in the full sun and I start to sweat. Dina doesn't seem to need any shade but she can see that I do. She goes into the house and comes back out with a large, black umbrella, like a giant bat's wing. She obviously doesn't go in for garden furniture.

She opens it up and hands it to me to hold it above my head.

As I sit here in its shade eating lamb meatballs, I reckon I must look like Dina's ancient great-grandmother. All I need is a shawl, a wheelchair and an ear trumpet.

I look at Harry and can see that he's laughing at me. I expect the swallows are giggling to themselves and can hardly wait to tell their babies how ridiculous I look.

After lunch, Dina says that as there are so many leaves in the compost heap, we could have a bonfire.

We cram as many of the leaves as we can into a kind of dustbin with holes drilled in the bottom for ventilation. Dina pours petrol from a can over the leaves and chucks a match in after it. For a moment I think nothing's going to happen but then there's a kind of controlled explosion and the leaves start to crackle and the flames shoot about six feet in the air.

For the next half hour we chuck dead plants and sticks and lawn cuttings and even a few logs into the bonfire until the bin starts to glow red and it gets too hot to go anywhere near it.

Dina looks really excited.

A huge tower of white smoke goes hundreds of feet straight up into the air. The swallows take no notice and fly right through it as though it wasn't there.

"There," says Dina, "we're sending a smoke signal to Rachel. She shouldn't have any difficulty finding us. They can probably see that smoke in Norwich."

My stomach turns over.

I'd completely forgotten that Rachel is supposed to be coming to tea.

Part of me hopes that she won't, even though that would be embarrassing now that I've told Dina about her. The other part of me hopes that she will.

Almost as soon as I have this thought, we hear a voice. "Hello?"

Harry immediately starts barking and runs off across the garden and round the side of the cottage.

When I catch up with him, he's lying at Rachel's feet having his ears tickled. She hasn't even had time to get off her bike; she's having to bend down to reach him.

She looks really nice. She's wearing olive green shorts and a dark blue T-shirt and she's got a baseball cap on.

"Hi," she shouts as I approach, "I'm glad I found you. Is this your dog?"

She takes her hat off and the sun shines in her red hair.

"No, he's my aunt's. Oh, and this is my aunt, Dina. Dina, this is Rachel."

Of course, I'm feeling really shy. But Rachel doesn't seem to be.

"Hello," she says, "thanks for asking me. I think your cottage is lovely."

Dina seems really pleased to see her. Strides over, shakes hands and screeches out a welcome at the top of her voice. I notice that she's got soot on both cheeks.

"Listen, I wanted to bring something, but I didn't know what to get, so in the end I got this from the shop in the village."

It's a sponge cake in a yellow box.

"I thought maybe we could have it for tea."

Dina's managing to look a bit pleased and a bit puzzled at the same time.

"Thanks, it looks lovely."

There's a silence for a moment because all three of us know that it doesn't. It's a Brenda special. All icing and sugar. It's a cake for toothless tractor drivers and old ladies who can't get their money in or out of their purses.

I haven't had a chance to explain to Rachel that Dina doesn't really do food (apart, of course, from sheep meat) – only cigarettes and alcohol.

"Come on round the back," says Dina putting the cake down on the doorstep. "Nick and I have been having a bonfire in the garden and we haven't quite finished. You can leave your bike here."

Rachel comes round and for the next quarter of an hour helps us to throw all the remaining bits and pieces into the dustbin burner which is now throbbing with heat and threatening to explode. She seems to be having a really good time and is nearly as excited by the fire as Dina.

She and Dina seem to have no trouble talking to each other. In five minutes flat, Dina knows about Rachel's family, where she goes to school, what subjects she's doing for her GCSEs and even that she's learning to play the violin, but not getting on very well with it.

91

There's a difficult moment when Rachel mentions meeting me and Gerry on the broad the other day. Dina's face goes a bit tight, but then the moment passes.

Women seem so much better at getting on with each other than men. I'm actually beginning to feel a bit left out.

Once we've burned everything that we can find in the garden, Dina suggests that Rachel might like to see round the cottage.

As we get to the door, there's an enormous red slug sitting right in the middle of the cake box, like some kind of hideous decoration.

"Ah," booms Dina, "*Arion ater*. Well, you're certainly not invited."

She bends down and pokes it with her finger and it immediately contracts into a ball and starts rocking from side to side.

She then flicks it off the box onto the grass. "I know I ought to kill them. The buggers eat half of everything I try to grow. But I just can't bring myself to do it. Besides, they make such a mess when you squash them."

Rachel seems to love the cottage and keeps saying how peaceful it is.

Dina looks pleased and suggests that we go out into the garden again while she prepares tea. "Perhaps you'll be able to manage without the umbrella this time, Nick," she stage whispers to me. Rachel looks a bit surprised and I feel stupid.

It feels odd to be sitting on the garden bench with someone else, although Harry doesn't seem to mind. He collapses and falls deeply asleep at Rachel's feet in a single moment. Rachel seems more comfortable than I am and tells me about her holiday.

She and her family are staying in a cottage in the village. They're here for two weeks and they're just coming to the end of their first week. They usually go abroad to Greece or Spain but Rachel's Mum has had problems with her ears and isn't allowed to fly at the moment.

She has a good moan about how hard they all are to live with and how noisy and badly behaved the younger ones are.

"What did you mean," she asks suddenly, "about your family wanting to run away from you?"

"Did I say that?"

"Yes, when we met yesterday."

For a moment I'm tempted to tell her about Mum and Dad. But I don't want a repetition of the other night with Dina. "Oh, nothing really."

And before she can ask me anything else, I tell her about the swallow chicks and take her to have a look in the shed. Of course, there's not very much to see, but while we're in there an adult bird comes in loaded with insects.

When we get back to the bench, Dina's already waiting for us. And you'll never guess what – there's a glass of wine in her hand.

"Has Nick told you about the swallows? I bet he didn't mention what a hero he was the other morning."

And while she tells Rachel about my attempts to patch up the roof in the pouring rain, I realise that it must be my day for feeling stupid. On days like today, it seems that you just have to put up with it.

Tea, to my amazement, proves to be a lamb-free zone. Dina seems to have put some real effort into it. There are smoked salmon sandwiches, cheese scones and what looks suspiciously like a home-made cake with blackcurrant jam. There are even some Christmas paper napkins. But there's no sign of Rachel's cake. Dina doesn't mention it and I know that Rachel won't. I notice that Dina has washed the soot off her face.

Dina eats precisely one quarter of a sandwich but makes up for it by smoking four cigarettes back to back while Rachel and I eat everything else.

The air is warm and soft and the sky is starting to turn yellow.

For a minute, it's as though the three of us are some kind of weird, dysfunctional family, with Dina as our bonkers Mum and Rachel and me as her two excessively well-behaved children.

Dina says she has some work to finish and suggests that Rachel might like to see the marsh. She asks us to take Harry with us.

Now that the light has started to fade, it's a bit spooky when we leave the garden. The mist is beginning to come in from the sea and the trees in the distance are turning blue. As usual, everything is very still.

Rachel says that it's beautiful.

In the field to the right of the track, we spot an owl moving up and down the hedge. In the fading light, it looks snow white and it seems to be flying incredibly slowly. It's like a large pale moth. No, it's more like a little mini ghost wafting slowly up and down the hedge line and from one corner of the field to the other.

Harry trots on ahead willingly enough. From behind, you can see how skinny his legs are, but his paws seem to be dancing across the ground.

When we get to the little wood at the end of the track, neither of us wants to go on. Although during the day it seems green and cool and welcoming, at night it seems murky and full of shadows.

Instead, we turn off at right-angles to the path and follow the ditch where I caught my fish. Something tells me that Rachel probably doesn't need a blow-by-blow account of my fishing expedition.

We've brought Dina's binoculars with us and as we look out towards the sea wall, we can see a small herd of deer lifting their heads to listen to something in a field of wheat.

And then, suddenly, we hear this loud honking noise as if someone is blowing on an old trumpet or bugle. About ten enormous birds appear from behind the trees, fly past us and disappear behind the hedge at the edge of the field. We only see them for about a couple of seconds and in the dim light it's hard to make out what colour they are. They seem to be a pale grey with darker ends to their wing feathers.

Neither of us has any idea what we are looking at. At first I thought they were swans or herons. But their colour is all wrong for swans and they don't fly like herons. They kind of shuffle across the sky.

We can still hear them bugling to each other but we can't see anything.

"Wow. They looked like something out of a Japanese painting," says Rachel. "What are they?"

"I think they must be flamingos," I say. "I didn't know you got them around here. Maybe they've escaped from a zoo or something."

By now it's definitely getting dark – the first few stars are out. And because it's so warm and still, the mosquitoes start to come after us. So we head back to the cottage.

Gerry's motorbike is parked outside, but there's no loud rock music being played. The atmosphere inside the cottage is tense, and we meet Gerry and Dina just inside the door. It looks as though he's about to leave.

"Hello, you two, what have you been up to in the dark?" he says with a nasty look on his face.

I introduce him to Rachel and he says he remembers seeing her on the boat but that "Jesus, your family were hard work."

No one says anything in response to this.

There's a bit of a silence, which I attempt to break by telling Gerry and Dina about the flamingos.

"They aren't flamingos, dick-head," says Gerry. "They're common cranes. They've been nesting in the Revenant area for the last 20 years or more. Besides, you don't get flamingos in Norfolk. This isn't Africa you know, even though it sometimes feels like it."

Why is he being like this?

Stupidly, I feel the need to defend myself. "Of course I know that there aren't any flamingos in Norfolk. I just thought they might have escaped from a local zoo."

"Well, zoos are something else we don't have too many of around here, in case you hadn't noticed."

Dina tries to come to my rescue. "I can see why Nick thought they might be, though. They are much bigger than any other birds around here. And the ways their legs hang behind when they're flying, they do look a bit like flamingos."

"Not to me and Rachel they don't. Still, we're not intellectuals like you two."

We all stand around not looking at each other and the silence goes on.

Eventually Gerry says, "Dina, any chance of a drink? I'm sure that Rachel could use a glass of wine after spending all that time on the marsh with Nick."

"No thanks, says Rachel firmly, "I don't drink." I get the impression she doesn't like Gerry that much. I want to say to her that he's not always like this — stupid and aggressive. That sometimes he can be really friendly and sensitive. But I can hardly believe it myself at the moment.

"Well, I do," he says.

"I thought you had to go," says Dina. "You were in a hurry to meet your mates at the pub a moment ago."

"Oh, I think I could bear to stay a little longer. It's not every day that I meet someone as pretty as Rachel."

I can hardly believe what I'm hearing. He's flirting with Rachel who is young enough to be his daughter, and I get the feeling he's doing it to spite Dina. Rachel says absolutely nothing. Doesn't pretend to laugh or flirt back. Just stands completely still.

"I'll go and get a bottle of wine," Dina says. "Nick, would you and Rachel like to join us?" This is the first time I've ever known her to be reluctant at the prospect of a drink

"Thanks, Dina," says Rachel, "but I think I'd better go."

"Well I suppose I should as well," says Gerry immediately. "Tell you what, Rachel, I'll give you a lift. I've got the motorbike outside. Where are you staying?"

"No, it's fine, thank you. I've got my bike outside."

"That's OK. I'm sure Dina won't mind if you leave it here and pick it up tomorrow. We don't want you cycling home in the dark now do we?"

"No thank you, I'll cycle back. I like cycling."

"I don't think you should do that," says Dina. "It's very dark at night here and you don't know the roads. Nick and I will give you a lift back. You can put your bike in the back of the pick-up."

"Thanks, Dina," says Rachel not missing a beat, "that would be lovely."

I want to punch the air. She may be only about 15 but she knows how to deal with Gerry when he's in this kind of mood. In fact, she's better at dealing with him than Dina is. Or than I am.

And having said that he's leaving, Gerry has to leave. He can barely bring himself to look at Dina and now that Rachel's given him the finger he decides to be a bit nicer to me.

"See you, matey. You'll have to come and spend some more time with me at the nature reserve."

"See you, Gerry."

And he goes. We hear the motorbike screeching up the gravel drive. We all stand there for a moment not saying anything, just listening to the bike's engine receding into the darkness.

Dina says, "Sorry about that," to no one in particular. We don't ask her what she's sorry about.

Dina's face has gone all slack and she's very careful not to look me in the eyes.

"I'll just go and get the truck's keys. Why don't you and Rachel wait in the sitting room?"

It was a really good day for all of us until Gerry went and spoiled it.

As soon as Dina's gone, Rachel whispers to me, "What an arsehole."

I try to defend him: "No, he's all right really. It's just that there's something going on between him and Dina. Some problem. I don't know."

"No, you're wrong," she says, "he's an arsehole. Let's not argue about it. Dina's lovely; he's a tosser."

"OK. OK."

When Dina comes back into the room, Rachel's really nice to her, saying what a lovely day she's had and so on.

You can tell that Dina's upset but that she's trying to make the best of things.

No one makes any mention of Gerry. He's clearly in disgrace. The trouble is that although I can understand why Dina and Rachel are cross with him, I can't be. I still think he's a good bloke, even if he's behaved really badly the last couple of times I've seen him. Anyway, I hate being disappointed in people or disapproving of them. That's what Mum and Dad have been doing to me since forever. I want to think that people are really nice.

With the three of us and Harry in the pick-up's cab, it's a bit squashed. The windows are down and Harry is lying across Rachel and me with his head out of the window, laughing at some private joke. Rachel, who's sitting between me and Dina, is pressing against my right side. It feels really nice.

The night outside the truck is warm and the air smells of earth.

We come to a racing stop outside the cottage that Rachel's staying in. You can see in through the kitchen window. The light's on and we can see her parents and her uncle and aunt sitting round the table, reading or playing cards or something.

Rachel asks if we would like to go in, but Dina says we ought to get back.

I don't know what to say next, but Rachel says. "Would you like to do something tomorrow, Nick? I can't make it in the morning because we're going to visit a windmill or something thrilling. But we could go to the beach in the afternoon... if you wanted to."

"Yes," I say, "that would be nice." What a wit. I surprise myself sometimes.

She kisses Dina on the cheek and says thanks and then we get out of the cab and I help her get her bike out of the back of the truck, with Harry supervising.

"Good night," she says and then kisses me on the cheek. I'm completely astonished. "See you tomorrow."

"Good night, Harry." She ruffles his ears. And then wheels her bike into the cottage's garden.

Back in the cab, Dina says, "I think she's really nice."

I nearly say, "And so do I," but I just manage to stop myself in time.

When we get back to the cottage, I check my phone and there's a text from Jack telling me that he and Emily have been up to the café in the broadway for a coke. He must be confusing me with someone who could care less.

There's nothing from Billy. Maybe he's been eaten by a crocodile.

And there's nothing from Mum or Dad. Maybe they're hoping that I've been eaten by a crocodile.

The best time to set a snare for a rabbit is the morning or the early afternoon.

If you leave it any later, your smell stays on the snare and the rabbits won't come anywhere near it in the evening...

Some of the old men say that when you make a new snare, you have to bury it for a week in cow shit...(I'm not allowed to say that)

or coat it with the soot from a candle.

But I don't believe that......

I think they say that because that's the way they have always done it.

... ...

Father says that I can only set snares by the beach. If I set them in the fields round the house I might catch a pheasant by mistake.

Then there would be trouble...

The soil by the beach is very sandy which makes setting traps harder.

Sometimes I set a hoop of wire across the rabbit run with a snare hanging from it. Sometimes I push a stake into the ground and attach the snare to it.

Four or five inches above the ground is best — the width of a man's fist.

The rabbit doesn't see the wire and pushes its head through the noose and is stuck.

... ...

The best time to check your snare is before dawn — just before it gets properly light.

The trapped rabbits crouch in the scrubby grass next to the snare...

Not moving... pretending to be dead.

...You have to kill them quickly though, because they always try to bite you.

Crossbar

The weather's still good this morning, the adult swallows are up and about, I can smell coffee and tobacco smoke.

It feels like it could be a good day, but I never really trust these feelings. It's best not to expect too much; then you're less likely to be disappointed.

After Harry and I have been for a walk, there's still more than three hours to kill before Rachel will be here.

So, I take *A Year At Revenant Broad* out into the garden and spread it out on the bench. In the sunlight, you can see how greasy and dirty the old red cover is – those must be the marks that people's hands have made over the last hundred years. It's so bright out here that when I open the book, there's a brownish tinge around the edge of the tiny handwriting where the ink has started to fade. Another 100 years and it might disappear altogether.

I've seen programmes on TV about archaeologists opening tombs only to see treasures that have lasted for thousands of years crumble away to dust as soon as they're exposed to the light and the air. I don't want this to happen to Dina's book so I make sure to sit between it and the sun, keeping it always in the shade.

With Harry dozing at my feet, I take another look at it.

I didn't realise when I looked at it before, how much it has to say about swallows. The first one arrived at Revenant Broad on 25 April 1896 and the last one was spotted on 3 September.

For some reason, I feel a need to give the writer of this diary a name and decide to call him Reg. One of the things that seems to have interested old Reg was the various places where swallows nest. In addition to the usual places like barns and the porches of churches, he collected stories of them nesting in a rabbit hutch, on the bedroom windowsill of a cottage in the village (the people who lived there kept their window open for the six weeks it took the chicks to hatch and fledge), in a broken tomb in the cemetery, under the seat on a rowing boat moored on the broad. He even mentions an item in the local newspaper about swallows nesting more than 50 feet underground in a disused tin mine in Cornwall.

He also tells a story of one pair of swallows who made their nest up against the corpse of a barn owl which had been nailed spread-eagled on a barn door at a local farm. There's a little picture of a cone of mud nestled up against the decaying body of an owl.

I have to admit I'm a bit shocked by this.

How could anyone do that to a barn owl? And why? Reg, who claimed to have visited the farm himself and drawn the picture from life, thinks that people did it to protect the barn from storms and lightning and evil spirits.

It also changes my view of the swallows in the shed a bit.

I realise that I've been thinking of them as if they were like humans. But, of course, they aren't. At first I think how could they be so indifferent and cruel as to use the dead body of another bird as a part of the structure of their nest. But that's stupid. They just have something in their little brains that says "MAKE A NEST. REAR CHICKS." And nothing else matters. They aren't cruel and they certainly aren't sentimental. They're just swallows. They're just doing what swallows do.

But I think I've had enough of this book for one day.

I'm having lunch (yes, yes) in the garden with Dina when Rachel arrives. She's wearing the same shorts and baseball cap as yesterday but a bright orange T-shirt instead of yesterday's blue one.

She chats to Dina for a bit and then we set off on our bikes for the beach.

It's about a two-mile ride, but a really easy one because the land is so flat. The sun is hot but there's more of a breeze than yesterday. We pass a couple of plantations of tall thin trees. The undersides of the leaves are silver and they flash like mirrors as they move in the wind. We pass a couple of pheasants ambling along at the side of the road – they're beautiful but have this completely mad look in their eyes. We pass cottages and a church built of jagged flints. We don't see another human being. Rachel is weaving her bike from one side of the road to the other and singing.

I tell myself that this is a good moment.

The little car park where Dina leaves the pick-up seems surprisingly full today. We get off our bikes and have to put them on our shoulders and climb over the line of sand dunes to the beach. There's a small weather-boarded hut nestling, half-hidden in the dunes, but it seems that no one's at home.

The beach is great – back to what it was before the storm. But, for a change, we haven't got it entirely to ourselves. A family has set up camp – complete with brightly coloured plastic wind protector and beach umbrella – next to a breakwater a couple of hundred yards away. Two little kids are digging in the sand.

We spread our towels out on the sand. Rachel slips off her shorts and T-shirt and is wearing a red one-piece swimming costume underneath. Her legs and arms are nearly as brown as Dina's but not as skinny. I feel a bit embarrassed and a bit breathless thinking about how soft and curvy she seems. I think she sees me looking at her legs. I look away.

Anyway, the good news is that I've remembered to put my trunks on under my jeans so I don't have to do that ridiculous hopping-up-and-down-on-one-leg-trying-to-get-out-of-my-pants-with-a-towel-wrapped-round-me routine that I treated Dina to the other day.

I get out of my clothes and am just starting to lie down on my towel when Rachel says "Come on," and grabs my hand and starts pulling me towards the sea.

Who am I to resist?

The water's great – freezing of course – and what's even better is that Rachel shows no signs of wanting to swim miles away from the shore so that she almost disappears. Instead, she's happy to mess about with the water up to our knees, splashing me and throwing enormous stones that smack into the sea with a "galumph" sound.

I watch her spinning round and round with her arms held out horizontally from her sides skimming the surface of the sea.

After about ten minutes it's too cold to stay in any longer so we lie on our towels to get warm. The thing about sea swimming is that it's great when you're in the water, but it's even better when you get out. It feels like every nerve ending in your skin is firing at once.

To begin with, we're both lying face down. I sneak a look at Rachel out of the side of my eye. There is the faintest blonde hair on her brown arms. Her fingers are long and brown and tapering and the nails look pink compared with her skin.

It's great lying here with the sun on my back, chatting to Rachel, sneaking the occasional look at her skin.

I get up on my elbows and look along the beach. The sea is flat calm and oily, barely lapping the sand. I can hear the children's voices from the next breakwater but I can't tell what they're saying. The gulls are diving out by the horizon, their wings shining in the sun. There are thin traces of cloud in the sky. The old magic is back.

As I'm looking at the dunes, I suddenly see a figure stand upright. And then, a couple of hundred yards away another one does the same. They're like the meerkats I saw in the zoo with

Gran. After a minute or two, one the figures disappears again behind the long grass. I keep watching and a few minutes later a third one stands up. What's going on? It's like they're signalling to each other. Maybe they're bird watchers.

I point them out to Rachel: "Do you think they're twitchers?"

"Don't be daft. They're gay. This beach is a famous gay pick-up place. It's where blokes come to meet other blokes."

"How do you know that?"

"My Dad told me. The local people are very cross about it. There have been articles in the local paper. Apparently, there was even a demonstration in the car park. You know, 'Keep our beaches for families' kind of thing."

"Oh." I don't know what else to say.

The sea is doing its usual trick of hypnotising me. As I listen to it rustling I can feel my eyes beginning to close.

I know Rachel is speaking, and it's a nice noise. But I haven't the faintest idea what she's saying. Her voice, like the sea, is fading further and further away.

"You're not listening are you?"

"What?"

"I said who's that kid? Do you know him?"

Her voice is back in focus now.

"What kid? Do I know who?"

"The kid who's sitting over there staring at us."

I roll over on my side. And there he is: the kid from the school playground. Just as dirty and just as scruffy as I remembered. He's wearing a dirty, torn shirt and shapeless black trousers and nothing on his feet. His parents should be ashamed to let him out like this.

He's staring at me and not blinking. And even when we make eye contact, he doesn't respond. Just keeps up the fixed stare. This is beginning to make me feel uncomfortable.

I whisper to Rachel: "I've seen him before. The other day when I was riding through the village he was in the school playground on his own. He seemed to be just standing there."

"Maybe he's lonely. There can't be many kids for him to play with around here. Let's ask him if he wants to come and sit with us."

"He's a bit young isn't he?"

"That doesn't matter. Besides, we can't pretend we don't know he's there."

I smile and say, "Hiya."

He looks intently at me for such a long time that I'm convinced that he's not going to reply."

But then he says, "What?" He says it kind of slowly. Sounds more like "*Whaart*."

"I said 'Hello'."

"Hello." Followed by another unblinking stare that seems likely to go on all afternoon. What is it with this kid? There's something about him that makes me uncomfortable.

"Would you like to come and sit with us?"

"Thank you." (Sounds more like "*than yew*.")

He gets up and walks over to us and then sits down again just beyond the edge of Rachel's towel. Up close, we can see that he's really dirty. His hair is filthy and his hands and neck are very grimy. His nails are broken and there's dirt under them. His clothes have been patched so many times that you wonder how they can hold together. Maybe it's just the dirt keeping them in one piece.

And he smells. Even though he's on the other side of Rachel from me, I can smell him. He seems to smell of sweat and earth and fish. It's a kind of sweet and dusty smell. I bet it's a while since he last had a bath.

I catch Rachel's eye and can see that she's noticed the smell. It would be pretty hard not to. You'd have to be wearing a gas mask and a full body protection suit not to.

Rachel speaks to him in a kind voice. "Hi, I'm Rachel, what's your name?"

"Sam." ("*Sem.*")

"Are you here with your parents?"

"No. They're at home." ("*Therrat hawm.*")

"Where do you live?"

"In the village." ("*Thur villaage.*")

Listen, I'm going to stop doing this. You get the point. The kid's got an accent. OK? You could cut it with a knife. He sounds like he's never been more than five miles from here. But forget about any more funny, phonetic spellings. I'll just translate as we go along.

"So, what are you doing here today?" asks Rachel.

"I came to see if the storm had washed anything up on the beach."

"What sort of things?"

"Cork. Bottles. Netting. Anything."

"And have you found anything?"

"Not really."

I'm beginning to feel a bit left out here, so I take over the interrogation.

"My name's Nick. I saw you in the school playground the other day. Do you remember?"

"I remember."

"Is that where you go to school?"

"Yes."

"And how old are you, Sam?"

"Twelve."

He may not be the world's greatest conversationalist, but he sure is one hell of a liar. He only comes up to my shoulder and he's so skinny. I bet he's no more than ten. In fact, if he'd said he was nine I wouldn't have been surprised.

He looks hungry and confused.

"Are you OK?" I ask.

"What?"

"Are you all right?" (I'm beginning to think he's deaf as well as dirty.)

"Yes, thank you."

I can see this conversation is going nowhere.

So I get up and build a small tower of stones about 20 yards away. Then the three of us spend time throwing stones at it to demolish it. Sam seems to be enjoying himself. He may not be much to look at, but he can throw like a man twice his size.

After about ten minutes we're all getting sweaty. Rachel and I decide to go for another swim, but when we ask Sam if he's coming in with us he looks terrified. "No. No. I don't go into the water."

"Why not?" I was thinking that a quick swim might do something for his smell. Even more so if he went in fully clothed.

I guess he hasn't got any trunks with him and is embarrassed.

But he looks like we've given him a real fright.

While Rachel and I mess about in the sea, Sam sits on the sand and watches us with absolute concentration on his face. He manages to sit completely still and never even seems to blink his eyes. He doesn't smile or say anything. It's almost as if he's trying to make sense of something. Work something out. But he does wave back when Rachel waves to him. It's that same, slow, serious wave that he gave me from the playground.

And when we get out of the water and start drying ourselves, he continues to sit and watch us.

It's only when Rachel calls to him that he comes back over to us. And then he sits down near the towels as though he's waiting for something. He seems to like talking to us, but he only answers questions. Never starts a conversation of his own. I wonder if he's quite all there. Maybe he's a bit autistic, like a couple of the kids at school.

By now it's getting cooler. The family by the breakwater have packed up their stuff and are heading back to the car. The meerkat men in the dunes seem to have packed it in – whatever *it* is – for the day.

Me and Rachel get into our clothes.

"Where's your bike, Sam?"

"What?"

"Your bike. Your bicycle."

"I haven't got one."

"Well how did you get here from the village?"

"I walked."

"But it's more than two miles. And how are you going to get back?"

"I'm going to walk."

"You can't do that."

"It's too far. You can't walk back on your own," adds Rachel.

"I do it all the time."

"But you haven't got any shoes."

"I don't need any."

"I'd better give you a crossbar."

"What?"

What's the matter with this kid – doesn't he speak English?

"You can have a ride on my bike with me."

"Thank you."

It's like trying to have a conversation with someone who is just starting to learn English from a phrasebook.

Now that I've got Sam sitting on my crossbar, I'm beginning to regret my kind offer. The smell that Rachel and I noticed as soon as he appeared is overpowering. His head is only a few inches in front of my face and the truth is that he stinks.

He smells of the dirt that seems to be ingrained in the back of his neck. But there's something else as well – like old fish or glue. And because I have the pleasure of looking at the top of his head from close to, I can see a number of red scabs under his badly shaved hair. How can his parents let him be like this?

I'm having to concentrate so hard on breathing through my mouth that I can barely ride the bike.

And Sam seems completely useless. I tell him to put his hands on the handlebars to keep his balance. But he hasn't got a clue and keeps jerking the handlebars from side to side and leaning the wrong way. We nearly come off about five times in the first minute.

"Can't you ride a bike?" I ask him.

"No. I've never been on one before."

"You must have been."

"I haven't."

He's shaking.

"Are you cold."

"No, I'm all right."

He has the same excited look in his eyes as Harry does when he sticks his head out of the pick-up window.

The ride back is very different from the ride to the beach. The mood has changed. The light is now quite dull. And Rachel isn't weaving about and singing. Things seem to have got a bit solemn and serious.

A whole load of enormous slugs seem to have decided to cross the road at the same time. (Maybe they've heard rumours about Rachel's cake and are going to see for themselves.) We have to concentrate on not running them over. I don't like slugs but it would definitely be disgusting to get one under my wheel.

We cycle past the drive to Dina's cottage, but for some reason I don't want to ask them in. So we carry on into the village. We go past the school and when we reach a road on the left by the church, Sam says, "Can I get down here please? This is where I live." So I stop the bike and he jumps down.

"Thank you," he says and sets straight off down the road without looking back. I notice that he seems able to walk on the gravelled road in his bare feet as easily as he walked on the sand at the beach. His feet must be tough.

"Bye, Sam," says Rachel. "Will you be all right?"

"Yes, thank you," he calls over his shoulder – still without looking back.

"Well," she says, "he's an odd little one."

"That's for sure."

I say I'll cycle the rest of the way to her cottage with her to keep her company. She says maybe I could come in and meet her parents. I don't really want to but say that that would be nice.

But as we get nearer the cottage, we can hear a man shouting. "I'm sick of those kids. No matter what you do for them it's never enough. And they're so badly behaved..."

Rachel looks embarrassed. "That's my uncle. The kids have obviously been living up to their usual standards."

"Listen, perhaps I'd better not come in after all."

"Maybe you're right."

As I stand here trying to think of what to say next, I realise that both days I've spent with Rachel have started off well but ended badly. Yesterday it was Gerry. Today it's Rachel's uncle shouting. But really, the problem started before that.

It started when Sam turned up at the beach. It's not that he did anything or caused any trouble. In his own funny way he seems to be quite friendly. But there's something about him that makes you feel sorry for him. He's so thin and dirty and helpless. It's like

111

he needs something that no one is giving him. Just to meet him
is to want to look after him. Being with him is some kind of weird
responsibility.

I don't say anything to Rachel about any of this but I'm sure
she's feeling it as well.

Rachel's uncle is still shouting and somewhere in the house a
kid is howling. The silence between Rachel and me has now
reached bursting point and because I can't think of anything else
to do I jump on my bike, say, "See you," and head off back towards
Dina's.

The air is much cooler now and I start to pedal fast to keep
warm.

The bats have begun to gather above the road.

I've only gone a couple of hundred yards when I hear Rachel
call my name.

I stop the bike and turn round. She's chasing after me.

"Listen Nick, I really enjoyed being at the beach with you.
Maybe we could do something else in the next few days. Can I
have your phone number? I'll call you."

She looks upset. I feel quite flattered.

I give her my number, which she says she will remember, and
watch as she cycles back towards the cottage.

Then I head off to Dina's. I can't help it, but I sing all the way
back. The road is so quiet that it seems important to make a lot
of noise.

"I saw a bird... *I saw a bird*
With a yellow bill... *With a yellow bill.*
It landed on... *It landed on*
My window sill... *My window sill.*
I coaxed it in... *I coaxed it in*
With a plate of spaghetti... *With a plate of spaghetti.*
Then I cut its head off... *Then I cut its head off*

With my machete… *With my machete.*"

I'm really looking forward to seeing old Dina. Bring on the lamb stew and the baby bottle of beer. I'm ready for them.

Father only comes to church with us on Christmas Day and Easter
Sunday...
He says that he has too much to do in the garden...
or that he has to fix the roof...
or cut wood...
Mother insists that the rest of us go.
She scrubs our faces until they are raw and shiny...

... ...

Nigel and Sarah and Arthur always make a fuss...
One or other of them is usually in tears before we leave.
And Mother is angry and her face goes tight.

... ...
...

There are four enormous gold candlesticks on the altar...
the floor is made of red and black checked tiles.
It's cool in summer and freezing in winter...
On hot days, the door at the back of the church is left open and I
can hear the bees humming.
Sometimes there are sheep grazing in the churchyard.
I can hear them tearing at the long grass...
Swallows nest in the porch...
I want to turn round and watch the things happening behind me,
but I know that mother wouldn't like it.
...Reverend Hooton has a kind face
but his sermons can be very long and complicated.
The light that slants in through the windows is filled with
swirling dust.
I can feel myself drifting off.
But if I fall asleep and my head starts to nod,
Arthur pinches me really hard.

... ...

I daren't look at him in case we both start to laugh.

The swallow is extremely capricious

I didn't sleep well last night, the first time since my first night here, when Dina and Gerry were at it like rabbits.

Dina and I sat up chatting about nothing in particular until about one in the morning. My eyes were closing for the last hour or so, but because she seemed happier than she's been for the last few days, I stayed up with her, while she worked her way through half a bottle of whisky, half a million fags and two thirds of her life story.

About ten minutes after I got back from the village, my phone rang and it was Mum. It was nice to hear from her but hard to feel much enthusiasm about what she was saying. But I did my best and asked her questions about the restaurants they'd been to and how Dad's work was going. She actually seemed to listen a bit more carefully than when I spoke to her the other night, but when I started to talk about what the beach was like I could tell that she was losing interest.

So I let her tell me about the beach near where they are staying, where women in bikinis roller blade up and down the promenade and where body builders flex their muscles in public.

The truth is the more I heard about her beach – apparently the water is so polluted that no one goes swimming for fear of skin diseases – the more I was glad that I was here and not there.

I don't think that I could lie and dream on a beach in California. I can't believe that an American sea would be able to hypnotise me in the same way as the sea does here. (Although, I have to admit I wouldn't mind seeing Rachel roller blading in a bikini.)

Everyone would be watching everyone else to see who was the coolest or thinnest.

Anyway, I let her go on and on about their beach and what they were doing because I could tell that she felt most comfortable talking about herself. I got the feeling that she was avoiding asking me about how I was doing in case I said the wrong thing like it was terrible and that I was unhappy. And then she would have to feel bad and feeling bad's not something that she or Dad go in for a lot.

What I didn't tell her was that I wasn't missing them or home at all. That I have started to feel settled here. Which comes as a bit of a surprise to me.

And then she said, "Jim would like a word."

"Hi, Nick, how's it going?"

"Fine thanks, how are you?"

"I'm great. We're having a great time. How's that sister of mine?"

"Dina's been brilliant," I say (I want her to hear this). "Her cottage is fantastic and her garden is fantastic. And she's been taking me to the beach and to the pub. And she's got a great dog called Harry. And we've got swallows nested in the shed and they've got chicks."

It takes a moment to realise that I'm blathering. Won't I ever learn? He only has to ask me a simple question and I start pouring out my heart to him. It's pathetic. He only has to pretend to be interested and I'm eating out of his hand. Harry has more dignity. I know he's not really interested. I can feel that down the phone from more than 5,000 miles away.

"I always thought she was a bit of a dry old stick, personally. She's probably got you eating veggie burgers and saving the planet."

"No, it's not like that at all. It's really nice." There goes my way with words again.

"Well that's terrific."

(Am I imagining it, Dad, or is there a note of disappointment in your voice? Am I imagining it or is part of you wanting me to say that I'm unhappy and missing you even though we both know that it wouldn't make any difference to anything if I did?)

There's a bit of a pause and then I say, "How's work going?"

And that seems to be a good question because he can go into this account of dealing with people at the studio and how the script is developing and which actors they've met and which producers have invited them to parties.

I like listening to his voice but I'm not really paying attention to what he's saying.

After a few minutes, the stories start to dry up. I'm a bit relieved.

Then he asks me if I'm spending all my time with "Old Dina" as he keeps calling her – even though she's his younger sister – or whether I'm hanging out with anyone else.

I don't think it would be a good idea to mention Gerry so I tell him about Rachel and for the last couple of minutes of the conversation he pretends that she's my girlfriend and teases me about when we're going to announce our engagement.

There's a bit of relief on both sides of the Atlantic that we seem to have hit upon a joke that we can share. *"When do we get to meet her parents? Have you decided whether or not to go for a church wedding? How many children are you planning on?"* And so on. It's kind of fun and has taken the tension out of the conversation.

"Do you want to speak to Dina?"

"No thanks, old sport, I've got to go now. Give her my love and tell her I'll speak to her next time. Meantime, you carry on having a great time. You're obviously having a much better time there than you'd have here with only boring old us for company. Lots of love. Bye."

That must have been one of the longest conversations I've ever had with Dad and neither of us really said anything.

I was a bit surprised to discover after I put the phone down that I didn't feel anything. Not sad. Not angry. Nothing.

When I finally got to bed, I couldn't get to sleep. The sheets seemed to have come to life and be determined to tie me in as many knots as possible.

I got out of bed for a while and sat by the window with the curtain open. The breeze had dropped and everything in the garden was still. Three quarters of a moon was hanging above the marsh and the air felt damp.

After a bit, I started to feel cold and got back into bed and fell asleep at once.

Almost immediately I had a dream about poor Sam. In the dream, Rachel and I cycled to the beach and everything was like it had been earlier in the day. The family were playing and talking in low voices by the breakwater, the meerkat men were bobbing up and down in the dunes, Rachel was wearing her costume and splashing me. Out towards the horizon, the gulls were diving. And just as we had done earlier in the day, we lay on our towels in the sun.

The difference in the dream was that this time I saw Harry coming across the sand in the gap between the dunes. He was barking furiously. I called to him but he took no notice of me. Instead, he ran down the beach and started nuzzling at something that had been brought in by the tide. I thought it must be a plastic barrel or sheet of polythene but Harry was barking so much that I thought I'd better go and investigate.

So I got up and walked along the tide line to where Harry was still barking. As I got closer I realised that what he had found was a body lying face down in the sand. The body was wearing Sam's terrible, patched clothes, its arms and legs were white and skinny and cold to the touch. I remember noticing a piece of seaweed clinging to the soaking trousers and two shells half buried in the sand next to the head. Beads of seawater were clinging to the stubble of hair.

I knew that I had to turn the body over even though I didn't want to. I knew that when I did I would see Sam's face but what I hadn't expected was that his eyes would be wide open and that he would be smiling.

I woke up in fright and looked at my watch: 1.50. I'd probably been asleep for less than ten minutes.

My heart was pounding.

I was so spooked by this dream that I had to put the bedside light on for a bit. I don't usually give much thought to dreams. They're just bonkers and don't mean anything. But this dream wasn't like that. There's something about Sam that makes me feel a bit sad and guilty and responsible for him in some way. I've just got this sense that I have everything and he has nothing.

I also have to admit that I was also a bit angry with him. I knew that it was stupid but I felt resentful towards Sam for disturbing my sleep in this way.

When I woke next at about 5.00 the bedside light was still on. I switched it off and rolled over on my side. I must have fallen asleep again because now it's after 8 o'clock and my phone's ringing.

Trouble is that I'm so dozy with sleep that I can't think where it is and while I hunt around the room I think at first that it must be Mum and Dad and then I think it's Rachel.

The one person I don't expect it to be is Gerry.

"Hi, matey. How are you?"

"Huh. I think I'm OK."

"Did I wake you? Sorry." (Well you certainly don't sound it.)

"It's all right." (Come to think of it, that didn't seem very sincere either.)

"I'm at the nature reserve today, and wondered if you'd like to come down this afternoon. I could show you round."

Of course, I say yes before I give any thought to how I'm going to explain this to Dina.

But, in fact, she doesn't seem to mind. Is pleased if anything.

"That's great," she says, "I can drop you off if you like."

I say thanks but I'd rather cycle and she just smiles.

The ride takes about half an hour and all the way I'm pestered by tiny black flies, which keep going into my eyes and mouth and up my nose. It must be the heat after the bad weather that's brought them out. In the end I have to cycle with my eyes almost shut, flapping one hand above my head.

I ride right through the village and then down a narrow winding road with cottages on either side with flowers growing on the grass verge outside their gates. It's like the owners of the cottages have staked a claim to this useless strip of land between their garden walls and the edge of the road. I make a right turn before I get to the broad itself and slide down a muddy, rutted track, following the hand-painted signs that say "Revenant Nature Reserve." They're decorated with a picture of a dragonfly.

I pass through some trees into a large open field with loads of picnic tables and chairs. Apart from where the tables are, the grass in the field hasn't been cut. It's way up past my knees and a kind of blond colour, dotted with pink and purple and blue wild flowers. There are half a dozen beehives sticking up out of the long grass.

A few families are sitting at the picnic tables and some little kids are running around in the grass.

There's a large wooden building with a thatched roof in the corner of the field with a veranda and double doors. There are two pots of red flowers on the porch.

A huge wooden dragonfly has been nailed to the veranda roof. I guess it's meant to look as though it's just taken off and is about to fly across the field. The truth is it looks like it's in the process of falling off the roof.

There's also a large sign, made out of sticks stuck to a board that says "Visitor Centre."

The doors are open, but inside it's baking hot and smells of wood. A woman behind a wooden counter is wearing the same uniform as Gerry was the other day, although, thank God, without the hat. She says hi and goes back to reading her book. As far as she's concerned, I can stand here as long as I like. She's making it plain that it's nothing to her one way or another.

The room is full of posters, of birds, of fish and of ducks. There's a photo of the visitor centre covered in snow under a bright blue sky. There are leaflets about the RSPB and a couple of gardens that are open to the public. One has a picture of two middle-aged men in bright shirts standing in front of what looks like a desert garden. I can't imagine what it has to do with anything.

There's also a small blackboard on which someone has chalked the names of all the birds spotted on the reserve today. "Two marsh harriers. Seven bar tailed godwits. Six stonechats. Four great crested grebes." And a partridge in a pear tree, for all I know. I'm sure it's all very important to someone but I also know that I would have no chance of identifying most of these birds if they landed on Dina's patch of lawn.

I still don't really understand why some people seem to want to tick boxes about nature; it's like they're trying to collect these birds. And the whole thing about birds is that they can't be collected.

I say hello to the lady behind the counter and tell her who I am and that I'm here to meet Gerry. She seems so laid back that I'm not sure that what I say is getting through to her. But in some way or another it must do, because she clicks on her walky-talky and says "Gerry, please come to the visitor centre, there's someone to see you."

She listens to some crackling noises: "He'll be here in a minute. I can't offer you a chair because there aren't any." Then

121

she looks at me and smiles. She has the palest blue eyes but there doesn't seem to be very much going on behind them. But it's no business of mine.

"Thanks," I say, "I'll go and wait outside."

"Good idea," she says, "it's so hot in here." But she says it in a way that suggests it has never occurred to her that it might be possible to do something about it. I start to feel tired just looking at her.

Before I fall asleep on my feet, I head on out and sit at the nearest unoccupied picnic table. The sun is warm and there's not much breeze. I can hear the families talking among themselves. A little pink and brown bird is nicking cake crumbs from under the table. Maybe it's a stonechat.

"Male chaffinch," says a voice. It's Gerry. He's wearing his khaki uniform and dark glasses but not his hat. I'm really hoping that he keeps it for the boat.

"Sorry I wasn't here when you arrived, but I was giving a short lecture on the mating habits of swans."

He smiles to show that this is a joke.

"Do they have interesting mating habits?"

"Not as interesting as mine." There's a bit of a silence – it's as if we both know that we don't want to go there.

"Anyway matey, do you want a coke or something?"

"Yes please, I'm really thirsty."

He disappears inside the visitor centre and reappears a few moments later with two cokes.

"So, you met Moon did you? What did you think?"

"Who's Moon?"

"My colleague. You know, Miss Dynamite in there."

I don't know what to say.

Fortunately, he takes pity on me and says, "Between you and me, I think it takes a fair number of chemicals to achieve such a state of bliss. And I'm not convinced that Moon is her real name. I bet she's really a Deirdre or a Gladys or something."

We sit and drink our cokes. I can tell that he's trying to be nice.

"So, how are your swallow chicks?" Just like Dina, he talks about them as though they're mine.

So I tell him that they seem to have survived the storm and that their parents are feeding them again.

Gerry seems pleased. He really is trying to be nice. No taking the piss. No calling me a dick-head.

"The reserve's got a little bit of a library," says Gerry. "I had a quick look through it to see what I could find out about swallows. I found this book by a bloke named Arthur Patterson. The book's called *Notes of an East Coast Naturalist*. It was written over a hundred years ago...

"Patterson lived just down the coast near Great Yarmouth and wrote dozens of books about the area. For some reason, he was also known as John Knowlittle. He was interested in everything – birds, fish, animals, everything. He was quite well known and if people found anything strange like a two-headed cod or an albino pheasant, they knew they'd be able to sell it to Patterson. Apparently, the local fishmonger used to save all the fish guts for him to rake through – he seems to have been particularly interested in fish parasites... Still, it takes all sorts, I guess.

"He used to correspond (I love that word) with other naturalists around the country, although I'm not sure how he would have wrapped up and posted a parcel of fish guts... At one point in his life he seems to have lost most of his money and had to make a living by travelling round Norfolk with a preserved 30-foot whale that had been beached at Gorleston. People used to pay to come to see it...

"Anyway, I thought I'd see what he had to say about swallows. I thought there might be some useful information in the book that might help you help the chicks to survive...

"Of course, there wasn't but he did have a lot of stuff to say about swallows, which I thought you might be interested in. Here, I made a few notes."

Gerry fishes around in his back pocket and comes up with a grubby sheet of paper.

"Of course, you have to get used to the way he writes, but he seems to have been interested in some of the weird places that swallows build their nests. This is what he said."

Then Gerry puts on this exaggerated posh voice and reads: "*The swallow is extremely capricious in its choice of locations for the building of its nest, the chief object of its solicitude apparently being immunity from the weather rather than suitability or comfort of the situation.*'"

I'm not sure what "capricious" or "solicitude" mean, but I wish that my swallows had read this book, then they might not have built their stupid nest right under a leaking, draughty roof.

Gerry is obviously having a bit of trouble reading his notes.

"Oh yeh, he reports that in 1878 a pair of swallows nested in the hold of an old ship, the 'Agnes', a brigantine from the days of Nelson, that had been scuttled and sunk at the entrance to a creek in Bleydon to divert the current. Apparently there were several feet of water in the hold and hardly any space between the surface of this water and the Agnes's deck, and yet the swallows successfully raised their chicks there. I like the way old Patterson put it, if I can read my bloody notes. Yeh, right, he said, that they were successful in raising a brood, 'notwithstanding,' (that's a bloody great word for you) '*notwithstanding the fact that at high water their tiny domicile was suspended in the centre of two thousand acres of not always placid salt water.*' I also like that bit about a 'tiny domicile', it makes me think of the marshman's cottage I'll show you later. Old Patterson went on a bit and had a pretty pompous way of expressing himself, but I think he sets up a really good contrast between the tiny, fragile birds and all that sea."

Gerry seems to run out of steam for a moment. "Blimey, I'm starting to sound like Dina." But this is somewhere else that neither of us wants to go.

"He also mentions a pair of swallows that built a nest in a shaft erected immediately over a main sewer for ventilation. Old Patterson has another of his phrases for it. Rather than saying it smelled of shit, he says it was – God, who wrote this? Right, he says it was *'probably the most offensive spot on earth they could have discovered.'* Apparently, they liked it so much that they returned to it year after year."

"I don't know about you" says Gerry, "but I take that as pretty conclusive proof that swallows don't have much sense of smell."

"He also talks about a pair nesting in the mechanism of a windmill, attached to the main shaft which turned through 360 degrees. This meant that when one of the parents flew off to fetch food, the nest wouldn't be in the same place when it got back. This didn't seem to bother them much. Because of the movement of the shaft, bird shit formed a complete circle on the mill floor…

"He even claims that a pair nested in the open top of a pint mug left on a shelf in a marsh shepherd's hut. He describes how they did it: *'The mouth of the mug appeared to have been first crossed by grass-bents, fastened securely by mud mortar to the edges. Upon this platform a nest as large as a shallow breakfast cup was constructed, and eggs laid therein.'*"

Gerry seems to have come to the end of his notes, and looks a bit embarrassed.

"Sorry to bore on about all that, but I thought you might be interested."

I realise that this is some kind of apology for the other night and that this is as close as he's going to come to saying sorry for the way he behaved.

"I think it is really interesting. It's great to know that swallows

125

seem to have this ability to survive in all kinds of unlikely places. That must give the swallows in Dina's shed a bit more of a chance."

"I'm not sure," says Gerry, "but I hope you're right."

"Anyway," he says, "do you want a look round?"

The reserve, which you get to by crossing a ditch and going through a gap in the hedge, seems to follow the edge of Revenant Broad. The ground is black and damp looking, but you walk on planks laid end to end. And they kind of bounce as you move along them. To each side are ditches full of reeds with feathery tops that catch the sunlight.

In some places, there is a kind of screen which looks as though it has been made of reeds woven together. Butterflies seem to like these screens, because there are hundreds of them sunbathing, slowly opening and closing their wings. They look like brightly coloured reminders of something pinned to a notice board.

As we walk along, a couple of tiny, brownish lizards scamper for cover. Gerry says they're common lizards, but I've never seen one before.

The ditch we're following turns away at an angle and passes through some dark trees, on the other side of which is a large wooden shed with a kind of jetty sticking out a few feet into the water. It's a hide for bird watching.

Gerry quietly opens the door. It's pitch black and very hot inside and our footsteps sound really loud on the wooden floor.

Gerry opens a narrow wooden flap and the sunlight pours into the room. We sit on a wooden bench and look through the slot, directly out onto a small lake. There are reeds all round it and several small groups of ducks. A heron is standing looking sad at one edge. There are huge white clouds in the distance. In the afternoon light, the water looks like crinkled silver foil as it moves and flashes. The sun is sending a narrow golden path right across the lake. The only sound is the "bip, bip" of some bird or other. You get the feeling that nothing has happened here for hundreds of years.

Gerry wants to talk again.

"Listen," he says, "I'm sorry about the other night. I shouldn't have said those things to you. I don't know what got into me. I guess you know that things aren't going too well between me and Dina at the moment. Maybe it was that. Anyway, I shouldn't have said those things to you in front of your girlfriend. I'm sorry."

"That's OK. And she's not my girlfriend. I've only spoken to her a couple of times."

"Thanks. I've just been really bad tempered the last few days. Things are never exactly easy between me and Dina. How could they be? She's a successful academic and I'm just a bloke who takes people out in a boat. But even if they aren't easy, we usually get on pretty well. But not the last couple of times we've met. You've been there; you've seen what it's been like. I just haven't felt the same about anything since the other day when we were out in Piranha. Maybe I drink too much. Maybe I just can't believe that she can like me."

"But she does. And she's been really upset since you've been having these arguments."

As soon as I say this, I feel that I shouldn't.

"Has she really?" Gerry seems pleased.

This was a big mistake. Who am I to get between them in this way? I can't make sense of my own life much less anybody else's. Let's face it, I haven't really got a clue about what Dina feels or thinks about anything. Same with Gerry. So, I start to back off a bit.

"Well, maybe 'upset' isn't the right word. Maybe it's just that she's been busy with writing up her lectures and is tired and things aren't going too well for her."

"What things?"

"I don't know really. I just feel that things haven't been going quite right for her. Maybe I've got it wrong."

Gerry looks at me. He doesn't seem quite so pleased now.

But I still feel that I'm in the wrong. I don't want to have to talk about their stupid relationship. Whatever I say is bound to be wrong. Why don't they just sort out their own lives? I don't want this responsibility.

"OK," he says, "sorry about all that. Let's move on."

When he closes the flap it's pitch dark once more.

As we leave the sun is so bright that I look down at the water below the jetty. It's brown and clear and sparkling. There are stones at the bottom and bright green, stringy weed. The water looks as if it would be warm to touch. I can imagine all kinds of insects and things wriggling about in that soft, warm mud.

It must be good to be them. They don't have problems with relationships. They don't have adults asking them for advice. They don't have to listen to Gerry's singing or be in the same country as his hat or worry about Dina swimming so far out from shore.

We walk on not saying very much. A few people are strolling around – mainly families but also a couple of blokes on their own with combat jackets in spite of the heat and expensive looking binoculars.

A heron flies over. Its wings beat so slowly that it looks as if it could fall out of the sky at any moment.

Through another stand of trees, we come across a tiny cottage, not much bigger than a doll's house.

Gerry says that it's a restored marshman's cottage. It has a tiny vegetable garden and one room downstairs with a black-leaded cooking range that takes up most of one wall. The floor is bare and there's a single high-backed chair in front of the range.

Upstairs there's just one bedroom with a wooden bed with a patchwork quilt and a tiny crib. There's also a hideous waxwork woman with glass eyes. She's wearing a Victorian nightdress. She's probably meant to look like someone's mum, but she looks more like the ghost of a mad axe-woman.

"Imagine having to live here with eight children and nothing to eat but eels," says Gerry. "And the mosquitoes used to be terrible. Poor bastards."

I don't think this can be the whole truth about the lives of the people who lived in this cottage more than a hundred years ago, but I'm sure Gerry's right as well. Their lives must have been very hard.

"Right," says Gerry, "I've got to get back on duty. There's one final tour party to show round today. I'll walk back to the visitor centre with you."

There's a group of about six people waiting at the visitor centre looking rather hopelessly at Moon who is looking rather hopelessly back at them. Gerry introduces himself and says he'll be with them in a moment.

Then he shakes hands with me and says goodbye. But he has changed since we were in the bird hide together. Then, he seemed genuinely sorry – wanting to make up. Now I'm not so sure. He has that arrogant look on his face, as if he's looking for an argument. "And remember to say hello to Rachel for me," he says in a voice that is not his normal voice and with a strange look on his face. And then he's gone – off with his tour party.

I say bye to Moon, who manages to focus on me long enough to reply, and leave. But no sooner am I out of the door than she calls me back.

"Someone was looking for you. A kid. He was here about half an hour ago. I'm not sure where he's gone."

"What kid?"

"About ten. Very dirty. Smelly. No shoes."

How did he know I was here?

"Did he say his name was Sam?"

"I don't think so. Sorry, I can't remember. He's probably outside."

But he isn't. I look everywhere, but no sign of him. I ask the family at the nearest table if they've seen a ten-year old boy with no shoes on. They say no and ask me if he is my brother and if everything is OK. I say no and that it is.

He must have met Dina somewhere and she told him where I was. I wonder what he wanted.

I expect I'll catch up with him on the road back to the village. But there's no sign of him.

... ...
I dream about a boy and a girl...
It's a dream that makes me happy
and sad at the same time...
They are older than me and taller and their skin seems to shine.

... ...
... ...
I see them through a fog or a blaze of light.
They shift and dance as if they were under moving water.
They are like angels.
They have magical powers
and I want to be with them.
I want to be like them...
The boy has dark hair — much longer than mine.
I think he has a kind, calm face
but I find it hard to focus on it.
... The girl has hair the colour of flames...

... ...
In my dream, they are always walking towards me...

...
But they never get any closer... ...

... ...
I try to move towards them but my feet are stuck...
I want to call to them but there's a stone in my mouth.
I wave and they wave back.

...
The boy is speaking.
I know that he is saying something to me.
But I can't understand what it is.
The roaring in my ears makes it sound like a foreign language...

... ...
They're not tears.

Time out of joint

As soon as I got back yesterday evening, I asked Dina if Sam had called, but she said no – no one had been.

"But then how did he know where I was?"

"Did you see Rachel on the way?"

"No."

"Well, it's a bit of a mystery. But maybe Moon got it wrong. She's famous around here for being a few sandwiches short of a picnic. Maybe it wasn't you this kid wanted. Maybe he met up with someone else and that's why he wasn't there when you came out."

"Yeh, you're probably right."

The weather this morning is warm and still but cloudy. I went on swallow patrol first thing and everything seems OK.

When Dina offered me a "trip into town" I jumped at the chance. I don't know what I was expecting – bright lights, good clothes shops, cafes, discos. But Stalton isn't really like that.

What a trip into town in these parts means is a trip to a small dump with a car park in the middle – a single shopping street, lots of small houses, and a load of old gimmers wandering around in pastel coloured raincoats.

Camden Market or Regent Street it ain't.

While Dina's in the bank and getting her usual "few bits and pieces" from the off licence, I have the chance to look round. It takes all of about five minutes.

Stalton consists of: a Balti house; a Chinese take-away; a fish and chip shop (open two lunchtimes and three evenings week); a baker's shop with pink iced buns in the window; a bank; a newsagent's with a whole load of beach stuff on the pavement –

buckets, spades, windbreaks, beachballs – even though the nearest beach is three miles away; a clothes shop ("gentlemen's outfitters") selling middle-aged clothes – hairy orange sports jackets, tweed trousers, sensible shoes – at what seem to be insane prices; a small supermarket with a name I don't recognise, selling mostly own-brand stuff like white bread, tinned peas and doughnuts; an estate agent's with pictures of horrible looking bungalows in the window; a bicycle repair shop; a solicitor's office; an antique shop with three huge pieces of brown furniture in the window and the price labels turned face down; a tiny library with about 20 books in it, most of them in large print.

And that seems to be about it. Apart from a few kids of my age who are riding bikes on the narrow pavement.

Don't get me wrong, though. This place has its exciting moments and today most of them are being provided by a pavement artist. Trouble is that he seems as odd as almost everyone else around here.

Who does he think is going to put money in his Tupperware box? There's not exactly a lot of passing trade in Stalton – just a couple of old ladies with shopping trolleys (even if they wanted to give him money – which they don't seem to – by the time they'd got it out of their handbags, the pavement would probably have eroded), a bloke pushing a pram with two babies in it and the kids on their bikes. It's hard to see how he's going to make a living.

Especially since he doesn't seem to have mastered the basics of pavement artistry.

For a start, he's doing it in the most dangerous way possible. He's lying full length across the narrow pavement with his legs sticking out into the road, forcing cars and vans to drive around him. I'm sure that isn't recommended in the pavement artists' manual.

And second, instead of large copies of famous paintings and ragged kids with enormous eyes, this guy is painting tiny, detailed pictures about the size of a photograph in ceramic paint. You can't really make them out at all unless you squat down and get close to them, which I don't want to do because it would mean getting close to this guy.

Anyway good luck to him.

I didn't realise that there is a small café at the back of the baker's shop, but I do now because that's where Dina has brought me for lunch.

The restaurant looks like it was kitted out in about 1960, but it has the incredible advantage of having non-lamb items on the menu.

I choose sausage, eggs and chips. Dina goes for a steak sandwich – protein and carbohydrate in the same meal, it must be a first. And, of course, she can't smoke in here. A fact which she tries to make up for by drinking strong black coffee.

This is a pretty dim place. No atmosphere. Crap food. But I'm really enjoying being here with Dina.

I tell her about the pavement artist – "I guess he must have escaped from somewhere."

But Dina tells me that he's really some kind of performance artist – "I read about him in the local paper. He's got quite a large grant from some organisation or another and he's going round Stalton creating all these tiny pictures that no one can see properly. Apparently, he's not painting them at random but following foundation lines of an eighteenth century high street. Some people seem to think his work is quite important; but not many of the people who read the local rag though. He's provoked quite a correspondence."

(For some reason, I remember that Gerry really likes this word.)

"People have been writing in saying that it's a terrible waste of public money to finance him. There was one letter saying that it was just vandalism – as bad as graffiti. (They don't get a lot of graffiti round here, but the kind of people who write letters to the paper seem to have heard of it and they're pretty sure that they don't like the sound of it.)"

In some way that I don't really understand, this changes things. I feel like I'm somehow in the wrong. This place keeps wrong-footing me like this. Cutting the ground from under me.

But I can see that it's funny as well and we both laugh.

It's really nice to be sitting here with an adult who seems to want to listen to what I have to say. Gran listens as well of course, but she always seems a bit vague, as though she's thinking about something else. Probably things like cathedrals and opera. But Dina's not like that. She has this way of giving whoever she's talking to her full attention – I noticed it with Rachel the other day. She looks straight at you and appears to be weighing up everything you say. She seems to think about it carefully before she responds.

Dina asks me if I want a pudding, but I say no thanks. I can tell that she's desperate for a fag and she lights up the moment we're outside.

On the way back we stop off at a pick your own strawberries place to get some for pudding tonight. For some reason there's a chicken pen right by the car park, with a load of orange chickens running round and round in frantic circles. They are exactly the same colour as the sports jackets in the gentlemen's outfitters in Stalton High Street.

As we're driving back to the village, it starts to rain. It's been cloudy most of the day, but there was no warning that this was going to happen. It suddenly goes from dry to pouring so hard that we can hardly see out of the windshield. And then the rain turns to hail. And the hailstones are the biggest that I've ever seen. They are whanging against the car like bullets. For a minute I'm scared that the windscreen is going to shatter.

There's a single flash of lightning, which turns the whole countryside white for an instant, followed by a roll of thunder that I swear makes my teeth rattle.

Dina says she can't see to drive and pulls over at the side of the road. For a minute or two the noise of the hail is deafening but then, almost as quickly as it started, it stops.

The road is covered about an inch deep in hailstones – it looks like snow in August. And when we set off again, the pick-up's tyres make a crunching sound.

As we approach the village, we can see that the road is flooded. Dina inches the pick-up slowly forward through the water which reaches almost to the truck's door. As we come out the other side, the water starts to dry on the truck's exhaust and the smell is terrible.

Dina says that as we're here, maybe we should call in on Brenda and Charley Maddox. In fact, I'd rather have her to myself, but I know she likes visiting them, so I say yes. I like them as well, but being with Dina is like being an only child. Of course, I am an only child, but in our house that means being a bit of a gooseberry.

Anyway, Brenda is in the shop, parcelling up some more baby food for another farm worker who seems to have walked here and brought a fair bit of the fields with him on his boots.

She says hello and that Charley will be delighted to see us, but to watch out because he's writing his newspaper column and it can make him bad tempered. "You'd think the silly old fool was writing for *The Times* or *The Guardian*, not page 22 of *The East Norfolk Gazette*. It's not exactly Pulitzer Prize territory. But he seems to take it that seriously."

I've no idea what the Pulitzer Prize is, but I do sort of understand what she means.

We duck under the counter flap and carry on through the back of the shop. We can see Charley in the purple summerhouse as soon as we go through the open back door.

And he sees us and waves.

He's got the door shut and the atmosphere inside is a bit tense. Although his face cracks a grin as soon as he sees Dina.

He's sitting in his usual chair with an old-fashioned portable typewriter on his knees. There's a sheet of paper in the typewriter although it seems to have more crossings out – XXXXXX – than anything else on it. There are several other sheets of paper rolled into balls on the floor.

"Hello, darlings," he says and holds his face up to be kissed on both cheeks by Dina and his hand out to be shaken by me.

"Sorry about not getting up Dina. But it's a bit of a palaver at the best of times and damned near impossible with this typewriter thing on my lap."

"Hi Charley, we just thought we'd pop in and say hello. We're on our way back from Stalton."

"Sounds thrilling," he says with a sour look on his face.

"Well it was," she says. "We sampled the culinary delights of The Baker's Dozen, I popped into the offie, and Nick saw the pavement artist that everyone's been writing letters to your esteemed organ about."

Charley is obviously trying to look cross, but not really succeeding. There's a light flickering in his eyes and he can't hide it. You sometimes see comedians doing this on TV. One starts to laugh at what the other one has said and has to hide the fact that he's laughing. Dad says it's called "corpsing."

"Bloody man," he says, "an obvious impostor. I've got more artistic talent in my arse – 'scuse my being so graphic my dears –

137

than he has in his whole body. And my arse isn't something you'd want to write home about. Not what you'd call pert any longer, I'm afraid. Mind you, I like the sound of this off licence. Did it sell alcohol by any chance? Did it have beer and wine and cigarettes? Were the bottles of beer arranged in little rows on the shelves, sporting their proud little labels? Were there bottles of wine in wicker baskets? Were there bottles of whisky and gin and vodka twinkling in the background? Did the whole place have that faint but wonderful whiff of the grape and the grain? Are they offering guided tours by any chance? Would it be a suitable holiday destination for me and that old bag Brenda?"

They both laugh.

"And speaking of which," he goes on in his wonderful voice, "I did open an amusing little Sauvignon Blanc a short while ago. £3.99 from the Co-op at Covington, but hang the expense. Perhaps you'd care to join me in a tiny glass."

He doesn't wait for an answer but pulls a bottle out from under his chair takes a glass from the little shelf behind him and fills it.

Then he gets his own glass from under the chair, clinks glasses with Dina and says "cheerio" in a very fruity, posh voice. They both drink.

"Sorry Nick, but there doesn't seem to be much call for soft drinks in these parts. I expect Brenda will be down soon with something."

I don't mind, I like just sitting here listening to them teasing each other and watching the sunshine in the garden. It's like the rain never happened.

"So, Charley," says Dina, "how's the column going?"

Charley immediately puts his angry face back on. "It's not. I know it's only a crapulous paper paid for by the adverts for second hand cars, but a man has his pride. I used to be a proper writer about a million years ago, when the earth was young. And now I'm reduced to writing crap for readers who are considerably more interested in house price rises than anything I might have to say about anything. My column, as you will know if you number yourself among my countless fans, is called 'Country Matters'. That's a laugh. It's hard to think of anything that matters less."

Although Charley now looks genuinely cross, I still get the feeling that he's enjoying this rant.

"Trouble is that I can't help but take it seriously. And I can never decide what I should be writing about. Should I be all fearless and hard edged and write about agricultural subsidies, the price of diesel or the fact that there's nothing for the local kids to do apart from take drugs and get each other pregnant? Should I be describing the plants in our garden and offering tips about how to get the best out of your roses? Or should I describe going on long walks – describing them being distinctly more possible than walking them – and report back on any wildlife I happen to encounter? The truth is that I'm buggered if I know and I'm even more buggered if I know why I care."

Dina quickly steps in to fill what seems likely to be only a moment's silence.

"So what are you writing about this week then?"

"Well that's just it, isn't it? I don't know. But I don't know in a different sense from my usual sense of not knowing. It's not so much that I don't know what to write about, but that I don't know what to say about what I want to write about."

"This is getting a bit philosophical Charley, and I think I'd need another glass of wine if I was required to get all philosophical." (At this point Dina holds out her empty glass.) "So, what are you getting at?"

"Well, perhaps you'd better have that glass of wine anyway.

139

And I'll tell you what, I think I'll keep you company... What I'm trying to say is that I want to write about what's been happening around here, but I can't quite put my finger on it, still less put it into words. Things are not quite... I don't know... they're not quite right. First of all there's the weather. I know British summers are not exactly famous for their consistency, but this year it seems worse than ever. One minute it's so hot and still that you feel like you're never going to be able to breathe in properly again. Then we get a storm that goes on for two days. Then hailstones the size of golf balls. What's next, a plague of locusts? It's only a matter of time before it starts raining herrings. But that's not it really. The atmosphere is different somehow. There's a kind of tension in the air. When I go into the shop (something I do as infrequently as possible), I can feel that the customers are feeling it. It's as though something is going to happen, and no one has the least idea whether it's going to be a good something or a bad something."

"I know what you mean," I say, "I felt that when I was with Gerry on the broad the other day."

Charley looks interested; Dina looks a bit fed up (Gerry is still clearly not flavour of the month).

"Did you now? Just goes to show what sensitive souls we are. And besides us, other people have been noticing that things aren't quite normal. Mrs Casey two doors up has a golden retriever which is normally the most docile dog in the world, but for the last week or so it's been barking almost non-stop. And it's been going into the garden and positively howling. She must have taken it to the vet's this afternoon or we'd be able to hear it. She can't understand what's wrong with it. And then there's this plague of flies that's been getting on all the fruit and vegetables. Old Hague, who's lived in the village for about 70 years, says that he's never seen anything like it. And Brenda told me at lunchtime that the hens at Manor Farm are only producing about half the normal number of eggs. In fact, some of them seem to have almost stopped laying altogether. And as if that wasn't enough, several people in the village have said that the house martin nests under the eaves of their houses have fallen off. They've come out of their front door in the morning and found the broken mud nests smashed on the ground with feathers and dead chicks scattered all over the place. What's most surprising about all this is that martins are generally good architects and build strong, secure nests. Barbara Pardew told Brenda that she thought there must have been an earthquake. Silly old tart."

"Well," says Dina, "I can see why you're having trouble writing about it. It doesn't really seem to add up to anything. Just animals suffering a bit with the heat and everyone getting a bit fed up with the weather changing all the time. It sounds like what we doctors call 'seasonal affective disorder'."

"I can see why you say that. But there's more to it than that. I'm sure of it, even if I can't prove it. There's something not quite right going on. It's like Shakespeare said about the time being out of joint. But as far as this bloody column goes, I guess I'll have to settle for a piece about the church bloody fete this weekend. Home-made sodding jam, a tom-bloody-bola stall with the same prizes as last year and the year before that, and teddy-bleeding-bears parachuting off the top of the church tower. It's bound to make for riveting reading. But, after all, what do they expect for the money they pay me?"

I hear the backdoor of the shop open and can see Brenda coming down the garden with a tray. I notice that Charley puts his half drunk glass of wine under his chair.

"Well," she says, "what do you think of old Ernest Hemingway here in the throes of creation? A miserable old scrote isn't he? Anyway, darling, love of my life, I've brought you all some tea. You can't drink white wine all day and expect to get away with it."

Brenda sits on the doorstep next to me and the four of us chat for about an hour. I'm not really listening to what they're saying but I like feeling part of things in this way. It's another of those dysfunctional families. Only this time, Charley is the Dad and Brenda and Dina are like my much older sisters.

When Dina says it's time for us to go, Charley cops his usual sneaky feel of her bum and Brenda winks at me. As she walks us back through the shop, she asks us in a way that is meant to sound casual, "How did you think Charley was this afternoon?"

"He seemed fine," says Dina, "but a bit preoccupied. I couldn't really get to grips with what he was saying about things not being quite normal. But it seemed to matter to him."

"I think he is really upset. Something's bothering him. I've never seen him like this before. But on the other hand, he is 92 and has been drinking too much for more than 70 years. So maybe it would be surprising if he *wasn't* a cause for concern sometimes."

"I'm sure he's fine. He'll probably settle back into his usual self once he's got his column finished."

"You're probably right."

Brenda kisses Dina and then gives me one of her soft, perfumey hugs.

But as soon as we've set off in the pick-up, Dina says to me, "I hope old Charley is OK. I think we forget how old he is."

"I think he's all right. I think I know what he was talking about. I know I've never been here before, but even I get this sense that things are a bit different."

Dina says, "You know that as people get older their memory can start to fade. I just hope old Charley isn't having a prolonged senior moment."

"No. I'm sure he's OK. He's just bothered by something that he can't explain."

142

"You're probably right," she says. "It must be difficult. It's bad enough being bothered by things that you can explain. As we both know."

I think this is a signal that Dina wants to talk about something important. Probably Gerry. But I don't, so I don't take the hint.

As we drive through the village, a fine, warm rain starts to fall.

I can see someone walking through the stubble in a field where they've just harvested the wheat. It takes me a minute to realise that it's Sam

Although he's a couple of hundred yards away and there's a hedge between us, I can see that he's still wearing the terrible old shirt and trousers and still has bare feet. He seems to be soaking wet. His head is down and he's plodding steadily towards the village. He must be on his way home.

"There's Sam, who I've been telling you about."

"Where?"

But by now the road has curved and as I look back, Sam is out of sight.

"I can't understand how his parents can let a little kid like that out on his own all day. Do you know them?"

"No, I don't think I know anyone in the village with a kid called Sam. But that's not really surprising. I'm a bit isolated out here and people come and go regularly in the village. If they're not pub people, then it's more than likely that I don't know them. I'll ask around if you like, but I'm not sure what difference it would make even if we did find out who they were. I can't exactly give them a lecture on childcare."

"No, I know. But it's just that I feel so sorry for him."

"Tell you what," yells Dina, "we'll give him a lift." She screeches the pick-up to a stop and then does a three-point turn at speed. But by the time we get back round the bend in the road, Sam's gone. We drive back about a mile but can't see him anywhere.

143

"He must have been heading for the woods," says Dina, turning round once again.

As we pass though the stand of trees on the road to the cottage, I can see what looks like smoke drifting around at the top of the trees. But then I realise it can't be smoke. It's too dark and it keeps changing shape like a shoal of fish.

Dina slows the pick-up down to take a look. "It's bees," she says, "they often swarm at this time of year. I guess they must be looking for a new hive. I'm not sure I've ever seen such a large swarm before."

As we watch, the bees swarm together to form a cylindrical shape like a pillar. But immediately they flatten out to form a saucer. The mass of bees is wispy at the edges as if the outlying ones are being flung off by the force of their mates' beating wings. But they soon rejoin the main shape, which is now a kind of swirling triangle.

We see three more swarms moving slowly and mysteriously over the hedges and the trees before we get back to the turn-off for the cottage. Dina says it's probably a good idea to close the windows if we don't want bees in the cab with us.

Fortunately, there aren't any swarms in the garden at the cottage, although we can see one moving slowly and uncertainly over the trees at the back of the marsh.

Harry is very pleased to see us, squirming and whimpering and doing his best to turn somersaults.

We sit at the kitchen table with the windows open watching the rain and eating all the strawberries we picked until it's completely dark and we can't see the bees anymore.

*Miss Stephens has a kind face
and hardly ever raises her voice.
... My desk is by the radiator
... which hisses like a snake when it gets hot.*

... ...

*Sometimes the heat and the hiss from the radiator make me want to go
to sleep.
... I have to struggle to keep my eyes open...
When it rains and we all come to school wet,
our clothes steam in the heat
and the classroom smells like an old dog...
I watch the raindrops sliding down the outside of the window...
and the low cloud over the fields and the marsh....
...We study Mathematics and English and History, and Miss Stephens
likes it when we bring things in for the nature table − feathers, dried
starfish, ferns, hazelnuts, owl pellets...
My favourite lesson is Geography...
We are studying the African Rift Valley...*

... ...

*Miss Stephens wants us to learn about the geological processes that
formed it...
But all I can think about are the animals that live there...*

... ...

*The elephants... lions... zebra... gazelle...
And above it all the hot,
burning African sun ... ...*

Why don't you sit with us?

Fantastic news: when I went into the shed this morning to check on the swallows, two of the chicks were sitting on the rafter. They don't look quite ready to fly and they've still got some of that baby bird fluff among their feathers, but they're stretching their necks out and flapping their wings. They look as though they might fall off the rafter at any moment, but somehow they never quite do. When one of the parents comes back with a beak-full of stuff, they both start this screeching noise and bob up and down and shuffle backwards and forwards on the rafter. Once the parent has transferred its load into the gaping gob of one of the youngsters, it's out of there in a flash.

I guess the other two chicks are still in the nest and I hope the parents remember to feed them. It would be awful if the idea got into their tiny bird brains that they only have responsibility for the two pushy chicks on the rafter. And believe me, I know something about how parents can ignore their young ones.

As I walk back across the garden, I can see that the bees are still twisting and dancing above the trees on the marsh. They obviously haven't found a better home yet.

Dina seems a bit more cheerful this morning and, as if to prove it, she's wearing a pale blue denim shirt instead of her usual checked working shirts. She's still wearing her boiler suit and wellies, but she looks almost dressed up by her standards.

She's drinking black coffee and smoking a roll-up. Two are stubbed out in the ash-tray on the table.

"Any plans for today, Nick?"

"Not really, I thought I might take Harry for a walk, if that's OK?"

My phone rings. I'm a bit worried it's going to be Gerry, but it's Rachel. "Hi, Nick. Are you OK? Listen. I can get away this afternoon. Are you free? Maybe we could do something."

I'm really pleased to hear from her and we arrange to meet on our bikes outside The Strangled Ferret after lunch.

Harry and I go on a longer walk than we've ever been on before. Maybe the fact that he was left at home yesterday has given him more energy than usual. Whatever, his feet almost dance across the grass that is still wet with dew.

It's warm and still, but there's no mist this morning.

As we walk towards the trees, I'm keeping one eye on the bees – I certainly don't want to get too close to them. At the far edge of the fields to our right I can see several other swarms moving around like smoke signals.

There's also loads of these little black flies around again this morning, which sting like mad if you get one in your eyes.

The marsh harrier is moving slowly up and down a distant hedge.

We continue right through the stand of trees at the far end of the marsh. Then I lift Harry over a wire fence and we skirt round the edges of two fields where the ripe wheat has not yet been harvested. There are loads of orangey-brown butterflies. We startle a rabbit, which dashes off with Harry in pursuit but he soon gives up and comes ambling back to me avoiding eye contact and with a look on his face that clearly says "Sorry about that, I couldn't help myself for a moment, it's my instincts you know, but everything's under control now."

The second field has a narrow ditch at the edge, which we cross on a plank bridge. The water is clear and teeming with little bugs and worms.

Just beyond the ditch, there's a ruined building that you can see from Dina's end of the marsh. It looks like it used to be a church or something. There's not a lot left now – just two walls about ten feet high. Mind you, they're about four feet thick. The walls are made of smallish, flat stones held together by a pale, crumbly cement. There are weeds and pink flowers growing out of them and all around their base is a mass of huge, dark, chin-high stinging nettles. (Charley was saying something to Dina about nettles yesterday. He's having real problems with them in the garden and, according to him, they only grow in places where people live or have lived. Never where they haven't. He says that they aren't a native English plant but were brought over by the Romans. And that they act like a distant memory of the people who used to live on the site. "All that remains of their hopes and dreams are a load of bleedin' old stinging nettles. There's a thought.")

Somehow, this doesn't feel like a very welcoming place. Harry is looking worried and I don't have any wish to hang around.

Two more fields and three more ditches later, we've arrived at the church near the beach car park. (It's much closer across the fields than by road.) When I first came here with Dina the churchyard was padlocked, but today the gates are open. Harry and I have a mooch around.

Apart from a narrow strip where the grass has been cut to make a path, it's been left to grow and is full of weeds, nettles and wild flowers. And it's covering many of the gravestones. The stones themselves are dark and covered in pale green and grey patches of moss or something. Many of them are flaking and some are cracked right through. Because of the grass, you can't read some of the names and dates, only the messages: "Beloved husband and father", "She is free and cannot be held in", "Gone before", "Called by God", "Not dead but sleeping", "Rector of this parish" and so on. And the dead have different names from us: Agnes, Prudence, Walter, Harold, Octavia and so on.

Most of the graves go back to the 1800s, but in one corner

there are some newer ones with white headstones. One is dated 1976. A few have flowers in vases and one has a rose bush planted in the middle of a stone frame.

But although this is a place of the dead, it doesn't feel spooky and unwelcoming like the ruins we've just been to. It feels peaceful and almost friendly. I know the sun's shining on it today, but I feel sure it would be the same even if it was raining and cold. Mind you, I'm not sure I'd want to come here on my own at night.

The church is open. I ask Harry if he'd mind waiting outside and he's happy to do so, flopping down with relief onto a fallen headstone for someone called Thomas Brewer who died in 1843, aged 71.

There's wire netting across the front of the porch, which I guess is there to keep out birds. There's a notice on an old notice-board saying that there will be a service of remembrance on Sunday 17 September at 10.00am (Rev Tim Downey will be conducting the service).

I turn the handle and push open the heavy wooden door. It's very small and dusty inside. There are about six pews on either side and no altar. On one of the windowsills there's a vase of dead flowers. The walls are painted white but covered in brownish water stains. In a couple of places the plaster or whatever it is has fallen off, exposing the stone underneath.

On the end wall is a huge wooden board on which the Ten Commandments are painted – five on the left and five on the right. But whoever did it, didn't plan it too well. By the time he got to commandments five and ten he must have realised that he was running out of space and so started writing much smaller. It looks like these two commandments – *Honour thy father and thy mother* and *Thou shalt not covet any thing that is thy neighbour's* – are less important than the others. There's dust everywhere.

I sit down for a minute and try to imagine what this church

149

used to be like. For hundreds of years people have been coming here for christenings, weddings and funerals; they've been coming at Christmas and Easter; they've made their way through the snow or on the hottest summer's days. They've sung hymns here and listened to sermons, they've slept and flirted and thought about other things. But I can't imagine them. These people aren't here anymore. They've gone. And all they've left behind is this sense that this is a good place to be in August at the beginning of the twenty-first century.

After a few minutes I collect Harry and we walk back to the cottage by the road. On the way we pass a thatched barn about the size of an aircraft hanger. There are a few cars parked outside so it must be open to the public. But we don't stop.

When we get back to the cottage, Harry is knackered and flops down on the back doorstep. Dina's gone out somewhere and left a note saying that she'll see us this evening and that lunch is in the kitchen. She's left a plate of lamb sandwiches on the table but she's forgotten to cover them with anything. So the edges have gone all crinkly and the bread is pretty stale. I manage to eat a couple and then feed the rest to Harry who seems to like them. He promises not to tell Dina.

I have to lock him in the cottage, but he doesn't seem to mind. I guess he'll take the chance of a nap this afternoon. I collect my bike from the shed and head off to meet Rachel.

She's waiting outside the Ferret when I get there and she looks fantastic. (In fact, she looks much prettier than the first time I saw her – how is that possible?) I think she must have just washed her hair because there seems even more of it than usual. It's reflecting the sunlight and she's not wearing her baseball cap today.

She waves when she sees me and I feel a bit self-conscious as I cycle towards her. But girls are good at this and she seems very sure of herself. "Hi, Nick. I'm glad you could make it."

"So am I." (I really should get an award for some of the brilliant things I say.)

"What would you like to do?"

"I don't mind." (Bloody marvellous.)

"I thought we could go swimming at the broad. Have you brought your trunks?"

Have I brought them? After that episode changing under my towel in front of Dina, I've practically slept in them. I've got them on under my jeans. But I don't feel like explaining any of this so I just say "Yes."

"Great. Come on then. Let's see how quickly we can get there."

With which, she sets off as fast as she can. I'm so surprised it takes me a minute to react. Then I set of after her. But she's pedalling really fast and she's got a new bike and I'm riding an old heap.

To be honest, it takes me a bit longer than I would have liked to catch up with her. By the time I do, she's through the village and out into open country, between fields.

When I do catch up, she slows down and we ride along together for a bit, while I try to hide the fact that I'm panting. Fortunately, she seems to be feeling quite chatty.

She's telling me some story about her family and the zoo they visited yesterday. "And that idiot Gerry said there weren't any zoos around here, shows how much he knows. We found one only about ten miles away. There was a treetop walk over the lion enclosure. It was really good. And speaking of Gerry, how's Dina? Not missing that jerk I hope."

I'm still trying to catch my breath, but I do my usual thing of trying to defend Gerry. "He's not so bad. I spent the afternoon with him yesterday at the nature reserve. I think he's a good bloke, it's just that there's something complicated going on between him and Dina."

"You're wrong. He's an idiot. But let's not talk about him."

I don't know why I bother.

I've never come to this side of the broad before. There's a small gravel car park (I wonder where the gravel came from) and a little jetty. But there's no one around. We leave our bikes. Rachel's got a padlock on a long chain, which we wind round both of them, but it's hard to imagine anyone TWOCing them from here.

Then we follow a narrow muddy path for about fifty yards before coming out at the side of the broad.

As usual, it's very still and the water looks milky, reflecting a pale blue sky. It's not as hot as when I came here with Gerry, but it still has that sense of being under a kind of spell. We can see a couple of yachts and a small motor cruiser out on the water. And I can just hear someone's radio. They're listening to music. But none of the boats seems to be going anywhere, and there are no signs of life aboard. I wonder if we'll see the *Piranha*.

The narrow muddy path seems to go round the edge of the broad, so we follow it for a bit. In most places there are reeds around the edge, into which little fishing platforms have been built. But no one seems to be fishing this afternoon.

In a couple of places though, there are gaps in the reeds and the water comes right to the grass, forming a kind of beach. And at the second of these, Rachel suggests we stop.

I take the towel out of my rucksack and spread it on the ground. Rachel's also got a bag with her, in which she's brought some chocolate and a couple of cokes. Trouble is that the chocolate is almost liquid when we unwrap it and it's impossible to get all the silver paper off. "I should have brought crisps," she says.

We sip our cokes and look out at the water, where the only thing that is happening is that a couple of ducks are cruising around and a seagull flies over making a mewing noise. The only sounds are the breeze ruffling the reeds and the water lapping at the bank and the crinkling of a few reddish dragonflies.

We talk for a bit about our families. Rachel tells me about her Mum and Dad. She says that she doesn't think their marriage is too secure and that they argue all the time. "I think that's why they had the twins," she says, "to try to patch up their marriage. I'm nine years older than the boys. For nine years, I was an only child, and I've always been one of those boring, sensible, well-behaved kids. Always did what my parents wanted. Never got into trouble. And then Donny and Rory came along and right from the word go you could tell that they were going to be the kind of boys who would fight and make a noise and behave badly. And they did and they have and now my parents are more stressed out than ever. I think that's why they asked my aunt, and her new husband along. The two other kids are hers not his. I think my parents thought that having other people around might ease the tension or something but it doesn't seem to have worked. In fact, it seems to have made things even worse."

I decide to tell her a bit about my family. I understand what she's saying about being boring and well behaved. That's what I'm like too. And it's a no-win situation. If you don't make a fuss you don't get noticed; and if you do make a fuss, then everyone is disappointed in you and makes sure that you know it. I tell her about Mum and Dad's trip to California and Dad's job, which she thinks sounds exciting and glamorous. I tell her about Gran in Italy and the cathedrals and art galleries, but I can't quite bring myself to tell her the real truth about my life, which is I'm the blemish in my parents' otherwise perfect marriage.

There are lots of reasons why I don't tell her. One: although I think it all the time, saying it out loud makes it seem more real. Two, Rachel might not believe what I'm saying. Three, even if she did believe me, I don't want her feeling sorry for me. Four, and this is the most stupid reason of the lot, I don't want to seem to be betraying my parents. As if they'd care. I'm sure that there are loads of other reasons why I don't tell her, but at this moment I don't want to think about them.

For a minute it's like we've both said everything that we have to say. I sit here watching a couple of ducks ambling across the space between the weeds. I turn to look at Rachel and see that she's looking at my face as if she's expecting something. I have no idea what it is, so I kiss her.

This is the first time I have ever kissed a girl and I want to be absolutely clear about why I'm doing it. I'm doing it because I have this weird idea that she might want me to. I'm doing it because a bit of *me* thinks that it might sort of want me to. I'm doing it because in a way I know that it's expected of me – you could say that I'm doing it because of Jack and Billy, and certainly because of Emily. And in an even weirder way, I'm doing it because of Mum and Dad – but I certainly don't want to go there, I'm not going to think that particular one through.

But just because I'm doing it for lots of complicated reasons doesn't mean that I'm doing it well; even I can tell that. For a start, our faces seem to be at the wrong angle and our lips don't exactly meet. Second, she seems to move her face towards mine as I'm moving mine towards hers, with the consequence that they kind of bump. And third, our teeth knock together. For a moment I can taste salt and lipgloss and then we move our heads apart.

I'm not sure who is more surprised, me or her. Neither of us seems to be able to think of anything to say.

If you pointed a gun at my head, I would have to say that it was nice. But if I'm really honest, I would say that it was also puzzling. I don't really know what to make of it.

The longer we sit here, the harder it is to think of what to do next. Should I say something? Should I put my arm round her? Should I kiss her again? Should I hurl myself fully clothed into the broad? Should I get up and run for the bikes? Truth is, I haven't got a clue.

Fortunately, we suddenly hear someone coming along the path. I think it must be someone walking their dog or maybe a fisherman. But it's Sam, looking even dirtier and sorrier for himself than usual. As he comes into view he stands still and stares at us.

Rachel is the first to react. "Hello, Sam," she says kindly, "were you looking for us?"

"Yes."

"Did you want anything in particular?"

"I just wanted to see you and Nick."

"But how did you know where we were?"

"I found your bicycles and I followed the path."

For some reason – maybe it has something to do with the kissing – I'm really angry with Sam.

"Are you following us?"

"No. I just wanted to see you both."

"I don't believe you. What about the other day? You followed me to the nature reserve."

Of course, I'm not really sure about this but it turns out that I'm right.

"I just saw you go past on your bicycle. I wanted to say hello. But the lady said she didn't know when you'd be back. I waited but you didn't come."

He's so passive and pathetic that I get even angrier.

"You're a liar, you must be following us. And I'm fed up with being spied on. I'm here with Rachel. We're too old for you. Why don't you go away?"

I'm not really expecting the response that this gets.

Sam's face just sort of collapses. He spends about ten seconds trying to fight back the tears, but then he lets them come. They're pouring down his face, creating tracks in the dirt.

Now I'm feeling angry with myself as well as him. How unkind is that? I've really upset a little kid who never did me any harm. What a hero. I want to say sorry but just can't seem to do it.

The tears are still running down Sam's face, there's snot coming out of his nose and his shoulders are shaking.

Rachel isn't saying anything, but I can imagine what she is thinking.

And then, without another word, Sam turns and walks off down the path in the direction he came.

I feel like I've kicked a kitten or stolen money from a blind person.

I've always known that the thing about Sam is how vulnerable and defenceless and needy he is. And now I've really upset him all because I was feeling a bit embarrassed about kissing Rachel so badly.

I turn to Rachel. "I didn't think he'd be as upset as all that. I was only saying that we were too old for him."

"Yes, I know," she says. But her eyes say something else.

We look at the water for a bit, and I realise that I've gone and spoilt another day. Is every day I spend with Rachel going to start well and end badly?

"I'm going to get him."

"OK. Good idea," she says.

I find him on one of the fishing platforms. He's sitting there with his legs crossed looking out at the water and he's still crying. He's like a painting with a title like "Misery" or "Dejection" or "Alone." And I'm responsible.

"Sam?"

There's no reply.

"Sam, what's wrong? Why are you so upset?"

"You know why. You told me to go away."

"But I didn't mean to upset you so much. I'm sorry."

And that is mostly true. But there is a tiny part of me, deep down, that isn't really sorry. There is a tiny part of me that gets really angry every time I see Sam. I say that he makes me angry because his parents so obviously neglect him. But that's not the whole truth. Sam himself makes me angry. It's because he's so hopeless and helpless. Because he's so dirty and smelly and thin and wears awful clothes and has scabs on his head and snot on his face. I know I ought to be kind to him and 90% of me wants to be. But the other 10% wants to say he's not my problem. The other 10% just wants to leave him to get on with it. Nice sort of bloke I'm turning out to be.

"Sam, I really am sorry."

He has stopped crying and turns towards me. "It's all right," he says, "I'm going to go home now."

"No, don't go now. Why don't you come and sit with me and Rachel for a bit. You know, we can have a chat."

Again, his response is much more extreme than I imagined it would be. His face lights up in a smile (I try not to notice how dirty his teeth are). His eyes shine. "Yes please," he says.

I hold out my hand to him and help him to stand up. It's like dealing with an animal as much as a human being. I feel like I'm now being kind to a dog I've just whipped. But Sam doesn't seem to bear a grudge.

When we get back to Rachel, she puts an arm round his shoulder and says, "Sorry Sam, we didn't mean to be so horrible it's just that Nick and I were... talking about something."

"It's all right," says Sam in his usual way. He's his own worst enemy this kid. A minute ago he was crying like he was going to burst but now that Rachel's being nice to him, he doesn't seem to respond.

"Why don't you come and sit with us?" she says.

And just like he did on the beach he sits close to us, rather than with us, and looks at us as if he's looking for something in particular.

"Are you OK, Sam?"

"Yes, I'm all right thank you."

"Would you like a drink?"

"Yes please."

Rachel hands him her coke. (I think this is very brave of her; I wouldn't want to drink out of the same can as Sam. God knows what germs he's carrying. And his smell hasn't got any better.)

He looks closely at the can for a moment, drinks from it and at once his face breaks out into another of those huge smiles. He's smiling so hard, it looks as if his face might come apart at the seams.

"It crackles," he says.

"Sam, haven't you ever had a fizzy drink before?"

"I don't think so."

I can't believe it. Either he's a very good liar or his parents are even worse than I had imagined. They probably make him drink some hideous herbal concoction of their own, like dandelion and dockleaf. Bloody hippies.

Before I can say anything else, he's finished the drink. "Thank you," he says solemnly, handing the can back to Rachel.

We sit for a while watching the water. A small black duck with a white beak goes past, making a blipping noise. For the sake of something to say, I ask Sam if he knows what kind of duck it is.

"It's a coot," he says.

And then, for the first time, he starts to speak unprompted.

"In the winter, people come to shoot them. They shot 427 in

one day last winter. My father let me go out on the boat with them. I helped to pick the dead birds out of the water."

This doesn't seem very likely to me. I think this Sam must live in a fantasy world. But there's something about that number – 427. It's as though I knew he was going to say that. What's so special about it? It's just an ordinary number and yet it's almost like I've been expecting it, as though I've heard it before. But I can't remember where.

"I know that they used to shoot coots, it says so in a book at my aunt's house, but I don't think anyone does it now. Are you sure about this?"

"Yes, I'm sure. I was there when they shot the birds. It was exactly 427 birds. My father told me."

He seems to be angry and upset that I'm doubting him. And that number's still bothering me. Where have I seen it before?

"What does your father do, Sam?" asks Rachel.

"He's a warden on Revenant Broad."

"Then you must know Gerry," I say. Rachel pulls a face.

"Who is Gerry?"

"He works on the broad as well. Tall, thin, very brown. He sometimes wears this awful leather hat."

"No, I don't think I know him."

I'm sure he must be lying. How can he not know Gerry if his father works on the broad?

"He's my aunt's boyfriend. Tells lots of stories. Spends lots of his time in The Strangled Ferret."

"What is that?"

"It's the pub in the village. You must know that."

"Oh, yes. I know the pub. I just didn't know that was its name."

"What's your surname, Sam?"

He doesn't seem to mind this interrogation.

"Wellsby. Sam Wellsby."

159

"OK, Sam Wellsby," says Rachel, "Nick and I are going swimming. Are you going to come in with us?"

And just as he did on the beach, Sam looks suddenly terrified. "No, thank you. I told you, I don't go in the water. I don't like swimming."

He's shaking with fright.

"I didn't mean that you had to come right in with us. I just thought you might like to paddle while we go in for our swim."

"No thank you. I never go in the water. I hate the water. I have to go now. I have to go home."

I've never seen anyone look so scared.

"It's OK," says Rachel, "you don't need to come in the water. You can just sit here and wait while we go in for a swim."

"No, thank you. It's all right. I have to go. I'm going now. Goodbye."

And with that, he gets up, turns his back on us and starts back down the path. Doesn't look round once. He's practically running. Having plonked himself on us uninvited, he can't get away quickly enough.

"Sam," Rachel yells, "will you be all right? How will you get back?"

"I'll walk," he calls back over his shoulder.

"Shall I go after him again?" I say.

"I'm not sure there's any point."

"I think there's something wrong with him. I mean, something other than the ragged clothes and the smell."

"He seems very unhappy to me," says Rachel. "He's just so sad and neglected. We'll have to make sure we're nice to him the next time we see him."

"Something about him makes me hope there won't be a next time," I say.

"What about that swim, then?"

The water is warm and brownish. We swim a few yards from shore and turn over on our backs watching the clouds move slowly across the sky. There doesn't seem to be anything else to say.

...
I'm flying through the air with the angel boy.
Travelling at a thousand miles an hour.
He's holding me up. Keeping me safe.
I am not afraid... ...
We are soaring.
Drifting.
... ...
The ground is rushing away beneath our feet.
And I am still not afraid... ...

... ...
The wind is making my eyes stream...

... ...
The fields and the hedges approach and retreat — a single blur.
I can't seem to focus on anything properly.

... ...
The angel is saying something to me...
Whispering in my ear.
I'm sure it is important.
Maybe it's a secret or a magic spell.
But I can't make out his words... ...

...
Only the sound of the wind... ...

They're only worms

There were three young swallows on the shed rafter this morning.

I'm embarrassed about how happy this made me.

They were stretching and flapping their wings, trying not to fall off, looking as though they owned the place. That means there's just one left in the nest. They're nearly safe; a few more days and they'll have made it. The parents look really harassed by their growing responsibilities, but continue to bring beaks full of scoff every few minutes to chicks who are nearly as big as they are. If the weather holds for a few more days, I think they'll be fine.

Rachel and I stayed at the broad for a couple of hours after Sam left yesterday. We swam around for a bit and I loved the feeling of the warm soft mud between my toes. Then we sat on the bank wrapped in our towels. It was so quiet and still. I didn't try to kiss her again and I didn't even sneak a look at her legs. But she was cool and chatted normally. In the end though, the mozzies moved in for the kill, so we got dressed and picked up the bikes.

There were more of the small black flies than usual, so there was no singing on the ride back.

We'd only gone about a mile, when I saw ahead of us on the road a small figure in bare feet plodding towards the village with his head down. What was he doing here?

He didn't turn round as we cycled towards him, but when we caught up with him, he turned towards us and gave us one of his huge smiles. But there's something sad even about his smiles.

Rachel said, "Sam what are you doing?"

"I'm walking home."

"But you left ages ago. What have you been doing."

163

"I've been walking."

"It can't have taken you all this time to get as far as this."

"It has."

"Won't your parents be wondering where you are? Won't they be worried?"

"No, I don't think so."

I could see this conversation was going precisely nowhere. Remembering what Rachel had said about being kind to him (and how bad I'd felt at making him cry) I said, "Come on then matey, jump on, I'll give you a lift back to the village."

He looked really thrilled and sat on my crossbar.

I tried to ignore the smell and the closeness of his scabby head and not think about his dirty teeth that were so close to my face.

Sam, meanwhile, was having a brilliant time. He seemed to have a better sense of balance than the last time. His eyes were shining and he was shouting, "Wheeee." It was a bit embarrassing really. But there was no one to see and I was really glad he was having a good time.

When we got to the turning in the road by the church, he said, "Please can I get down here."

"Wouldn't you like me to give you a lift all the way to your house? Is it down here?"

"Yes, I live down here, near the church. But no thank you, I don't need a lift."

"Are you sure?"

I really wanted to see where he lived. Maybe meet his parents, find out what sort of people could treat a kid like this. But he made it pretty plain that he didn't want me to go to his house, and I couldn't see how I could insist.

So I stopped the bike and he climbed off.

And just as he did a couple of days ago, he set off down the lane without looking back.

Rachel called to him. "Sam, would you like to meet up with us tomorrow? We could do something."

"Yes please, I would like that."

"All right then, let's meet at the broad tomorrow – same place as today. We'll see you there at about three o'clock. What would you like to do? We could go for a walk or maybe we could go out on a boat. You choose."

"I don't want to go out on a boat. Could we go fishing? I like fishing."

"OK, fishing it is."

"What?"

"Yes, we'll go fishing."

"Good." He turned to go.

"Have you got your own fishing stuff?" Rachel called.

"What?"

"Your own fishing rod?"

"Yes."

"Goodbye then Sam."

"Goodbye Rachel. Goodbye Nick."

And with that, he was gone.

"Why did you do that?" I said. "Why did you invite him to meet us tomorrow?"

"I don't really know. I'm sorry. I just couldn't help myself really. I said it before I knew I was going to say it. But don't worry. It's all right if you don't want to come. I can meet him on my own and watch him fishing. I told you I was a right little goody two-shoes. As if I didn't have enough trouble putting up with my own brothers, without adopting another one."

"I know what you mean," I said. "He makes me feel like that as well. And of course I'll meet you. I've even got an old fishing rod, not that it's much good."

I cycled back to the cottage with her and then said I had to go.

She looked straight at me and said, "I enjoyed the kiss."

I muttered something about me too. Where do girls get this confidence from? It's like nothing fazes them. I took off as quickly as I could on my crappy old bike and I didn't look back.

In the evening, Dina and I went to the Ferret. I guess she went to see Gerry but, amazingly enough, he wasn't there. Was this the first time ever? I think I'd imagined that they wouldn't open the place until Gerry turned up. A small posse of loonies was sitting at one of the tables and we joined them. The atmosphere was a bit strained. I guess these people really think of themselves as Gerry's friends rather than Dina's or maybe they were a bit embarrassed by how mean he was to her the other evening.

Anyway, everyone chatted about this and that in a polite sort of way and the pints disappeared and the fags were smoked. At one point, I asked if anyone knew the Wellsby family. But no one seemed to.

"They've got a boy of ten or 11 called Sam. I think his dad works on the broad, they live in one of the cottages by the church."

But still nothing.

Not that I should have been surprised, the brains of this lot are so full of booze and tobacco and endless chat, that it's amazing that they can remember their own names and where they live. Let alone where other people live.

I had begun to think that this was it, when one of the loonies (multi-coloured ringlets, horrible orange jumper that he might have knitted himself) said, "Are you sure he lives in Church Lane? There are only a few cottages there and I thought they were all weekend places. I didn't think anyone lived there full time."

"Well that's where he says he lives."

"Maybe they've just moved in then."

I was about to say that I didn't think that was likely, but the conversation had already moved on and was all about second homes and "incomers" and how they are pricing local people out of the property market. So I gave up. But I was more sure than ever that Sam's lying to me. The only question is why?

There was a break in the conversation and Dina asked, "Anyone know where Gerry is tonight?"

She was trying to sound casual but I knew – and I think everyone else knew – that she'd been wanting to ask this since we arrived.

The loonies looked at one another a bit uncomfortably and then the one with the ringlets – the self-styled expert on who lives in Church Lane – said that apparently Gerry had got completely rat-arsed at lunchtime and fallen over when he was supposed to be guiding a party around the reserve. Unfortunately, his boss was there and sent Gerry home. He made a real fuss about going on his motorbike but they wouldn't let him and in the end Moon drove him home in the reserve's van.

"So, he's probably sleeping it off at the moment," he said. He had a stupid smile on his face as though he thought that Gerry's had done something really cool rather than just lived down to Rachel's opinion of him. "He seems to be drinking rather a lot at the moment."

"Well that's not exactly a personality change," said a loony lady (some kind of blanket over silver boots, tons of eye make-up). "Gerry always did like a drink or 20."

"Yeh," said another lady (green streaks in her hair, white string vest over pink T-shirt), "he did. But he seems somehow different at the moment. I dunno... bothered about something. Upset. I dunno... What about you Dina, you must have noticed?"

Dina started to say something about how he must be working too hard (which I was sure no one believed) but it didn't matter because loony lady number 2 had already closed her eyes and was apparently thinking of something else. Probably about something that's happening on the Planet Krypton.

After a bit, Dina said it was time for us to go. We said goodbye to the loonies. To be fair to them, they were nice enough, almost jolly; but I still got the sense they were glad we were going. Although he was at home pissed, Gerry was still managing to spoil the evening.

As soon as we got into the pick-up, Dina said the most stupid thing I have ever heard her say. I think she must have realised how stupid it was even as she said it because her voice was so quiet. "Do you think we ought to stop off at Gerry's to make sure he's all right?"

How many ways are there of saying "no?" Of saying, "No, actually, I don't think that's a good idea. I think it's a truly terrible idea. In fact, I doubt if anyone in the history of the world has ever had such a bad idea before. It's completely useless. It's pants. A chocolate teapot of an idea."

What I said was, "No probably not. He's probably asleep and even if he isn't, he might be a bit embarrassed at knowing that we know about him getting drunk and being sent home."

What I meant was that I was sure that if we went there, Gerry would be horrible to Dina. I just knew it.

"Perhaps you're right." I couldn't tell whether it was relief or sadness.

On the drive back, I was worried that she was going to start pouring her heart out about Gerry. Give me all the ghastly details of their relationship. But if she was tempted, she resisted it.

The windows were down and the night was warm and damp and I could almost hear and feel things growing in the hedgerows. There was no moon and you couldn't really see anything outside the beam of the pick-up's headlights as it lit up the road ahead.

Once back at the cottage, we let Harry out into the garden for a pee and Dina poured herself a large drink and followed him outside.

I found her on the bench sucking on a roll up as if her life depended on it (rather than the opposite) with Harry sitting at her feet. She was absent-mindedly tugging at his ears and he looked like he was settling in for a good long session of this.

I sat down next to them. Now that we were out of the car, I could see that the sky was a pale green colour. There were no stars.

"Hi, Nick."

"Hi. Are you OK?"

"Yeh, I'm fine thanks. Contrary to what you might think, I'm not out here getting all upset about Gerry. For some reason, that all seems a long way away. I was actually thinking about your Dad."

"Dad? Why?"

"I was just thinking that some people have a talent for making you feel in the wrong all the time. Gerry seems to do this to me a lot at the moment – Oops, sorry, I said I wasn't going to talk about him. Well, your Dad's a bit like that. He's just so perfect, and so successful and everything comes so easily to him. When I was little, I used to think that he was wonderful. Not that I saw much of him, he lived with your grandmother, while I lived with my mother (she was his Dad's second wife). But he used to come to stay for holidays. I thought he was so glamorous that I tried hard to impress him. But I don't think he noticed. Once, when he was staying (I think he must have been at university), I wrote a story for him. I must have been about eight, and I wrote it in my best handwriting and illustrated it with some poster paints. It was only about four pages long but I made a cover for it out of cardboard and silver paper. I presented it to him at supper one evening. He said all the right things about how honoured he was and how he

169

would always treasure it and so on. He said he'd read it and let me know what he thought. So, for the next few days I was on tenterhooks, I was desperate for praise from him. But he never said anything. I reminded him a couple of times and he always said that he hadn't had a moment but the he was really looking forward to it. When he left, I went into his bedroom like I always used to do. I used to love to lie on his unmade bed and smell the sheets... Maybe I shouldn't be telling you this, let me know if it gets too uncomfortable... Anyway, I used to lie there and have this fantasy that somehow we could be married when I was older even though he was my half-brother. Sometimes I would fall asleep in his sheets and dream about him. Anyway, this particular time I searched the room, not really telling myself what it was I was looking for. And sure enough, under the bed, I found my story. I was only eight, but I didn't have to be told that he hadn't even opened it, that I had given him a gift which meant absolutely nothing to him."

I had to fight down this urge to defend Dad. How ridiculous is that? "Yes, I know," I said, "he can appear a bit self-centred at times. But he's never deliberately unkind or angry. It's just that sometimes it seems like other people have nothing to do with him. Like he lives in this charmed circle with himself at the middle and that no one else can really get through, not even Mum although she comes closer than anyone else."

"But that's not my point," said Dina. "Even though I knew he hadn't read it, I blamed *me*, not him. The fact that he hadn't read it meant that there was something wrong with it, not that he was failing an eight year-old girl. It obviously wasn't good enough. Because he couldn't be in the wrong, I must be."

"I know what you mean. He has the same effect on me."

"I sometimes think that my whole life has been shaped by him, even though he couldn't care less. I sometimes think that's why I became an academic – to impress him. Not that he's the least bit impressed. He only seems to value the things that I don't – money and glamour and eating meals with famous people. I'm sure that he thinks what I do is a waste of time. And the biggest problem is that I can't always convince myself that he's wrong. Once again, it must be me who's wrong."

"Listen, Dina, Dad knows how clever and successful you are. And I'm sure he's very proud of you." (Actually, I'm more or less sure he's never given it a moment's thought.) "And I really like being here. And I like the way you live. It's much better than hanging out with a load of Z-list celebrities in California."

At least that's true. If someone offered to fly me to California tomorrow to join up with Mum and Dad, I'd say no. I've got too much to do here. Harry needs walking. There's the swallows. There's Rachel. There's Sam to be sorted out somehow. There's Gerry and Dina's relationship to be got right. This is where I need to be at the moment.

Dina said, "Listen Nick, sorry, I didn't mean to burden you with all this. He's your Dad after all and I guess things are complicated enough for you without having to worry about me. Forget it. In fact, I don't really know what came over me. Telling you all that. It's not like me. I'm usually a person who keeps herself to herself."

"It's OK, I'm glad you told me. I do know how you feel."

So we sat there for a while. I could just hear the wind over the marsh and Harry's regular breathing. Then I said good night and before I could think about it gave Dina a hug and felt her bony arm on my shoulder and smelled the tobacco and whisky on her breath. I don't know what's going on – I've never done so much hugging and kissing in my life.

When I got back to my room, I checked to see if there were any texts for me, but there weren't. I sent a text to Billy in Africa but I couldn't think of much to say, so I just said hi really and mentioned that I'd met someone called Rachel. I started to send a longer text to Jack about Rachel and how much I like her, but in the end I deleted it because it didn't seem to have anything to do with him. So I just texted hi to him as well.

Anyway, this afternoon Rachel and I met up with Sam and it was a total disaster.

I asked Dina what she thought would be good bait for pike and she said maybe worms would be an idea. I wasn't sure that this was quite right but I couldn't think of anything better. So, while Harry watched over my shoulder, I dug up about 40 from one of the compost heaps. The swallows and the dragonflies kept me company.

I don't really like handling worms, but I got used to it and put them in a plastic bucket with some damp earth. Then I took the old fishing rod to pieces and tied it to my crossbar, hung the bucket and the old tackle box with the flies in it over my handlebars and set off to meet Rachel at the Ferret.

She was looking great and chatted about this and that as we cycled to the broad. We left our bikes in the same place as yesterday and walked round the edge of the broad to our little private beach. Sam was waiting for us when we got there – sitting on the ground looking out over the water as if he was thinking of something else or seeing something out there that the rest of us couldn't.

When he saw us he smiled, but I swear he looks worse every time I see him. Dirtier. Thinner. Paler. Scabbier. Smellier. More pathetic. It almost looks as if he's ill or fading away. What is the matter with his parents? I feel I've got to do something about him. There must be somebody who can help. Maybe he should be in care. There must be social services around here. He can't just be left like this, it isn't right. He's so sad and so neglected.

Rachel was all bright and cheerful and gave him a chocolate bar, which he ate as if he was starving. And when she dug a can of coke out of her rucksack and handed it to him, his smile was as big as I've ever seen it. He seemed to be having trouble opening it – I noticed that his nails were bitten down almost to nothing – so I opened it for him. He drank from it with this puzzled, blissful look on his face.

"Where's your fishing rod?" I asked him.

"I forgot it. I'm sorry."

"Well, never mind," said Rachel, "Nick's brought his, we can all use that."

It wasn't until I'd fitted the two pieces of the rod together that I realised I was going to have to put a worm on the hook. And I really didn't want to do it. Nor did Rachel. But Sam said he'd do it and he simply held the worm between two fingers in his left hand and passed the point of the hook through its body twice. When the hook went into its body it curled up and wriggled like it had been electrocuted. I felt sick. I didn't want to look at Rachel. Sam didn't seem to be in the least bit bothered.

He offered to hand the rod back to me but I said, "no, you go ahead."

So he cast the line out into the water and sat back on the ground with the rod across his knees watching the little red float dance up and down.

We all sat and watched the float for a while and nothing much happened. After about ten minutes, Sam brought the line in, tore the remains of the worm off the hook and threaded another one on and cast it out again. It was the first time I'd seen him do anything and he did it expertly. All in one movement. But it was horrible – once again the worm curled up in silent agony as soon as the hook went into it. But once again, he took no notice.

After another ten minutes, he brought the line in again and changed the worm in this same unthinking way, cast it out again and handed the rod to Rachel. At first I thought she was going to refuse, but she smiled and took it from him.

The three of us watched the float for a while as it moved in the water. At one point I thought there might be a bite – the float moved in an odd way – but nothing came of it. I was feeling really drowsy, sitting in the warm sunshine, doing nothing, watching the float ride the little ripples at the edge of the broad and the specks of light flashing on the water's surface. (It seems that I get dozy all the time at the moment. I'm not normally like this.) I think I could have fallen asleep, but then Rachel suddenly shouted, "Sam, what the hell are you doing?"

Sam looked up, startled, tears in his eyes. "Nothing."

He'd found a length of line in the old tackle box and was threading the worms on it, but the really horrible bit was that he was threading them lengthwise.

He was using a thin pointed device for removing hooks from a fish's mouth and forcing it in at one end of a worm, down the whole length of the body and out the other end. It was disgusting. There were already four worms on the line and Sam was in the process forcing the thin piece of metal through the body of the fifth.

Rachel was really angry. "I said what the fuck are you doing?"

Tears started to roll down his cheeks. "I'm making a bab for eels."

"What," Rachel shouted.

"It's for catching eels. They can smell the worms' blood. You put a hook in and you can catch lots."

There were tears in Rachel's eyes as well. "How could you do such a thing? How could you be so cruel? I can't believe you."

I could see why she was so angry but I could also see that Sam didn't know what he'd done to make her angry.

"They're only worms," he said. "They can't feel anything and the eels like them."

"What do you means they're only worms? That's no reason to torture them. And who are you to say that they can't feel pain? Of course they can."

174

"I thought you would want to catch some eels."

"I don't. I don't care about stupid eels or any other stupid fish. But I just hate cruelty."

"I don't understand," said Sam, looking helpless, the tears still falling.

"Well I'm sick of it and I'm sick of you. We met you here this afternoon because we wanted to give you a good time. Well, I don't want that any more. In fact, I wish you'd go away."

It seemed to me that, in her own way, Rachel was being as cruel as Sam, but it didn't seem like a good idea to tell her so. Seeing him standing there with tears streaking his dirty face, seeing his body curl up and tremble, was almost like watching him having a rope forced through his body from one end to the other. Like he was wriggling and bleeding like a worm.

Sam dropped the threaded worms. Looking totally miserable and hopeless and defeated, he turned and without another word set off down the path between the reeds. It was like he didn't have the strength to stick up for himself. Just gave in. Just went.

There was a bit of a silence. I guess both of us were thinking that we'd twice sent Sam away from this place.

Rachel said in a small voice, "Could you please do something about the worms?"

I tipped the remaining worms in the bucket onto the ground but I didn't know what to do with the ones already on the line. Getting it out of them would be as bad as threading them in the first place. I couldn't think of any way of killing them quickly, so in the end I just threw the line and the piece of metal and the worms into the broad where at least we wouldn't have to look at them.

Neither of us said anything for a bit. I could see why she was upset but, to tell the truth, I did think she'd overreacted a bit. After all, like Sam said, they were only worms.

"That didn't go very well, did it?" she said, with a sort of half

175

smile on her face. "Poor Sam. But it's just that I can't bear seeing things hurt. It was bad enough putting worms on a hook but seeing them threaded like that was just horrible. I guess you think I'm a bit of a bitch – and it was me who said we should be nice to him."

"I don't think he realised that he was doing anything wrong."

"Well he should have done. What's the matter with him?"

"I think he wanted to catch some eels for you. I think he thought it would be a nice thing to do. I don't think he thought about the worms."

"That's right," she said, "make me feel guilty. Put me in the wrong."

"I don't think you're in the wrong. Like I said yesterday, he really pisses me off as well. He just seems to bring out the worst in us because he's so useless and dirty and weird."

"Come on then," said Rachel after a minute or two. "I suppose we'd better catch him up."

So we packed up the fishing gear (the pikes of Revenant Broad were safe for another day), collected our bikes and set off back to the village.

The flies were worse than ever. There were great clouds of them getting in our eyes and mouths, up our noses and in our ears. It was vile. We kept expecting to see Sam stomping bare-foot along the road.

Rachel was trying to explain it away. "I shouldn't have reacted like that, I guess. He's only a kid and he lives in the country and things are different here. I should have just asked him to stop and not do any more. But it was like the sight of him made all this anger come out of me. It wasn't really his fault. I hope we catch him up."

But we didn't. For what seemed like the first time in ages, he was nowhere to be seen.

Typical. Just when you want him, he's not around. I thought

back to what Dina had been saying about people who put you in the wrong. Sam was like that. First it had been me and now it was Rachel who was feeling guilty about him.

I cycled back with Rachel to the cottage she was staying at, but said I wouldn't go in.

I didn't tell her, but I had a plan. I was going to call in at Sam's house on the way back to Dina's. I had an excuse: to check that he was all right. And then I would get to see where he lived and maybe meet his parents. I knew that I wouldn't say anything to them about how neglected Sam was, but I think I thought that just knowing he was meeting other kids might encourage them to do something about him.

I realised that I was coming to think about it like that: What's to be done with Sam?

So when I came to the lane by the church, I turned into it. Running along the right hand side was a field of pale stubble. About 50 yards from the main road on the left were three cottages in a row. They had thatched roofs and the fronts had a checker-board pattern of pink and purple bricks. All three had little front gardens and there was no sign of anyone in any of them. The first one in the row had all the curtains closed and it was obvious no one was at home. I knocked on the doors of the other two but there was no answer. I called out "hello" in case there was anyone in one of the gardens, but I didn't really expect a reply. You can always tell when you are calling at a house where no one's in. You can feel the emptiness through the door.

So, Sam had been lying to me. I knew it. Wherever he was, he wasn't here.

On summer nights the marsh is a magical place…
The moon rides the clouds like a ship at sea.
The mosquitoes drone and zizz.
Owls call
and everywhere there are mysterious splashes.
The breeze makes the reeds rustle…
… like someone rubbing dry fingers together.

… …

When we pass the ruined abbey I always whisper a prayer to myself
and stay close to Father.
The air seems colder there… …

…

Father tells me stories about ghostly monks walking the marsh on moonless nights.
He says that they walk in single file around the edge of the ruins, chanting mysterious words to the night air.
He says that they are wearing brown robes
which flap in the wind and sound like the reeds… …

…

But then he puts his arm round my shoulder…
And he laughs… …
And I feel safe.

Shore thing

I can't open my eyes, the light behind the curtain's too bright. I can hear Dina moving about downstairs but I can't be bothered to get up. As I lie here half asleep, I'm trying to think about Sam and Rachel and Gerry but my thoughts keep getting mixed up. It's so warm and I'm so sleepy.

In the end, however, the fact that these thoughts keep getting mixed up gets on my nerves and forces me out of bed.

I go to the window. The sky is the palest blue and the garden is filled with butterflies and dragonflies. And here's the best thing: I can see four swallows. *Four*. It's bloody marvellous.

Two of the chicks must have started to fly.

The four of them are swooping and darting and making secret patterns in the air and I can't really tell which are the chicks and which are the parents.

A couple of days ago they couldn't make it off the shed rafter, and now they are brilliant fliers, whizzing around as if they'd been doing it all their lives. If humans were like that, babies would go from crawling to running a marathon in about ten minutes flat. Where does this fantastic control come from? What must the wiring in their brains be like? What does it feel like to flick in and out of the shadows at such speed and without putting any effort into it?

I get dressed, visit the hedge down the lane and check out the shed. The third chick is on the rafter, sticking its neck up as far as it will reach and flapping its wings frantically. If willpower could get it into the air it would be long gone. But there's no sign of the fourth chick. I guess it's still in the nest. I hang around in the shed for a few minutes but the parent birds don't call in with any food like they usually do. I think they must be encouraging the two remaining chicks to leave the nest and the shed.

And I can see their point. Who would want to stay in this stuffy darkness if they could fly over the garden? Even though they don't fly very high, they must be able to see for miles across the marsh to the sea.

Dina and I have breakfast in the garden – toast for me (which always means a bit for Harry) and fags for her. The flies are a bit of a pain but there's enough of a breeze to stop them being impossible. There's still a large swarm of bees coiling and uncoiling above the trees – now a giraffe, now an ocean liner, now an iceberg, now a giant sewing machine, now William Shakespeare's head.

"I've been thinking about your disastrous fishing trip with Sam. I think what he was trying to do with those worms was a traditional way of catching eels. The marshmen used to do it. Maybe Sam's read about it somewhere. But I don't think many people use it now because it seems so cruel. People's views of things change and maybe we're more sensitive now than we used to be. I guess that's why Rachel was so upset."

"Yeh, I think he was trying to do something nice, just got it all completely wrong. I didn't tell you that I tried to call in on him on the way back here." (I almost said "home" without thinking.) "I went down Church Lane but there didn't seem to be anyone in any of the cottages. All three felt empty."

"Well, Brian did say that he thought they were all weekend cottages."

Brian of the multi-coloured hair and hideous jumper.

"But if Sam doesn't live there, then he must be lying to us and why would he do that?"

"Could be for lots of reasons. He's ashamed of his house. He's frightened of his parents. He doesn't want them to know that he's hanging out with older kids. He doesn't trust you – you did say you weren't very nice to him a couple of days ago. I don't know."

"I guess you're right. If I met his parents I don't know that I'd be able to stop myself saying something about the state of their kid. So, it's probably as well I don't know where they are. I wish he wouldn't lie to me though. I don't like thinking that he feels he can't trust me."

Harry starts to bark and we hear a van coming down the track. The postman appears round the side of the cottage – "Mornin', thought I might find you here."

He's got a bundle of stuff for Dina and a postcard for me from Gran.

Before he goes, I ask him if he knows the Wellsby family who may have moved in recently.

"Sorry, no, never heard of them. Friends of yours?"

"They might live on Church Lane. They've got a boy called Sam. You might have seen him in the village. He sometimes plays in the school playground. No shoes."

"Doesn't ring any bells with me. And they definitely don't live on Church Lane, unless they're travelling under an assumed name. Spies are they?"

Just what I need – a postman who fancies himself a bit of a comedian.

After he's gone, Dina says, "I've had a thought. Maybe Sam's adopted or fostered or his mother's married again or something. Maybe he has a different name from his parents and that's why no one's heard of the Wellsbys."

I guess this could be true, but for some reason I don't really believe it. There's something more than that going on.

Gran's postcard is from Verona:

"Hi Nick, I hope you're having a lovely time in Norfolk. The old bags are continuing to break young men's hearts

> *throughout the length and breadth of Italy. Tonight, we'll*
> *be getting dressed up and going to see Aida in the*
> *amphitheatre. There's a rumour about real elephants but I*
> *don't believe it. I'm really looking forward to you coming*
> *to stay in two weeks or, if the Italian post is as efficient as*
> *usual, two months ago. Say hello to Dina for me. Lots of*
> *love, Gran."*

"In two weeks," and the postmark shows that the card was posted a few days ago. That's a bit of a shock. It's hard to imagine not being here. There's so much that needs to be sorted out. The thought of leaving makes me realise that this is the only place I want to be at the moment.

I can hear my phone ringing up in my bedroom but I don't want to answer it. It can't be anyone I want to talk to right now.

When I do go up to my room, it turns out to have been a call from Rachel. She's left a voice message saying that she can be free in the afternoon if I want to do something.

The truth is I don't. I certainly don't want a day like yesterday with all that arguing and shouting and crying. I think I'll have a day on my own. I decide not to call her back.

Harry and I spend the morning on the marsh. We make camp in a patch of long grass and I lie on my back with Harry's head on my stomach and watch the sky moving over my head. It's very quiet, a few birds fly over but I can't hear any singing in the hedges. Harry breathes and twitches in his sleep.

At lunch (I won't bother describing it) I ask Dina if she'd like to go to the beach this afternoon. She says that she'd love to, but she's got to get some work finished first.

"It has to go into the post this afternoon. Tell you what, though, why don't you and Harry go on the bike and I'll drive down to meet you as soon as I'm finished?"

As we cycle towards the beach, with Harry's back feet in the basket and his front feet on my shoulders, I can't help but think that he's a lot less smelly than Sam.

Two women in a car wave as they pass. Harry smiles at them and I'm sure he'd wave a paw if he could. I can't wave back either because I don't dare take my hands off the handlebars.

We've got the beach to ourselves today. The sea is oily and flat under a sky with feathers of clouds breaking up towards the horizon. The water laps against the shore with a whisper.

I've brought a tennis ball and throw it for Harry who immediately forgets he's an old dog and tears after it like a puppy. (Dina says some men are like this. Give them a ball and the years drop off them.) He has this wonderful run – ears back, low to the ground, excitement coming off him in waves. The sand is good for him to run on because it's so easy on his paws. He brings the ball to me and drops it at my feet. Then he goes into a crouch, waiting for me to throw it again.

We do it four or five times. Then he catches the ball but doesn't bring it back. He's saying, "Thanks, that was great, but it's enough for now. I'm shagged." Then he settles down to chewing the ball on a damp patch of sand, minding his own business.

I walk over to him and rub his stomach while he groans with satisfaction.

I have this sense we're being watched and as I turn towards the sea a shiny black head with great liquid eyes emerges about ten yards from the shore.

It's a seal and it's very curious. It's obviously never been told that it's rude to stare and it watches us very carefully without blinking, as if judging us. And then, having made up its mind that we're really boring, its head slips below the water without a ripple and it's gone.

What hasn't gone though is this sense of being watched.

I go back to my stuff and spread the towel out on the sand. I'm not brave enough to go swimming on my own so I'll just lie here on seal watch.

I can't shake off this feeling that I'm not alone. Harry doesn't seem bothered – he's still playing with the tennis ball.

I get up on my elbows and look back at the dunes. I'm almost certain I see a head duck down behind the sand. For a minute I think it might be one of the meerkat men but them I'm certain it's Sam. Bloody Sam. Spying on me again.

I shout out, "I've seen you Sam. You might as well come out."

But nothing happens except that Harry looks a bit surprised.

"Come out Sam. I know you're there."

Still nothing.

I get up and walk back to the dunes, but he's not there. There's no one.

I must have imagined it. I feel a bit stupid. I'm glad there was nobody here to hear me shouting. It's well uncool shouting "Sam" to a completely empty beach.

But I still feel as though someone's watching.

After a bit Harry sits up, barks once and dashes off to the gap in the dunes.

It's Dina.

I ask if she saw anyone while she was driving here but she says no.

She gets out of her clothes and is about to dive in when I say, "Dina, do you always swim so far out?"

She looks surprised – "I guess so. Why?"

"It's just that I get nervous. I don't know. I'm stupid really, but it's like I think you're not coming back or that something is going to happen to you out there. I'm sorry."

"Don't be sorry. But I love it out there, between the sky and sea, with the land behind me. When I was a kid, my ambition was to swim out as far as the horizon. There's nothing to be nervous about, I'm a strong swimmer and the current here is towards the shore not away from it."

"It's just that you look so small when you get away from the shore."

"Well, promise that you won't worry today, and I'll promise not to go too far. OK?"

"OK."

And with that, she's gone heading straight from the shore. But when she's gone about 100 yards, she stops, treads water and turns round and waves to me. Her skinny brown arm looks so frail against the blue of the sky, but I can see that she's smiling. I wave back.

She heads out to sea again, but stops after a bit and waves again. It's like she's trying to stay in touch even while she's out there on her own. I wave back. This is better than the usual experience of watching her disappear. But not much.

And I'm still relieved when she gets back and flops onto the sand next to me. She's so brown, that the beads of water on her back look blue.

"How was it for you?" she says and smiles.

"Scary. Brilliant. I don't know."

"Well that's OK then. Maybe you should come out with me next time."

"No thanks. I'm not a strong enough swimmer. Besides, I like being next to the shore. I've just had a thought – 'shore' sounds the same as 'sure', as in certain. And I like things to be certain. Maybe that's why I don't like seeing you all the way out there. Because things are not sure out there. I guess that makes me a bit of a wuss."

"Listen, Nick, it certainly doesn't make you anything of the sort. I'm flattered by your concern."

We lie in silence for a while. There's enough of a breeze off the sea to make my skin feel cool, so I cover myself with a towel. Dina just lies there roasting in the sun. Harry rolls over on his back and kicks his legs in the air. The sea laps and sucks. Nothing happens.

Dina rolls over on her back but she doesn't kick her legs in the air. Instead, she lights a fag and blows smoke into the sky.

"And now it's my turn to be sorry. I'm sorry about telling you all that stuff about your Dad. He is your Dad after all, and I didn't mean to make you uncomfortable."

"It's fine. You didn't. I understood what you were saying. It's just that even though I *know* he isn't as perfect as some people seem to think, I sometimes can't *feel* it. He only has to show an interest in me or anything I'm doing, and I roll over like old Harry there. It's pathetic."

"Yeh, me too. Isn't it just?"

We both laugh.

The hair on the back of my neck is prickling.

"Dina, I've got this sense that we're being watched. I've had it all afternoon."

"Sorry, I can't feel anything. Maybe it's just all this space getting to you."

"Yeh, probably."

We stay on the beach much longer than ever before. The light starts to fade. The horizon turns from purple to yellow and the sea from blue to grey. So time hasn't really stopped even though it feels like it has. Night is falling at the edge of the world.

"Come on," Dina announces to the whole of Eastern England, "I need a drink."

We load the bike into the pick-up and the three of us climb into the cab. We all smell of the sea and warm sun. My hair is stiff with salt which has also left a pale tide mark on my forearms.

186

Dina has to drive a little slower than usual – still about twice the speed of an averagely sane person – because of the thick clouds of flies that smear themselves across the windshield. Not just the little black ones but much larger, juicier numbers. You can hear them hit the screen and they leave their guts in a little transparent mound like a blob of glue.

In the end, Dina has to put the wipers on in order to see at all – millions of tiny corpses form a line at the edge of the screen.

"Horrible things," she says, "I'm glad we're not walking."

A cloud a bees is screwing itself up into a detailed replica of St Paul's cathedral in one of the fields as we pass.

When we get back, there's a bunch of 50p front garden flowers and a punnet of strawberries on the doorstep. And a note written in pencil on a tissue. It's from Rachel. It says: *"Called in but you were out. We'll be at the pub tonight. Rachel X."*

"Shall we go?" asks Dina.

"I don't really want to. Could we just stay in this evening?"

"Did you and Rachel have a row yesterday?"

"No, it's nothing like that. I just don't feel like seeing anyone."

"OK, I'll start supper. Why don't you check your swallows?"

It's warm and still in the shed and absolutely silent. There's no sign of any birds but that doesn't necessarily mean anything. I'll have to come back in the morning to take another look.

It's dark when I walk back to the cottage. The lights are shining out into the garden. I can see Dina in the kitchen creating one of her 101 magic things to do with lamb. (What I'd like to do is bury the remainder of that poor frozen sheep somewhere out on the marsh. I'd have to put a stake through it though, to stop it coming back as mince or kebabs or something.)

I stand and watch for a minute as she takes a quick swig from her glass of red wine and then stands at the sink peeling something. The radio's tuned to some classical music station and she's singing along with it. She hasn't got exactly what you'd call a brilliant voice but she can hold a tune and I can see from here that she's enjoying herself.

For the moment at least, she's happy and that makes me happy too.

We have supper in the garden, but it's cooler tonight, so we have to wear coats. The mist is rising on the marsh and a small piece of moon is doing its best to light the sky. The trees make a sighing noise in the breeze.

As I sit here, I can't believe that in a little more than a week I'll be gone. The marsh will still be here, and the moon and the stars and the wind in the reeds will still be here, but I'll be at Gran's. I can't handle this, so I decide not to think about it.

It's obviously a special occasion because Dina doesn't insist on the one small beer rule and lets me have a second. I don't know what the occasion is, but I think I approve of it.

Dina goes back into the house and comes back out with a couple of blankets which we wrap around ourselves and snuggle back into our chairs. The stars are brilliant but occasionally hidden by scraps of cloud.

We sit out until the blankets get wet with dew.

And now I'm back where I started – in bed worrying about things.

I can hear Dina snoring in the next room, but I don't think I'll mention it to her tomorrow.

I'm thinking about Gerry – is he really a good guy or is he cruel and unkind?

I'm thinking about Rachel. There was a text from her saying sorry about yesterday. Will I kiss her next time I see her?

I'm thinking about Sam. What can be done about him? Why is he so weird? Where does he really live? And then there's that thing he said about shooting coots. 427 he said. He was very precise. What is it about that number? Four plus two plus seven makes thirteen. But that isn't it. Maybe it's a prime number. There are three nines in twenty seven but what about the four hundred? No it, can't be a prime because seven sixes are forty two and seven ones are seven. So, 427 is seven times 61.

It's really bothering me, but I'm too tired to deal with it.

I'm thinking about Jack, and Billy, and Emily... I'm thinking about swallows and seals... and the sound of the sea... and the clouds of bees that seem to be able to take on any shape they like... and the gulls that live out near the horizon... and the time it takes Charley Maddox to get out of his chair... and the feel of the sun on my back... and dragonflies and slugs... and the loonies... and how 61 and seven are both prime numbers, I think, but so what?... and the marsh harrier... and old ladies taking lizards out of their purses very slowly... and nests falling from rooftops... and owls and nettles... and perfumey hugs... and hailstones... and Harry in posh restaurants in California... and Mum and Dad running through the reeds with their eyes shining... and sheds with newspaper roofs... and Gran and Dina swimming out to sea... and the pavement artist drawing a huge picture of my lovely golden fish in the middle of Stalton High Street... and a hundred grey cranes nesting on the cottage roof... and lamb chops... and... and...

*On the first Saturday in November all the boys meet at the head
keeper's cottage.*
The keepers are there with their guns and their dogs.
*At ten o'clock, we walk over to the patch of wood near the big
house.*
Everyone is very excited and chattering.
Some of the dogs are shivering
*and pull at their leads and embarrass their owners who hiss at
them...*

...

The guests are all waiting at the wood.
*Each keeper looks after one or two of them and helps them get
set.*
... Some of us boys are to act as stops...
*...We stand around the wood to stop the pheasants escaping into
the fields.*
The rest of us are beaters...
At the head keeper's whistle,
the beaters move into one side of the wood,
yelling and banging the trees...
A beautiful cock pheasant breaks cover.
The guns crack,
but they miss and he gets away...
Three others take off. The guns crack again and again.
The birds crumple in mid-air.
They land in the stubble with a thud.
They bounce,
flutter
and lie still.

Such nice young people

When I open the curtain this morning it's raining. A fine warm drizzle. It's a bit of a relief after the heat of the last few days. Harry is lying full length on the deckchair and his coat looks soaking wet but he doesn't seem to mind about the rain.

As I'm lying here still trying to sort things out in my head, my phone rings. I'm guessing it's Gerry but it's Rachel. "Hi Nick, I'm sorry about the other day. I really lost my cool with poor Sam. I guess I spoilt it for all of us. I was hoping to see you and Dina in the pub last night. Your loony friends were there, but no sign of Gerry. Not that I'm sorry about that."

She's talking very fast and sounds a bit nervous. Surely she can't be. She's normally so cool.

"Anyway, I went with Mum and Dad and my aunt babysat the kids. We had quite a nice time until the people there started singing. I remember you told me about that. You won't believe it, there were actually grown-ups with their fingers in their ears singing. I don't know what they were hearing, but it wasn't what the rest of us were hearing. Anyway I'm sorry and I wondered if you were avoiding me and would you like to do something today?"

She really does sound nervous.

"There's nothing to be sorry about," I say. Just what Dina said to me yesterday.

"I understand why Sam makes you angry, he has the same effect on me. And of course I'm not avoiding you. I just spent the day with Dina and we had supper late and sat in the garden and then it was too late to go to the pub." I'm not sure how convincing this sounds.

"So what about today?"

"It's raining."

"Yeh, but not much and it said on the radio that it's going to clear up. Everyone here is planning to go to the beach this afternoon. Let the kids exhaust themselves by running around. We could go out somewhere on our bikes. Come on, I'm only here for a few more days."

"Sure. OK. Where do you want to go?"

"I thought it might be a good idea to get away from Revenant, otherwise we're likely to run into Sam again. Even though I feel sorry for him, I need a day off. Tell you what, let's meet at the pub about one o'clock and I'll bring a picnic. We don't need to go too far, but let's just get away from here for a bit. My parents have got an OS map of the area, I'll bring that with me."

"OK, sounds good. See you at one."

"Great, I'm really looking forward to it."

"Me too." (Who was that speaking? Sounded like the world's wittiest man.)

Dina pretends to be all upset when I tell her that I'm meeting Rachel. She puts on this whining voice and says: "So, you're abandoning me for another woman. I was good enough for you yesterday when you had nothing better to do, but first chance and you're off with your fancy piece. Leaving me alone with nothing to do but black lead the coal cellar."

"Maybe, we could go to the pub this evening," I say, "maybe Gerry will be there."

"OK," she says, "but on one condition."

"What?"

"You're buying the first round."

"I'd be honoured."

Rachel's right, the rain stops and it starts to clear up.

By the time I set off, the sun's shining. The ride to the village is a bit of a pain though because the flies seem worse than ever and the rain has brought the slugs out – they're all over the road and I can't avoid them. I can feel them as they go under the wheels. It makes me shiver every time I ride over one.

The trees are all dripping and as I cycle under one I get a great splash down the back of my neck. It's freezing. There is no breeze at all and the air feels thick and heavy.

Rachel seems pleased to see me – she even thanks me for coming – and gives me a hug, which is pretty hard to do when you're both straddling bikes. She's got a rucksack on her back, which I guess has our picnic in it.

"It shows on the map that there's a broad at Coningsby. It's the only one left in private ownership. It's got a picnic area and there's a boat you can go out on. It's about three miles away. Shall we go there?"

"Sounds good."

This time, though, when Rachel does another of her racing starts, I don't bother to try to catch her. I know when I'm beaten and this old bike is never going to win any races.

In fact, I like ambling along slowly, watching her disappearing into the distance. In a funny kind of way it makes me feel grown up, like I'm her Dad or something. It's definitely not like watching Dina swim out to sea.

After a bit, as I knew she would, Rachel turns round and cycles back to me, and then we go on together at the only pace this old wreck is capable of – extremely slowly.

To begin with, the flies are awful but as we get out of Revenant and into open country, they start to thin out a bit. And the air feels different as well – clearer, easier to breathe. It's like we're leaving the spell behind. I start to feel like I've got more energy.

Cycling around here is great because the land is so flat. We pass fields in which the wheat has been harvested and the straw gathered into these huge rolls. In one, a tractor is already turning over the stubble. In another, half a dozen calves come to the gate to look at us. Pigeons scramble out of the hedges, their wings clapping, as we pass. Blackberries are beginning to ripen in the hedges. We pass a church with a round tower and a thatched roof and an overgrown graveyard. There's a pub next door with a car park and some tables. But there don't seem to be any customers at the moment. A bit further down, there's a cricket pitch with two sight-screens, a small wooden pavilion and a scoreboard showing 123 for 8. There are hardly any cars and we don't see another bike.

We've gone about two miles when we see a green bird a bit smaller than a pigeon flapping about in the middle of the road. It's a woodpecker with a red head and a wicked beak and an insane look in its eyes. It tries to run away from us, but falls over and turns a circle on its back. It seems to be stunned. It must have been hit by a car or a lorry. I try to pick it up, but it lets out this weird scream and tries to peck me. I don't want to go too near that beak – it looks like a dagger. In the end, I half push and half shoo it to the side of the road where it tumbles into the long grass. I can't see it any more but I can hear it thrashing around. I guess its chances aren't very good, but I don't see what else I can do.

There are tears in Rachel's eyes.

A bit further on, there's a sign for Coningsby Broad Car Park. We turn off the road and cycle through a stand of trees with silvery trunks and feathery leaves. There are two or three cars here, and we lock the bikes to a tree.

In front of us is a large open field of mown grass that runs down to a little river. A yacht with a brown sail is making its way along the river but because of where we're standing it seems to be sailing through the fields.

There are loads of swallows zipping up and down, only a few feet above the ground. It's amazing that they never crash into each other. Even when it looks like they must collide, they don't slow down (can they slow down?) they just tilt their wings a fraction and dip away from each other. Every time they do this they go "tswit." It's like they're saying how easy it was and how clever they are. And they sure are. It occurs to me that I've never seen a dead swallow on the road, even though the pheasants seem to be queuing up to be knocked down. I just hope that the swallows back in Dina's shed are half as smart as these ones.

There's a huge house at the top corner of the field, with a formal garden round it. It seems to be some kind of study centre, but there's no one around. In the opposite corner at the bottom of the field, a muddy footpath leads through some trees.

We head away from the river along this path. The sun is filtering through the trees making the light green. There are large yellow and pink flowers like giant primroses growing up out of last year's dead leaves. A pigeon clatters away in panic. Two elderly ladies, who might be sisters, walk by and say hello to us as they pass. We smile. I can almost hear them thinking, "Such nice young people."

The path leads to a small fence and a large metal gate in the shape of a spider's web with a huge iron spider in the middle. A giant metal fly has just been caught in one of the web's outer spokes and now it's trapped there forever.

Just outside the gate is a small, grey wooden kiosk with a very smartly dressed middle-aged lady inside. "Hello," she says in a voice that could cut glass (she sounds even posher than Dina and almost as loud). "It's a pound (*pined*) to come in, but awfully good value. Or you can buy a ticket for two pounds (*pineds*) fifty (*fifteh*) that entitles you to a boat ride. I'd go for that if I were you. It's really jolly good."

So we do. I don't suppose that anyone has ever argued with this lady in her entire life and I'm certainly not going to. Even Rachel seems a bit scared of her.

Taking care not to touch the great fat iron spider, we open the gate and are in a small garden with brick paths and flowers spilling all over the grass. Another couple of old ladies, who seem to be exactly the same as the first two, are sitting at a table eating ice-lollies.

We go through another gate, and there in front of us is Coningsby Broad. It's smaller than Revenant Broad and surrounded by trees which in some places come right down to the water's edge. It also feels different from Revenant. The light is dancing on the water and the trees are moving in the breeze, their leaves flashing. The water is the colour of honey. There's no spell here.

This feels like someone's garden. It's not like Revenant which always feels like a wild, slightly dangerous place. This feels safe and well looked-after. There's nothing mysterious about it. It's impossible to imagine anything bad ever happening here. I'm sure that even the pike, if there are any, are well behaved and certainly wouldn't dream of eating anyone's pet dog. They'd probably swim in formation for the entertainment of the old ladies.

There's a small wooden jetty and moored to it is a beautiful, old-fashioned boat. It's hard to imagine anything less like the good ship Piranha.

The Piranha is a dirty, plastic bucket. This boat – The Saratoga – is lovely, all dark wood and gleaming brass with a small cabin at the front. It lies really low in the water.

Standing on the jetty is a bloke wearing white trousers, white shoes and a yellow and red striped blazer. He's also wearing a white yachting hat with a peak. I never thought I'd say it, but it's even worse than Gerry's leather cowboy hat. He's obviously meant to be dressed as they would have when the boat was made.

He waves to us. "Do you two want to go out for a ride? It's really quiet today and you could have the boat to yourselves."

Rachel looks at me and then says that would be great.

We may be the only people wanting a ride but the bloke in the blazer still asks to see our tickets and then punches a hole in them with something that looks like a pair of pliers.

The engine makes a gentle chugging noise and we slowly edge out to the middle of the broad. Compared with the Piranha, this is luxury – a stretch-limo of a boat. Rachel settles herself back into the stripy cushions that are stacked on the little deck and says, "This is the life." I feel a bit embarrassed.

The water is only a couple of feet deep and there are patches of yellow lilies. There are thousands of dragonflies and I can see shoals of little golden fish that might be rudd. On the far side of the broad from the jetty is an old wooden boat house that's about ten times the size of the marshman's cottage. As we get near it, we can hear a whirring noise which turns out to be an automatic fish feeder fixed to its side. Every couple of minutes, a slot in the feeder turns and drops food into the water. Seven or eight enormous fish are lazily jostling each other to grab it as soon as it hits the water. "Carp," says blazer man.

We drift around for half an hour or so – probably because old blazer has nothing else to do – and watch the swallows as they dip down to drink. Like everything else they do it's fantastic and skilful. If they hit the water at the speed they travel, they'd really hurt themselves. But they never do, they just skim the surface with their beaks open and hardly make a ripple. Their whole lives seem to be like this – always on the edge of disaster, always in danger of a crash, or the weather. They're so frail, and yet they couldn't care less. Just belt through their lives at full speed as if they hadn't got a worry in the world. So, not much like me really, and particularly not like me when I'm on that old boneshaker of a bike.

When he drops us off at the jetty, blazer man says, "Goodbye, Sir. Goodbye, Madam," in a silly voice.

"Goodbye, twat," whispers Rachel. I try to stop myself from laughing and make this snorting, gagging noise. I daren't look back at the man or his blazer.

We have our picnic sitting at one of the tables in the garden. Rachel's brought cheese rolls and apples, crisps and cokes. I'd practically forgotten that it is possible and legal to put something that doesn't come from some part of a lamb into a sandwich. We don't talk much while we're eating, but then I don't feel that I need to.

After lunch we wander about the garden for a bit, but it's boring. Maybe you need to be an old lady in a flowery frock to understand gardens. So, in the end, we sneak past the posh lady and the gate and wander round the woods.

Near where we came in, the trees go right down to the river. There's a wire fence at the edge of the wood, but someone has already trodden it down. So we step over it and lie on the bank watching the river flow slowly past. Here as well the air feels different from Revenant.

We chat about this and that and then I can't put it off any longer, so I kiss her again. It's not quite as clumsy as the first time – our mouths meet in roughly the same place and there's no banging of teeth – but to be honest it's not quite as interesting as the first time.

As far as I can tell, Rachel is kissing me back, or maybe she's trying to escape, or suffocating, or wanting to make a run for it, or laughing or trying to say something. I don't know.

And now that I've started I don't really know how I'm going to stop. I suppose I could pretend to faint, or say that I can hear someone coming.

I wonder what Rachel's thinking at this moment. Probably the same as me.

It goes on for a bit, and so I put my hand in her shirt. It's warm in there and I can feel her bra strap. But I have to admit I don't really feel anything else. What I mainly think at first is: "I can tell Jack and Billy about this." And then I think that would be really uncool.

But it's enough to put a stop to things. Rachel pulls away. "Listen," she says, "do we really have to do this? I like you a lot and kissing's OK but this all seems a bit pointless. Shall we give it a rest?"

Blimey. I don't really know what to say. I sort of agree with her. Part of me is disappointed but another part of me is relieved. After all, I only met her a few days ago. There are so many things I don't know about her, all this sex business seems a bit sudden.

"OK," I say, "you're right. We don't need to do this."

"Great, although I wouldn't say no to the odd kiss."

And just to prove the point, she kisses me very gently and very briefly on the lips.

It's weird because neither of us seems to be embarrassed now that we've stopped. We're more relaxed than before. It's like we've got something out of the way and that there's no longer anything preventing us from being friends. I'm really pleased about that, although still a little curious about what's in her shirt. But we'll put that on hold for the time being.

A little ball of bright blue and orange flicks up the river and disappears into the reeds – it must be a kingfisher. Another tiny life that seems to be lived at frantic speed. We take this as a signal to leave.

As we cycle back towards Revenant, it's like travelling back into a dream.

The first thing we notice is that the flies seem to get worse. Then there are the swarms of bees – the Eiffel tower, a cement mixer, a bunch of grapes – that don't seem to be able to settle. And something in the air changes. It becomes, thicker, murkier, stranger. Something is waiting to happen. I don't know what. But I do know what old Charley meant when he said that the time was out of joint.

And guess who we see as we reach Revenant village; guess who's standing in the school playground doing nothing and waving to us, just like he was the first time I saw him? Why is he always on his own?

We stop our bikes and say hello and he walks down to join us.

"Hi, Sam."

"What?"

"Hello."

"Hello."

"What are you doing here?"

"This is where I go to school."

"Yes, but what are you doing."

"Nothing."

"You must be doing something."

A van drives past and honks, it's Brenda, who must have been out doing some deliveries. Parcels of junk food for elderly country folk. She waves and we all wave back.

"Yes," says Rachel, "you must be doing something."

"This is where I go to school. This is where I learn things."

For God's sake.

"Do you think Miss Stevens is here today?" he asks.

"I shouldn't think so, it's the summer holidays."

"Oh, yes."

I think that maybe Sam likes school because it gets him away from his parents and his home.

"Do, you like school, Sam?"

Why does every conversation with this kid seem to turn into an interrogation?

"When I'm able to come here."

What's that supposed to mean?

I notice that he doesn't say anything about the other day, or the worms or Rachel getting so upset. In fact, come to think of it, he never talks about the previous times that we've seen him. It's like he starts from the beginning every time. It's not that he doesn't recognise us, but that he can't remember or isn't interested in anything we did.

I offer him a lift into the middle of the village and he practically jumps onto my crossbar. Well, at least the smell hasn't got any better. Maybe I'd miss it if it did go away; but I don't think so. Even if it is a part of Sam, it's a part that I could do without.

And just like all the other times, he is so excited. You'd think we were travelling at the speed of sound rather than wobbling along at about three miles an hour. I let my eyes slip out of focus a bit so that I don't have to look at his poor scabby head.

Just as we're about to pass the Maddoxes' shop, Rachel wants to stop to get us all drinks and something to eat. I know that she really means that she wants to get something for Sam but he doesn't want to come in.

He goes from being really happy to really worried and upset in no time flat. "No. No. I can't go in there, I haven't got any shoes."

By now, he's looking so frightened that we don't bother arguing with him. Rachel says he should stay outside with the bikes and you can see the relief on his face.

We go into the shop and the thing on the door goes "ping." Brenda looks up and smiles: "Hello, my two lovelies."

I introduce Rachel.

"Have you had a good day?" asks Brenda. "Where have you been?"

"We spent the day at Coningsby," I say, "and then we met Sam at the school on our way back. He's the kid I was talking about the other day. The one whose parents let him wander about in a terrible state. He says they live in Church Lane but no one seems to have heard of them. He was with us when you drove past a minute ago."

"I don't think I noticed him, my darling. I only saw you and the lovely Rachel here."

"He was standing right between us."

"No, I must have missed him. But I was listening to a play on the radio and watching the road and worrying about that silly old fool I'm married to, so not surprising really. Why don't you ask him to come in?"

"OK."

But when I get back outside, there's no sign of him. He's vanished. The road is empty.

A weird thought is starting to form in my head, but I push it back down. I don't want to go there. It's ridiculous.

"He's not there," I tell Brenda.

"Well, maybe he realised that he was late for tea or something and has gone home," she says.

This sounds reasonable, which is exactly why I can't believe it. Nothing to do with Sam seems reasonable. People are always coming up with perfectly ordinary explanations of his weird behaviour but that's only because they've never met him. If they had, they'd know that Sam and perfectly ordinary explanations don't go together. Wherever he's disappeared to, I'm prepared to bet it's not because it's tea time, or because he's going to a judo class or anything like that.

But I don't know how to say any of this to Brenda, so I just say, "You're probably right."

Rachel gives me a look that says, "What are you talking about?" I shrug.

We try to buy a couple of cokes, but Brenda insists on giving them to us for nothing. She does, however, let Rachel buy one for Sam in case we run into him.

"How's Mr Maddox?" I ask.

"Oh, I think you can call him Charley. The honest answer is not too good. He still seems to be upset about something but he says it's nothing. He had words with the editor of his paper. You remember he couldn't decide what to write his column about. Well, in the end he sent in two – one about the church fete and one that seemed to be mostly about flies and wrecked birds' nests. Well, not surprisingly, the editor said that he could use the fete piece but not the other. I heard Charley shouting down the phone at him, which is really unusual – he generally restricts his shouting to the summer house. But why don't you go and say hello to the old timer? He'd be really pleased to see you."

And I suppose he is really, although he's changed.

Of course, as soon as he sees Rachel he decides to stand up and shake hands with her. I swear that I could count up to 30 while he unwinds himself from his chair, and another 30 when he coils back into it and drops the last couple of feet.

I can tell immediately that Rachel really likes him. And what's not to like? As Dina says, he's a lovely man.

But he's different from when I last saw him a couple of days ago. It's not that he looks older – he's so old that he couldn't really look any older – he just seems to have shrunk into himself a bit. He doesn't seem to have his normal spark and there's this confused look in his eyes. Whatever is bothering him has really got to him.

Rachel tells him about our trip to Coningsby Broad and he laughs about the guy in the blazer and his "Goodbye Sir, Goodbye Madam."

When she tells him about the terrifyingly posh lady on the gate, he surprises us by saying that he knows her. "That's Sarah Manters, her husband owns the broad. Not that he's here much; seems to spend most of his time in London making money. I've known her for donkeys' years, I used to teach her brother in the days before I escaped from school. And you're right. When you first meet her she is scary. But when you get to know her better, you realise that you were absolutely right to be scared."

For a moment the old light is in his eyes, but it soon fades as if being spiteful about her was too much of an effort. He's trying to entertain us, but it's clear that he's feeling pretty subdued.

When we leave, he apologises for not getting up again.

We say goodbye to Brenda and decide to cycle to Church Lane to see if Sam's there. But he isn't. The houses look as empty and shut up as before. Nobody lives here. In fact the only sign of life is the crows in the trees by the churchyard. For some reason they're making a hell of a noise, screeching and chattering at one another.

Again, this weird thought comes into my head – for a minute I think of talking to Rachel about it – but in the end I decide against it.

Teddy comes to the beach with me after a storm...
... We bend our faces into the wind
and screw up our eyes against the dazzling light.
Weed is scattered all up the beach.
... Teddy says that it is called "sea wrack."
I like that word. "Wrack" is like "wreck."
... It makes me think of pirates and giant clams and mermaids.
... Of rippling sand at the bottom of clear, warm, blue seas.
... The blown sand stings our faces.
We gather bits of driftwood
and old rope
and cork floats
and lumps of tar
that the sea has left behind...
We pile them up with bits of netting and pieces of bleached
paper...

...

Clouds cross the sky and gulls are blown around like leaves.
Teddy has brought a magnifying glass with him...
He focuses a tiny white sun on the wisps of sea wrack and dried
paper until they begin to curl and smoke...
We pile on more bits and pieces very carefully
until the flames break out into the sunlight...
At first, you can hardly see them.
But soon we have a wonderful bonfire roaring and crackling on
the beach...
... We dance around it like madmen, shouting and laughing.

Let's get you home

This morning there's a thick mist over the marsh. But the garden is clear and there are five swallows in the air. At first I thought there were only four, but now I'm sure that there are five. That only leaves one in the nest.

I'm so pleased that my heart feels like it's going to burst. And when I tell Dina, she seems almost as pleased as I am.

"That's fantastic, Nick. And they owe it all to you risking your neck on the shed roof in the gale." I don't know about that, but it's nice that she said it.

But my great mood goes into a nosedive when I'm in the shed. I expect to see the remaining chick on the rafter, but it isn't there. I suppose it must still be in the nest. Maybe it's asleep. But then I hear this rustling noise on the floor in the corner.

At first I think it must be a mouse, but then I realise that it's the last chick. It must have fallen.

It tries to escape when I try to pick it up, but it hops and flops and jams itself into the corner.

When I do finally catch it, I hold it as gently as I can in both hands. It's bigger than I imagined but lighter. Its bones are full of air. Its wings sweep back in this fantastic curve and its blue black feathers sparkle even in the dim light. Its tail is like the flights on an arrow but not as forked as those of the parent birds. It has a creamy, white belly and a reddish-brown throat. Although it tried to escape from me, it doesn't seem frightened now that I've caught it. It sits in my hands without struggling, moving its beautiful head from side to side, opening and closing its beak. It has these really empty black eyes which flick backwards and forwards as it checks out first one corner of the shed and then another and then the window.

I've never seen a bird as beautiful as this before. It's fantastic.

But now that I've got it, I don't really know what to do with it. How am I going to get it back into the nest without putting it back on the floor first? And I don't want to do that. A dusty cold floor is no place for such a beautiful animal. Everything about it says flight and air and freedom.

So I carry it carefully back to the house. As I walk across the garden, two swallows – the parents I guess – dip down around my head as if to make sure I mean their baby no harm.

Dina loves the chick. She lightly strokes its head between her thumb and first finger and it seems happy to let her do so.

At first I feel a bit jealous, but then I realise that the swallow isn't responding to her; it's not allowing her to make it comfortable. Its world and ours are so different that there can't be any contact. It is just tolerating her touch or maybe it hasn't even noticed.

Whatever, she comes back to the shed with me and fetches down a small step-ladder which is hung on the wall. From this I am able to place the chick back in its nest. It seems happy to be back. It just sits there and stares into my eyes.

"Come on," Dina whispers (I didn't know Dina could whisper), "I think we should leave it. We don't want to handle it too much. Its parents are probably still feeding it." And as if to prove her point, one of the birds flies in and disappears into the nest. There's a few seconds of screeching noises and then it reappears and is gone before we can focus on it properly.

Trouble is that when I check after breakfast, the chick's back on the floor again. It allows itself to be picked up and admired without any protest. Its tiny black eyes flick around the shed. And it doesn't complain when I put it back in the nest. Just sits there waiting to see what's going to happen next.

But I'm beginning to get worried. It may be in danger on the floor. There are bound to be rats living in the ditches and there

207

may even be a fox around, although I've never seen it. What's to stop them killing it? I can't shut the shed door or its parents won't be able to get in to feed it. But if I don't shut it, the chick might flutter outside and put itself in danger.

In the end, I make a kind of barrier across the door with a load of logs from the woodpile. The parents can get in and out, but it can't get out. At least, not unless it flies over the pile of logs – which would be fine by me. Harry has been watching me do this, but he doesn't seem very interested in the chick. Which I guess is a good thing. Do dogs eat birds as well as rabbits?

Dina says that she wonders if there's something wrong with it. If it can get out of the nest, why can't it fly? Maybe it's damaged in some way. Maybe it's the runt.

I don't want to hear any of this. I guess all I can do is check on it every couple of hours and hope for the best.

After I got back from Coningsby Broad last night, Dina and I had an early supper (it was a curry, something beginning with "l") and then she disappeared for a while to get ready for our trip to the pub.

When she came back downstairs, she was wearing a long black skirt – the first time I've ever seen her in anything other than dungarees – with a checked work-shirt over the top. She'd put some lippy on, and this time she'd managed to get most of it on her lips. (I get the feeling she's not very good at make-up) and she'd brushed her hair until it shone. I guess in her strange way, Dina's quite beautiful, if you like that kind of thing. Not my type though.

She seemed a bit nervous and said, "I'll just have a quick drink before we set off. And you'd better have your beer now, because you'll only be able to have soft drinks at the Ferret." So, she poured herself an enormous whisky which disappeared in about two gulps.

We were just going out of the door when the phone rang.

"Could you please get it, Nick," she said. I guess she was worried it might be Gerry and that he might be in one of his moods.

But to my amazement it was Dad. This is the first time in nearly 15 years that he has phoned me – it's always been Mum and then he comes on the line at the end. It's almost like he's noticed for the first time that I exist.

"Hi, Nick, just wanted to see how it was going."

"Fine, thanks, it's great."

"Not too bored?"

It's like he wanted me to say yes, to say that I'm not having a good time. Well, if he wanted that, he shouldn't have sent me here in the first place.

"No, not bored at all. There are loads of great walks around here, and places to cycle to. And I've been out on boat rides. It's great having a dog. And I've met the people who run the shop. He's called Charley and he's very old and – I think – very intelligent, and he's published novels."

Come to think of it, I probably couldn't have said anything worse. By telling Dad about his writing, I've made poor old Charley sound like competition. And although Dad is a successful writer for television, he's never published a novel and maybe that counts for more. Dad can be really rude about the writers who publish books that aren't read by many people but which win prizes. But maybe that just means that he thinks writing novels is somehow better or more important than writing for TV.

"Well that all sounds great."

But he didn't sound as though he meant it. In fact, it sounded like he's jealous of Dina. This means that in a way he doesn't want me to be happy when I'm not with him, never mind that half the time he doesn't want to be with me. I'm not saying that's what he thinks to himself, but it must be behind this conversation.

He asked about his "future daughter-in-law" and I told him about our trip to Coningsby Broad but I didn't tell him anything about Sam.

He told me a bit about how his script is developing. In the episode he's working on, the gay lawyers have a problem about whether or not to hire a chef who is not gay, but who is nevertheless a good chef. I think I laughed in the right places.

And then Dad said something that nearly knocked me over: *"It's really quiet without you, Nick and we're looking forward to seeing you when we get back."*

Well that's the first I'd heard of it.

"Yeh, I'm looking forward to seeing you both as well," I said although I'm not quite sure how true this is.

"OK," he said, *"can you put Dina on for a minute? I'll speak to you soon. Lots of love. Bye."*

I handed the phone to Dina.

"Hi Jim, sorry but it has to be quick, I'm cooking supper... No, he's fine. Having a good time. No, no... I'm sure he's not... Seems to me he might have the makings of a country boy... No, of course there's nothing wrong with London... No, I'm sure... Plenty of things for him to do, cycling, the beach, trips with Rachel... I think he's looking well on it... Yeh, he seems to be getting by without TV... OK, speak to you then...Hi, Liz, We're having a great time, How about you?... Great. Shall I put Nick on?... OK, bye."

She handed the phone back to me.

Mum and I chatted for a few minutes. She's not as intense as Dad, but I get the feeling with her as well that they would prefer me to be having a less good time.

She said that they would call again in a few days.

"Dina," I said, "you told Dad that you were cooking supper, but we ate it an hour ago."

"Did I? I must have meant that I was thinking about planning tomorrow's supper."

We both laughed.

That was a conversation that needs some thinking about. I guess that Dad's feeling uncomfortable about things because he doesn't really know much about how Dina lives and what things are like round here. He's used to regular meetings with friends and dinner parties and expensive restaurants. But maybe hearing about Dina and what we're doing is a reminder that some people don't want to live the same way as him. Maybe that's why he seems to want me to want the same things as him, not the same things as Dina.

And if I'm really honest, one of the reasons I love it so much round here is because it's so different from Mum and Dad's world.

For the very first time in my life, I felt like I had the upper hand in a conversation with Dad. That I was on top. That he wanted something from me more than I wanted something from him. Is it a good feeling? Abso-bloody-lutely. Will I go back to being bottom dog as soon as they're back? Probably. But it will never be quite the same again. I really feel I've done some growing up in the last couple of weeks. And quite a big part of this is due to the lady here who I've promised to buy a drink.

The Strangled Ferret is heaving. You can hear the noise from the car park and you could cut the cigarette smoke into blocks. Mind you, I don't know what you'd do with them if you did.

We haven't seen Gerry for a few days, but he's back, looking pale under his tan and thinner than ever.

He seems to be trying to be nice – he kisses Dina on both cheeks, shakes hands with me, strokes Harry's ears (Harry immediately curls up under his chair as if Dina and I didn't exist), finds us a couple of chairs – but there's still a dangerous look in his eyes.

I hope Dina has seen it.

But in fact it's a pretty quiet evening. At least, it's as quiet an evening as you would expect to have with a load of pissed people all shouting their heads off and not listening to each other.

Gerry says to the table, "I bet you don't know what the people who lived by the coast used to use to catch rabbits."

"Ferrets," says someone. "Terriers," says someone else.

"Not a chance," says Gerry drinking half his pint in one gulp. "Some of them were too poor to keep dogs or ferrets. They had something closer to hand and free."

No one can guess.

"They used crabs," shouts Gerry, demolishing the rest of his pint, "bloody crabs. Much better than ferrets."

Of course, no one believes him.

"I'm telling you it's true," he says lighting a roll up, "they used to bring crabs from the shore, stick a stub of lighted candle on their backs and stuff them down a rabbit hole. The candle was supposed to make the crab move faster and frighten anything in the burrow. After a couple of minutes a terrified rabbit would come whizzing out to be trapped. They must have preferred being killed and cooked to having to deal with a big old crab in a dark rabbit hole."

Half his audience thinks it's a wind up; the other half thinks it's a disgusting story.

"That's really gross," says one loony (straggly beard, nose stud, dungarees). "But I think you're confused. Rabbit is the best bait for catching crabs, not the other way round."

"No," says Gerry, "I have absolute confidence in my sources."

"If you think that's horrible," says a second loony (velvet jacket, incredibly tight jeans, huge boots with steel toe-caps), "my toads story's worse. I read somewhere – although I can't remember where – about a cocker spaniel in Texas which used to spend hours licking the cane toads in the garden in order to get high. In fact, she liked the hallucinogenic toxin in the toads' skins so much that she sucked all the colour out of them. Turned them into albino toads."

This is followed by more shouts of disgust, more buying of pints, more lighting of fags, more shouting of horrible stories – a blue-tit eating the brains of a sparrow, a pigeon with a dead and rotting chick stuck to its leg, a house martin walling in a sparrow that's stolen its mud nest, a pet turtle whose body collapses and turns into turtle soup overnight, the skeleton of a cat with its front leg caught in a hole in a tree.

And so the evening passes.

Gerry is drinking steadily but although he hasn't caused any trouble so far, I get the feeling that he'd quite like to.

Dina isn't saying much but she seems to be OK.

I can't relax because I'm worried about what's going on between them, even though it's got nothing to do with me. I just want to make sure that if Gerry does start being horrible, I can stick up for Dina and maybe make him turn on me instead like he did the other night. Fortunately, it isn't necessary even though there seems to be this tension between them.

It's about eleven o'clock, my face is burning from the heat, my brain's jumping from too many cokes and reeling from too many stories, my eyes are stinging from all that cigarette smoke. Maybe it's the strain of trying to keep the peace between Gerry and Dina but I'm done in.

Dina must have noticed because she says I look tired and asks me if I want to go back.

"No, it's OK. I'm fine."

"No it's not and no you're not. I'm ready to leave. I never thought I'd say it, but I'm getting a bit fed up with this place. Just let me finish my drink."

That takes about two seconds.

"Right," she announces to the table, "that's us. We're out of here. Night all."

Chorus of goodnights from any loonies who happen to be paying attention.

Gerry gets to his feet but doesn't look too steady. "Shall I come with you?" has asks. He seems to be both challenging and pleading at the same time.

"No thanks, love" says Dina lightly, "we're both done in. I don't think we'd be very good company. Another night."

There's nothing for Gerry to do but sit down again and start working his way through yet another pint, which has mysteriously appeared at his elbow.

I feel a bit sorry for him.

Going outside into the night air is like jumping into a cold bath. It's wonderful. The stars are blazing and bats are hawking for insects around the car park, flicking in and out of the lights. An owl is hooting somewhere behind a stand of trees.

At least it's wonderful until we get to the pick-up.

While Harry is having a huge pee against the truck's wheels, I noticed that Dina is crying. Absolutely quietly, but there are tears on her cheeks.

This is worse than watching her swimming away from the shore because this time it's me who's out of my depth.

"Dina, I'm really sorry," I say putting my hand on her arm.

"Sorry, Nick. I shouldn't be putting you through all this. I just couldn't help myself. I don't know what's the matter. It's just that there's something wrong between Gerry and me at the moment, and we don't seem to be able to put it right. You remember what Charley said about the lady who thought there must have been an earthquake. Well, that's what I feel like."

She sniffs, wipes her eyes on her sleeve and smiles.

"Still, I'm glad that I said no to Gerry – he's had it too much his own way for too long in that department."

I really don't want to think about what this might mean. I already know much more about their relationship than is good for me. I'm too young and too sensitive and too inexperienced. Besides, it's all so disgusting. They're so old. They ought to know better.

But what I do know is that I hate it when Dina's unhappy, however good she normally is at hiding it.

"Come on," she says, "let's get you home."

And that's really what she says: "home."

Teddy is my best friend…
He has the same birthday as me.
Mother says that we are as alike as two peas, but I don't think so.
My eyes are blue but his are green. His nose is pointier than mine
and I have more freckles.
… He is full of jokes and stories, but I am too slow to think of
jokes.
Sometimes he makes me feel stupid.
… In the summer, his skin goes brown but mine goes pink.

… …

…

On hot summer days
we lie in the fields at the edge of the marsh and talk about the
future.
Teddy lies on his back and looks at the sky.
He is going to be an engineer, he says,
and build huge bridges across roaring rivers.
His bridges will be famous around the world.
He will make his fortune and marry a beautiful wife and live in
a light and airy house with armfuls of beautiful children…
… I don't know what I'm going to be.
Sometimes I think I will be a teacher.
Sometimes a farmer.
Maybe a poet…
But I can't imagine a beautiful woman wanting to marry me.

… …

… …

Teddy says it doesn't matter if I don't know what I want to be.
There's no hurry, he says…
There's plenty of time.

Do you know where home is?

This afternoon, Dina and I went into Stalton again. She took the pick-up; I took the bike. Harry was left to look after the cottage.

We arranged to meet at The Baker's Dozen for tea, although I can't quite get used to the idea of Dina taking tea.

It was threatening to rain but never did. One after another these huge purple clouds tracked across the sky. They looked capable of drowning the whole area, but in the end did nothing. There were flickers of lightning out over the sea, but no thunder. It felt like the sky was about to fall in.

And the flies were terrible, I could hardly open my eyes at all, my nose, ears and mouth were full of the horrible things. I could feel them in my hair and they were stuck to my arms. I was wearing a white T-shirt but within a couple of minutes of leaving the cottage it looked like it had some kind of black pattern on it. In about five minutes, I was wishing that I'd gone with Dina.

And the roads were again covered in slugs, which must have thought it was about to rain. Thousands had been squashed by cars and tractors but there were plenty more where they came from. In fact, there were so many of them coming from the grass verge at the side of the road, that it almost looked as if they were on some kind of mission. The massed ranks of east Norfolk's disgusting slugs marching off to battle. Anyway, I did my best to avoid as many as I could.

There were loads of magpies and crows hopping around, stuffing their faces with as many slugs as they wanted.

Cycling was no fun. The only way to keep moving was to fix my eyes on my front wheel and the patch of road a couple of yards in front of it. I only really looked up when I heard a car coming, and every time I did so thousands more flies decided to make their home in my face.

In one place, the road turns sharp left and almost immediately sharp right. I could hear a car coming from the direction of Stalton, the driver was changing gear as the car approached the double bend. I had no choice but to look up and as I did so I caught sight of Sam standing by the side of the road looking at me.

I was so shocked and surprised that I almost lost control of the bike, and as the car came round the corner, I swerved right across in front of it. Fortunately, the woman driving it had slowed right down and was able to drive onto the verge at the side of the road. She almost drove into the hedge.

She wound down her window and shouted, "For Christ's sake be careful." She looked really scared.

I was trembling. "I'm sorry," I said, "I stopped to talk to my friend."

"I've no idea what you're talking about. Just be careful." She drove off.

I half wheeled and half pedalled the bike off the road.

All this time, Sam hadn't moved. He was just standing there staring at me.

"Sam, what are you doing?"

"Nothing."

It was getting harder and harder to resist this stupid thought that kept coming into my head.

"I mean what are you *doing* here. Other than almost getting me killed."

His smell was stronger than ever and it was coming off him in waves. He looked even more miserable and neglected than the last time. It was like there was, I don't know, less of him every time I saw him.

"I'm going home, I think."

"What the hell do you mean you think? Where have you been? Why are you here?"

"I don't know where I've been. I can't remember. I think I've been walking. I think I've been looking for rabbits."

"What do you mean you can't remember? And why would anyone be looking for rabbits in the middle of the afternoon?"

"For food."

"Never mind the rabbits. Why can't you remember where you've been? Are you ill? Have you had an accident?"

"I don't think so."

The more questions I asked him the more upset he got. He was crying again – that seemed pretty much normal – and his skinny, filthy little body was trembling all over.

"Come on, Sam. Come and sit over here by the bike."

He sat down but it still looked as if all the sadness of the world had somehow ended up in this one kid.

"Sam, are you sure you're all right? Do you think you're well?"

"I don't know."

I was getting more and more certain that I was right. But what I was right about was impossible.

"Sam, listen, do you know who the Prime Minister is?"

"I don't want to talk about that."

"Were you spying on me at the beach?"

"I don't want to talk about that."

"What's your favourite television programme?"

"I don't want to talk about that."

"What music do you like?"

"I don't know."

"Do you know what year it is?"

"Yes."

"Well, what is it then?"

"I don't want to talk about that. Leave me alone."

When he said that, I really lost my temper. "Leave *you* alone," I shouted, "that's just what you've never done since I first met you – leave *me* alone. And you won't leave Rachel alone either. And now you tell me to leave you alone."

He didn't respond.

"Sam," I said in a quieter voice, "I'm really worried about you. I think there's something wrong with you. I'm not sure what I can do to help. Do you know what it is? Shall I tell you what I think? Can I help you in some way?"

But this made him much worse and he started to howl like a wounded animal, rocking backwards and forwards as he sat there. It was clear that I wasn't going to get any sense out of him while he was like this.

I didn't know what to do.

Why wasn't there anyone else around? Not a single car had passed in either direction since I'd been nearly run over.

Suddenly Sam stood up: "I want to go home now."

"But Sam, do you know where home is?"

"My name is Sam Wellsby. I live in Church Lane, Revenant."

"No you don't. Your name may be Sam Wellsby, but you don't live in Church Lane. They're bloody weekend cottages in Church Lane. No one lives there."

I really was trying to keep calm but kept losing my temper.

"It's OK Sam, calm down. Stay here for a bit."

"No, I'm going. I need to go home. I'm going to Church Lane. My parents are waiting for me."

He started to walk the way I'd just come and because of the bend in the road he was out of sight in a few seconds.

I stood there for a minute, trying to get my head straight. Trying to work out what to do next. I couldn't just let him walk back to Revenant. He wasn't safe out on his own. I couldn't expect him to cope with the traffic on the road. (Even while I was thinking this I was wondering where the traffic was.)

On the other hand, if I was right about Sam none of that mattered. But I couldn't be right about Sam. It was ridiculous. He was just a little kid needing help. I ran after him. But when I got round the curve in the road, he was nowhere to be seen.

I wasn't really surprised.

By the time I got to Stalton, I was feeling terrible. Sweaty. Sick. Shaky. My clothes were sticking to me and I had a splitting headache.

As soon as Dina saw me she knew that something was up.

"Are you OK, Nick? What's happened?"

She was sitting at one of The Baker's Dozen's Formica tables with the inevitable cup of black coffee in front of her. In spite of everything, it made me smile. Only Dina could describe one cup of coffee without any milk or sugar as "tea." I sometimes wonder if she really is surviving on a diet of fags and booze. Maybe she's some new kind of human being who doesn't need carbs and vitamins and proteins to keep her going.

Her asking me this gave me a problem. How much should I tell her? Even I can see that the things I'm thinking about Sam are not your everyday kind of things. Not the kind of things that make people say, "Oh yes, I see, so that's the problem is it? Really. How interesting. I never would have guessed. But I'm sure you're right."

It would be hard for her to believe me or take me seriously. And I really don't want her not believing me.

So, I decided to take it gently.

"I think maybe I cycled too fast and got too sweaty – it's so humid. And the flies were terrible and made it hard to breathe."

It was ridiculous – I was this close to crying. But I told myself I'd done more than enough of that for this holiday. And given how fragile Dina is at the moment, she might have joined in. And that would have given the other diners at The Baker's Dozen – three old ladies in cardigans and a kid with purple hair playing a game on his phone – something to talk about. Strange looking woman and idiot boy weeping over single cup of coffee. No thanks. Anything had to be better than that.

"Well sit down and let's get you something to drink. You look knocked out. Maybe last night's catching up with you. You're right, it is really humid. Did you see the lightning? I thought of coming back to get you but when it didn't rain, I thought you'd be OK. I didn't really notice the flies though. It must have been worse on the bike."

Dina called the waitress over – a girl of about my age with white dreadlocks and a brown nylon apron – and ordered a large glass of lemonade and a doughnut.

"I think maybe we need to get some sugar into you."

"I saw Sam again, you know that kid I keep running into, about a mile down the road."

"Oh, yes."

I could see that Dina was not exactly overwhelmed by this piece of information even though my brain can't seem to focus on anything else. It didn't immediately seem odd to her, or surprising or something worth writing to *The East Norfolk Gazette* about.

And of course, in a way, she's right. There is nothing special about a kid standing by the side of the road. But she's also wrong. I think there's something very special about this kid. But I can't think how to put it into words.

"Yes, he was just standing there. He said he'd been out looking for rabbits and was on his way home."

"I see."

This was clearly not setting off any alarm bells in Dina. She didn't seem about to leap out of her chair shouting "extraordinary" and knocking her coffee over and making the teaspoons rattle on the other tables. To her, it's just another country kid out looking for rabbits, doing what country kids do.

And of course she's right. But, at the same time, she couldn't be more wrong.

"And it gave me such a surprise when I saw him, that I nearly came off under the wheels of a car. The driver stopped. She was really angry with me. But when I tried to explain that I'd stopped because I'd seen Sam she said she didn't know what I was talking about."

This got Dina's attention, but not in the way I'd been expecting. She looked really worried. But she wasn't worried about the woman in the car or Sam. She was worried about me.

"God, Nick you've got to be careful. There's not much traffic on these roads, but that's part of the problem. No one will be expecting to see you. It's really important to concentrate all the time. Imagine what might have happened. And I'm not even sure that that old bike is safe. I think you'd better come back in the pick-up with me."

I just couldn't seem to turn the conversation in the direction I wanted it to go. I wanted to say something that would stop Dina in her tracks. I wanted her to understand what amazing things had happened this afternoon just outside Stalton. But to her, the events I was describing were just ordinary except where they were ordinary and frightening at the same time.

I decided not to say any more for the moment, but to think about the best way to get her to listen to me. There wasn't any urgency.

Besides, I quite liked her being concerned about me. Not if it meant she was going to object next time I tried to take the bike out. But otherwise it was fine.

So we sat there for ages, until Dina was so desperate for a fag that we had to go outside. I was starting to feel better – maybe the sugar had done the trick.

We headed off for the pick-up, Dina dragging on a roll-up as if trying to set a new world suction record, me wheeling the old bike.

A couple of hundred yards further down, the pavement was blocked by the pavement artist – wearing women's clothing today – who was lying full length across it with his feet in the road, working on another of his tiny pictures.

Dina whispered to me, "There's a man dedicated to extending the concept of pavement artistry." Which made me smile.

But we didn't stop, just took a detour round him by stepping into the road.

Suddenly, he didn't seem so weird.

Amazingly enough, absolutely nothing surprising happened on the way back to the cottage.

Dina drove quite slowly for her – only about three times as fast as anybody else on the road. My story about nearly crashing into the car seemed to have scared her.

Sam didn't jump out from behind a hedge or suddenly appear round a corner.

The flies didn't completely cover the windscreen making driving impossible.

We didn't skid off the road on the bodies of all those slugs.

It didn't rain blood.

There wasn't a tornado.

I could hear the old bike rattling around in the back of the pick-up. I watched the hedges and trees whizz past. I could smell earth and musty flowers. The lightning was still flickering out to sea but we couldn't hear any thunder. As we approached the cottage, a swarm of bees was doing a perfect impression of a whale blowing out a fountain of water.

Things were pretty ordinary really.

As soon as we got back, I tried to call Rachel. I really needed to talk to her.

Her phone rang for ages and then a voice I didn't know said "*Hello?*" very uncertainly.

"Hello, could I speak to Rachel please?"

"I'm sorry, she's not here. Who's calling please?"

"It's Nick, I'm a friend of hers. I'm staying at my aunt's house just outside Revenant. I was hoping to talk to her today."

"I'm her aunt Jody. Everyone's gone out. I could hear a phone ringing somewhere in the house and I just found Rachel's phone on her bed. She must have forgotten to take it with her. They've gone into Norwich for the day and I'm not sure what time they'll be back. I didn't go because I had a headache and I had to do some shopping for tonight's supper and..."

I got the feeling that if I didn't say something quick, Rachel's aunt would probably treat me to her entire life story, starting from the moment of her birth and finishing yesterday evening.

"Could you please ask her to ring me when she gets back. It's quite important. It doesn't matter how late it is."

"Yes, of course, is there any message?"

"No, thanks. But it would be great if she could call me."

"Sure. OK."

Before supper, I went out to check the swallows.

As soon as I got to the shed I could hear scrabbling on the floor, but it was too dark to see and I had to go back to the cottage to get the torch.

I found the last swallow chick in the corner, covered in dust and cobwebs. Its bright, mad little eyes continued to flick around the shed and it seemed all right, but it made me really angry. Why would anything so beautiful roll about in the dirt instead of heading into the air where it belonged? It was like it had no sense of how precious its life was and how easily it could get itself killed. Why did it keep coming down onto the floor? Was it trying to fly and failing? Was it just curious? And were its parents able to feed it down here?

The dirt and the dust were like insults. And this stupid little baby bird didn't know or care that it was being insulted. But I did.

I put the step-ladder under the nest and very gently picked up the chick. It made no attempt to struggle as I put it back in the nest. It was like it had been waiting for me to come back and help it.

Next thing I knew, I found myself talking to it. I was saying things like: "Now, I want you to stay there and get some sleep. The world is a dangerous place for a little thing like you. There are rats and foxes. Stay off the floor. Wait for your Mum and Dad. They'll help you. You could be flying in a day or two not rolling about on the crappy floor of a crappy shed. Don't waste your life. Play your cards right, and you'll be skimming over the marsh in a day or two. Eating lovely insects and feeling the sun on your feathers. And then it won't be long before you're off to Africa. Just think of that."

So maybe it wasn't the bird that was so stupid after all.

The problem was that I could see this going on for some time – the chick jumping out of the nest and me putting it back, on and on until something terrible happened. I'm glad there was nobody there to hear me.

Dina is concerned when I come in to dinner and tell her what's been happening. She says that it's probably best to keep checking and keep putting it back in the nest if necessary. She can't think of anything else to do.

We try to sit out in the garden so that Dina can have a ciggie, but the mist that's already covering the marsh starts to pour through the trees like smoke and into the garden. Within ten minutes, it's really thick. We are surrounded by dripping noises and our blankets are soaking. The light is nearly gone and we can hardly see each other through the murk. Apart from the constant dripping, there's not a sound to be heard.

It's definitely time to go indoors.

... ...
I'm so tired...
... And I dream all the time...

... ...
... It's hard to tell dreaming from waking...
Every time I close my eyes, the world swirls around...
behind my eyelids.
... Memories drift in... ... and out again...
... Shapes form and dissolve.

... ...
In my dream, there is a truth that I can't... discover,
... something I want to remember,
but can't quite grasp...
... It remains... just beyond reach...
Fades away before I can make it out... ...

... ...
I know that I need to remember it......
But I can't... ... ...
It is as though I am searching for a secret...
... A secret that everyone knows...
except me...
... ... A secret that is so important,
that not knowing it frightens me.

... ...
But I'm also afraid... ... ...of
... knowing it..

... ...
I cannot do this on my own.

... ...
...
I need the angel boy... ...
... to...
... help... ...
...
me...

Welcome

There's someone in my room.

I've just woken up. It's the middle of the night and there's someone in my room. I know there is, although I haven't yet opened my eyes to check.

I can't hear anything – no movement, no breathing. No one has said anything. No window or door has opened. No floorboard has creaked.

But there's no doubt about it, there's someone here.

And, what's more, I know who it is.

My heart is beating so hard it feels like it's going to explode and hurl me out of bed.

Part of me wants to scream and wake Dina.

But the other part of me has been expecting this for some time, and I know I have to deal with it, no matter how scared I am.

But I still haven't opened my eyes – that's going to be the hardest part. Harder even than not calling out for Dina.

I can feel the cottage settling into the ground. I can feel the press of the peat on the marsh. I can feel the scrap of moon shining behind the mist.

And now I *can* hear something – a faint dripping noise. It seems to be coming from a long way away. I'd like to believe that it's the bushes dripping in the mist in the garden but I know that it's coming from this room.

Opening my eyes and accepting what I'm seeing is the scariest, most difficult thing I've ever done in my whole life.

Sam is sitting at the end of my bed, looking out of the window.

He's soaking wet. His clothes are clinging to his body and the water is coming off him in streams.

I'm fighting down the panic. I think that if he were to move or even look at me, I'd be out of bed like a rocket. Out of this room. Away from him. Howling for Dina.

But as long as he sits still and doesn't look at me and doesn't speak, I can just about cope. After all, I've been waiting for this, expecting it, knowing it was going to happen, since that first day on the broad with Gerry. I didn't exactly know what it was, but I knew that it was coming.

Very slowly, I sit upright in bed. I don't want to frighten Sam or startle him.

That's a laugh; me not frighten him. He doesn't seem too bothered about frightening me.

I don't want to make things worse than they already are.

And for a minute, nothing happens. My heart continues to thump and I don't dare to speak. And Sam continues to sit there, looking out of the window at something I know I wouldn't be able to see even if everything wasn't clouded with mist.

When I've seen Sam in the daylight, I've always had this sense that he was disappearing before my eyes. I feel that much more now. It's like he doesn't have any edges, like he's melting into the air. Like he's too frail to exist. Like if you looked at him sideways and let your eyes slip a little, he wouldn't be there at all. It's almost like you can see through him.

"Sam," I manage to whisper although my voice shakes all over the place. "Sam, are you all right?"

There's no answer – and I guess it *was* a pretty stupid question.

"Sam, can you hear me?"

Whatever he's looking at through the window must have all his attention because he's taking no notice of me.

"Sam, is there something you want from me?"

No answer.

"Sam, do you know that you're dead?"

No answer.

"Sam, is there anything that I can do to help you."

No answer.

You wouldn't believe that a situation like this could go nowhere, but it can.

What can I say? How can I reach him? How can I make a difference?

I have to continue to fight down the panic long enough to think this through.

I can feel the blood beating in my ears.

Sam doesn't move. Just one touch, I think, and he'll dissolve, fall to bits.

Just one touch and he'll be gone forever.

And then I know what I have to say. It's bloody obvious. How can it have taken me so long? I think Rachel's been close to it all along. She may not have had the same suspicions as me about Sam but she seemed to know what he needed, how to talk to him, apart from when she got so angry.

"Hello, Sam," I manage to croak. "It's good to see you." (This is without doubt the biggest lie I've ever told in my life.) "Welcome."

And this seems to do it. Very slowly his head starts to turn away from the window. Again, I have to fight back this urge to leap out of bed and run for it or scream for Dina.

I know that he's no threat to me, but believe me it's not easy being around him like this.

Our eyes meet although I'm not sure that he's really seeing me. I've never seen anything as sad as that lost, frightened look in his eyes.

And then he seems to recognise me. And ever so slowly a shy smile lights up his whole face.

We sit there, eye to eye, not saying anything. And the whole world seems to have come to a stop. Me panting with fright and him dripping wet and trembling in and out of existence.

And then... I can't believe this... then I must have fallen asleep because it's the morning, Sam's gone, the bed and the floor are dry and the sky through the window is clear.

There's a bee bouncing noisily against it trying to force its way inside and I can hear birds in the garden.

My phone's beeping. It's a text from Billy, who's seen a rhino. At least I assume it's a rhino because the text actually says he's seen a "shimm." So, he's either not looking when he's texting (when I type in "shimm" it says "rhino" on the screen) or he's discovered an animal previously unknown to man. Which, after the night I've had, wouldn't really surprise me.

The thing is, I couldn't care less. I've seen something that Billy hasn't and Jack hasn't and Emily hasn't. I've seen something that no one else has seen. Well, no one else except Rachel.

The thing is, I've seen a *ghost*.

I check the shed and, sure enough, the daft little chick hasn't taken any notice of the talking to I gave it last night. It's on the floor again and dusty and cobwebby. It's got so used to being picked up that it no longer tries to escape from me. It just allows itself to put gently back into the nest. It shows no signs of going to join its brothers and/or sisters and parents in the sky.

I guess I'm just going to have to be patient. Like Dina says, I'll have to prove to it that I'm ready to put it back in the nest more times than it can flop onto the floor. It's got to learn that the only way of stopping me picking it up is to fly out of the door.

Dina asks me if I'm OK and says I'm looking a bit pale. I'm bursting to tell her about last night but I haven't got a clue how to begin.

Instead, after breakfast I ring Rachel. She's in Stalton shopping with her Mum.

"Hi Rachel, it's Nick. Listen, can you get away? I need to talk to you?"

"What about?"

"I don't want to say over the phone. But it's really important. Can you get away?"

"Well, Mum and I are meeting the others here for lunch, but what about this afternoon? Shall I come to the cottage around four? What's it all about?"

"No, really, I don't want to say at the moment. I'll tell you as soon as you get here. Listen, did you get my message last night?"

"Yeh, my aunt said you wanted me to call. She said it sounded really urgent and that you sounded a bit stressed. But I rang and rang and nothing happened. I thought maybe you'd switched your phone off. I just couldn't get through at all, not even to your voice mail."

I can't understand this. I'm sure she's telling the truth, but my phone was switched on and it must have been working because I got that text from Billy and his bloody shimm.

"I don't know what the problem was, but thanks for trying. And I guess your aunt was right – I was stressed – but I promise I'll tell you about it as soon as you get here. I'll see you about four."

"Can't you give me any idea of what it's all about? I'm going to worrying about it all day."

"No, sorry, it'll be best if I tell you face to face."

"OK see you later. But I think you're being really mean."

She may be eaten up with curiosity, but I could explode. I so badly want to tell someone about what's happened to me.

About a hundred times in the next hour I nearly say something to Dina, but something is holding me back. And that something includes the fact that she wouldn't believe me in a million years – she is a scientist after all. And even if I didn't think she might have me locked up for talking gibberish, I wouldn't know how to get started.

If I'm honest, I'm scared to say anything about it to her. Scared she'll think I'm soft in the head.

Just as Sam doesn't seem to do normal; so Dina doesn't seem to do mysterious.

So, in the end I take Harry out for a walk. We take the same route as we did the other day, but I decide to give the ruined abbey (or whatever it was) and the nettles a miss. Somehow, I don't think I want to go there today. It was haunted and depressing enough even before I'd seen a ghost. (I've seen a ghost.)

The air is thick and still, but Harry doesn't seem to mind and he skips along beside me. He doesn't even seem very bothered by the flies taking up residence on our faces.

The hazy sun is making the marsh and the fields look whitish. A few pigeons flap over and we see the marsh harrier flying along a line of hedges and then settling on what looks like an impossibly thin branch which bends and swings under its weight. In the distance we can see a few sheep grazing on pale blue grass. A little deer runs across a field of stubble — probably startled by us. Harry seems to know that there's no point in chasing after it.

I walk slowly because I don't want Harry to get too tired and because I'm trying to make the time pass.

We go past the church near the beach, but this time we don't go in. Seeing a ghost really changes the way you think about things. And one of the things I'm thinking is that today of all days I don't really need a trip to an old, overgrown graveyard. I can't imagine why.

Just like we did the other day, we walk back to the cottage by road.

All the time I'm thinking about Sam — what else would I be thinking about? Who is he? I suppose that should be, "Who *was* he?" Why isn't he happy to stay dead? (Is anyone happy to stay dead?) Why has he chosen me and Rachel? Why did he come to my room last night? What does he want from us? How can we help him? Why is he soaking wet? Why is he so dirty and smelly? Come to think of it, I never heard of a ghost being smelly. Or drinking coke and eating crisps for that matter. Or riding crossbar on someone's bike. What makes people come back as ghosts? What does he need? How can I help? How can I make him less sad?

The next couple of hours seem to last forever. I sit in the garden with Harry watching five swallows – still only five – swoop and swerve like they're having the time of their little lives. I've been keeping a look out for the slow worm, but I've never seen it again. Dragonflies whirr round and round and hundreds of browny-red butterflies doze on the flowers, their wings moving in and out like beating hearts.

And even when Rachel does arrive, I don't get a chance to talk to her straightaway.

She's brought another bunch of 50p garden flowers – you can hardly get into the cottage for all the flowers that she's bought and I've bought. She also seems happy to sit and talk to Dina for hours about all kinds of girly things – families, what they did yesterday and so on.

In the end, I can't stand it any longer and I interrupt and say, "Rachel, shall we go for a walk?"

Both of them look really surprised and not very pleased. But Rachel agrees to come.

"I was really enjoying talking to Dina," she says as soon as we get outside. "What's the matter? What's so urgent that it can't wait? After all, you've kept me guessing all day and now you can't seem to wait an extra minute."

"I'm sorry, but it's really important."

"So what is it then?"

"I don't want to tell you here. I'll tell you in a minute. Let's go out onto the marsh."

We wander up the path into the marsh with the hedge on the right and the ditches on the left. It's very still and the flies are bad. I don't even know why I wanted to come out here.

We sit on the grass by the ditch in which I caught my rudd. Little, long-legged beetles are stirring up the water's surface between the patches of lilies. The branches of the trees in the little wood are not moving.

Trouble is that now I've got her here, I don't know how to begin.

"Rachel?"

"Yes," said with a bit of a sigh.

"You know Sam?"

"Yes," even more impatiently.

"Have you noticed anything odd about him?"

"Have I noticed anything odd about him? That's a bit like asking me if I've noticed anything hideous about Gerry. Of course, I've noticed something odd about Sam. If there's anything about Sam that *isn't* odd I haven't spotted it. But so what? What are you getting at?"

"Have you wondered about why he's so odd?"

"You mean apart from smelling terrible and looking so miserable and talking in this bizarre way and torturing worms? I suppose, I think he's very unhappy and probably has awful parents and maybe he has some kind of illness. I don't know. But where's all this going?"

I can't put it off any longer. "He's odd because he's dead. He's a ghost. He's haunting us for some reason. He turned up in my room in the middle of the night. He's trying to reach us."

Complete silence. Rachel's looking at me as though I've just made some terrible joke. "Nick, what's this about? That's not even funny."

"No, listen, I promise I'm not joking. I'm really serious. He came to my room and sat on the end of the bed and smiled at me when I said it was good to see him. And he was sort of transparent – you could almost see through him. And he was soaking wet and looking at something out of the window. And then I went back to sleep and in the morning he was gone and the bed was dry. I'm sure there's something he wants from me but I don't know what it is."

I can tell that this is not going down well and I'm dreading the moment when I stop speaking.

"Nick, I don't understand. What's the point of all this? It's not funny. Sam's a poor little kid who looks as though he needs loving and looking after. I'm not sure that I think he's very nice, but that's all he is. So, why don't you give all this a rest and let's talk about something else?"

It's so frustrating that she's like this. But I guess I'd react in just the same way if she was telling me the things I'm telling her.

I try to prove the point.

"But don't you see how it all fits. For a start, only you and I have ever seen him. When Dina and I passed him in the car one evening, I pointed him out to her but she missed seeing him. Then there was the other evening when we came back from Coningsby. You remember that Brenda drove past us when we were talking to Sam in the road, but she said afterwards that she'd only seen you and me. But she couldn't have missed him in spite of what she said about listening to the radio and all that. And do you remember how terrified he was at coming into the shop? He said it was because he hadn't got any shoes, but I think it was because Brenda wouldn't be able to see him. And then yesterday, I was cycling to Stalton and he nearly got me run over by appearing at the side of the road. The lady driving the car said that she didn't know what I was talking about when I said I stopped to talk to a friend. She obviously couldn't see him either. I'm sure only you and I can see him."

Would I take this stuff seriously if I were in Rachel's position? Absolutely not. No way.

"So, Sam's the invisible boy is he? And what's this about you nearly getting run over?"

"I know this doesn't make any sense, but I swear I'm telling you the truth. And it's not just that nobody else has seen him. It's clear that he doesn't belong to this time."

Everything I say sounds more and more ridiculous. I guess the best thing is not to give Rachel a chance to say anything back about. So I blunder on.

"Just think. Half the things we say to him he doesn't understand – ordinary things like 'hi' and 'OK' and 'cool'. Why not? And then he says he's never had a fizzy drink before or eaten crisps. Why not? His clothes are terrible and he's dirty and his hair looks like it was cut with the kitchen scissors. Why? And he's never been on a bike before. Why not? And he doesn't know anything about music or who the Prime Minister is. And he won't even say what year it is. Why not? I think the answer is that he's been dead for a long time and that a lot of the things we take for granted are confusing and frightening to him. Maybe that's why he won't come swimming. Maybe that's why he talks about shooting coots and why he skewered those worms the other day."

Rachel's gone from looking a bit fed up to looking quite worried.

"Nick, I'm beginning to think that you're serious about this. Are you sure you're OK. You must have just dreamed about Sam being in your room last night. I remember you telling me about that dream you had of finding him washed up on the beach."

"Yeh, that dream was obviously really important. It was trying to tell me something. I didn't know that at the time, but I do now. Maybe it's a kind of code. But if it is I can't work it out."

I'm going to have to slow down a bit, take it easier. Rachel's looking as though she'd like to run for it and who could blame her? She's looking nearly as spooked by me as I was by Sam.

"Nick, you're not trying to tell me that dreams are messages from the spirit world or some rubbish like that are you?"

"No, but everything fits. Just think about it. No one we talk to knows anything about him or his parents. He says his name's Wellsby, but no one's ever heard of the Wellsbys. He says he lives on Church Lane but we know that he doesn't. No one does. He says he goes to the school in the village, but he doesn't seem to know anything about school holidays and he says he only goes there when he can. What does that mean? No one goes to school only when they can. The law says you have to go. But maybe when he was alive, things weren't so strict. Maybe he had to work on a farm or something."

Is this convincing? Not really.

"So, the fact that he's lying about where he lives proves he's a ghost, does it?"

"No, of course not. Not on its own. But if you start to add all the things together it makes sense. Something odd's been going on for weeks. Everyone says so. I think old Charley can sense something, even though he doesn't know what it is. Then there have been all the flies. And the weather and birds' nests falling from roofs. I think everyone feels that something is wrong, but that a few people have a stronger sense of it than others. It's upsetting lots of people in ways they can't explain. Maybe that's why Gerry has been so strange and horrible."

"So, now poor old Sam's responsible for Gerry being a tosser is he? Couldn't be that Gerry makes a perfectly good job of being a tosser all by himself? I know you've always tried to see his good points, but maybe he just doesn't have any."

"No, I'm not saying that. I don't know what I am saying really. I just think that some people are more sensitive to Sam's presence and that it confuses them and makes them behave in ways they don't normally. You remember I told you how upset Charley was when he tried to write about what was happening?"

"Nick, I'm getting a bit scared. You can't expect me to believe any of this. And it's not funny in case you think it is."

"Rachel, I absolutely promise that I'm telling the truth. Why would I lie? And I swear to you that when I woke up last night Sam was sitting on my bed. Maybe that's why you couldn't call me. I know this is hard to believe or even take seriously, but I promise that's what really happened. I know Sam is a ghost."

"So, not only is he the invisible boy, but he forces Gerry, who's really a lovely bloke, to behave like an arsehole and now he even has the power to make phones not work."

I never thought this was going to be easy, but I never thought it would be as hard as this.

"OK, have it your own way. I'm lying. This is all some stupid joke. But will you at least come with me to see Sam again? Maybe we can find out what's really going on."

"I'm not sure that I'd feel safe with you out on our own."

"Please, Rachel, it's really important to me."

"OK, when do you want to go?"

"This afternoon. Now."

"But Dina's asked me to tea."

"We'll make an excuse."

There's a bit of an atmosphere between us by the time we get back to the cottage. Dina looks puzzled when I announce that we're going out on the bikes. But she doesn't say anything about tea or try to stop us.

Rachel doesn't talk much on the ride to the village. She obviously thinks I've been trying to make her look like an idiot. Knowing something that you can't tell anyone because they won't believe you unless they're as bonkers as the thing you're trying to tell them is a right pain.

I can't think what to say. There doesn't seem to be much point in trying to change the subject. No point in talking about the weather or what Rachel and her family are planning to do tomorrow.

Of course, when we get to the school, Sam's not there.

So, we cycle down to Revenant Broad. By now the light is beginning to fade. The air is so thick that it feels like it could choke you. It's like it's touching your face and clinging to your clothes. It makes you feel breathless. Even Rachel seems to feel it. She's gone very quiet.

I don't know why, but my heart's beating really fast as we dump the bikes and set off down the path by the reeds. The broad is reflecting a sky that's gold and grey at the same time. A thin trickle of mist has started to form at the water's edge. There isn't a sound. No bipping of coots; no panic of pigeon wings; no wind stirring the leaves. Nothing.

I swear I can feel the weight of the air on my head and shoulders. It's trying to cover me like a blanket. It's trying to push me down into the peat. It's smothering me.

Rachel takes hold of my hand. "Nick, I don't like this."

Nor do I, to tell the truth, but I think it's important to keep going. It's just really hard to do so.

Suddenly, Rachel's hand grips mine really tightly. I can feel her nails digging into my palm, which has suddenly got all sweaty.

"What's that?"

Ahead of us we can hear a splashing noise and then something crashing about in the reeds.

Rachel stops and starts dragging me back. "Nick, I don't want to go any further. I want to go back to the bikes. Come on."

Well why didn't you say so? We turn and practically run back to the bikes. Whatever's up ahead, I don't think is going to ask us to tea.

We don't say anything as we quickly unlock the bikes and start cycling back to the village.

It takes a few minutes for my heart to stop thumping and then I say, "So, you're still sure that there's no such thing as a ghost? You still think I'm making all this up? You didn't think anything spooky was going on at the broad."

She's a bit calmer now. "OK, so I admit it, I was scared. The atmosphere was horrible. And you've been going on about ghosts, and that must have upset me. Sure something felt wrong, but that doesn't mean I have to believe everything you say about Sam."

"So, what was making that noise up ahead of us?"

"I don't know. It could have been a swan or a heron or something. Or maybe it was a fisherman packing up his gear."

"Do you really believe that?"

"I don't know what I believe."

"Well, if you think it was a fisherman, where was his car? Tell you what, let's stop the bikes and wait. He'll have to come past us. It shouldn't be long. It's nearly too dark to fish."

Rachel has no intention of doing anything of the sort. She just keeps cycling. And I know how she feels. I'm having to use all my willpower not to cycle as fast as I can away from whatever it was.

We start to feel a bit better as we get nearer the village, but not all that much better. But things do at least seem a bit more normal here.

Rachel says she wants to go home. Whatever she says, she was clearly frightened down at the broad. But I persuade her to come with me to Church Lane to see if Sam's there.

Of course, he's not. The three cottages are empty. No one's been here.

As we cycle past the churchyard, the crows or rooks, or whatever they are, are going mad. Shrieking their heads off and flapping from one tree to another. It's like they're laughing and jeering at us.

Rachel is pretty quiet and doesn't say much when I drop her off at her cottage.

I have to admit that riding back on my own to Dina's is not exactly the most fun thing I've ever done in my life. I have to resist this urge to look back over my shoulder. It's almost dark and the air is thick and clammy just like it was by the broad. As I approach the cottage, I can see the mist swirling in from the marsh – it looks like the tide coming in. And just like at the beach the other day I can't shake off this sense that I'm being watched. The flies are as bad as ever, but I'm almost getting used to them.

I realise that I can't tell Dina about Sam, she's bound to react in the same way as Rachel. If Rachel who's the only other person to have seen and dealt with Sam can't take me seriously, then how can I expect Dina who's never seen him to?

And as I think this it occurs to me that there is someone else who has seen Sam – Moon. Moon not only saw him but she also talked to him and even took a message. I'm going to have to go and talk to her. See if she can tell me anything.

I lean my bike against the shed wall. The mist has made everything seem damp and chilly. I can hear the moisture dripping from the trees and bushes. I check the shed but as far as I can tell the swallow chick isn't on the floor. I go back to the cottage for the torch, come back and climb the step ladder. I peek into the nest and the chick is sitting there all alone, breathing quietly and looking straight into my eyes. This is the first good news I've had all day. "Just make sure you're out of here first thing in the morning. I expect you to fly around the garden 100 times before breakfast. Checking out time is 9.00 am."

It's so cold in the cottage that Dina says we'll have a fire. She piles sticks and coal into the fireplace but when she lights it the smoke, instead of going up the chimney, comes straight back into the room. She holds a sheet of newspaper across the fireplace to encourage it to burn better, but the smoke just goes on pouring into the room.

Dina says that it's often hard to light a fire when you haven't had one for a few weeks. The chimney gets damp and won't draw. I think the problem must be the mist, after all, there's nothing to stop it getting into the top of the chimney. We've probably got a whole chimney full of mist. My eyes are streaming and I can taste the smoke at the back of my throat, although Dina doesn't seem too badly affected. And anyway, she seems to like breathing in smoke. Even pays for the privilege.

In the end, she runs upstairs and comes back with her hair dryer, which she plugs in and points directly up the chimney. She says that once the air in the chimney gets warm, the fire will start to draw.

And she's right: after a couple of minutes the warm air wins out over the cold mist and the fire starts to roar and crackle and the flames shoot up the chimney.

If only dealing with ghosts was as easy as that. But something tells me that pointing a hair dryer at Sam isn't going to make him go away.

The trouble is that the fire's now so hot and the room's so small that it's boiling. I take off my jumper and sit here in my T-shirt. But Dina seems to love it. She lies full length on the floor close to the fire and closes her eyes, just like she does on the beach.

She looks like some strange skinny cat. I can smell the flames singeing her clothes.

… … …
…
…
… …
I think she may be angry with me…
She is shouting but I can't hear her words…

… … …
… …
I'm frightened…
… but I haven't done anything wrong…
… … I think

… … …
…
Her hair flames in the sunlight…
… … Her eyes are angry

…
Fire and ice… light and dark…

… …
…
… The angel boy is kind
… … and his voice is soft…
… … I want to fly…
… through..
… the air with him…
… again… … …
And never…
… touch the ground…
… … again

… …
… … I'm frightened…
I haven't done anything wrong.

… … …

So much less of him

I wake with a start. He's back. I know that because I can feel it. I know it even though there's not a sound to be heard apart from the drip of the mist in the garden.

I know it even though I haven't opened my eyes yet.

In fact, when I got to bed I didn't think I'd be able to get to sleep at all. Not only was I half boiled alive from Dina's fire, but my head was full of ghosts. Was Sam going to appear again tonight? Was he going to haunt me forever? And if so, was I doomed never to get another night's sleep?

Was I doomed to wander the earth forever tormented by a lost soul?

Well, to be honest, that seemed a bit unlikely. Whatever Sam was, I couldn't imagine him really frightening anyone. As long as you could get use to the idea of him being a ghost, you could go back to feeling sorry for him and angry about the state he was in. If – and I'm ready to admit that it's a pretty huge IF – if you could learn to live with the fact that he's dead, then there's no reason to be any more frightened of him than of the mist.

I was so hot that I opened the windows wide, but one look at the mist which had crept right up to the walls of the cottage and I shut it again. There may not be any reason to be frightened of it but that doesn't mean that I want it in my room. In fact, I think it's pretty amazing that I came to bed at all after what happened last night. So, I'll shut the window if I feel like it.

I know that Sam doesn't need a window or a door when he decides to come visiting, but sleeping with the window open would have taken far more nerve than I've got at the moment.

Anyway, he's back and I'm trying to pretend I'm still asleep.

I'm putting off as long as possible the moment when I sit up and have to deal with a dripping-wet ghost at the end of my bed. There's nothing in any of my GCSE courses that gives any clue about what you're supposed to do in a situation like this. But even keeping my eyes shut takes a fair bit of nerve.

Although I don't want to see what I know I'm going to see, I'm even less keen on not knowing what the thing I'm not wanting to see is doing.

For all I know, Sam could be hanging from the ceiling or whirling round in circles or constantly changing shape like the bees. And that's a pretty bad thought. He could be creeping up on me ready to grab me in an icy grasp – except, of course, that I know he isn't.

When you have a bad dream it's such a relief to wake up and open your eyes and see how everything in the room is normal. Only this time, when I open my eyes I know it's not going to be normal.

Not unless being paid a midnight visit by a dead person fits in with your idea of what's normal.

But in the end, I have to. And there he is.

I say, "There he is," but to be strictly accurate, I should say, "there he nearly is."

There's so much less of him than there was last night.

It's not a person or even a ghost sitting at the end of my bed. It's the idea of a person, the idea of a ghost.

A something-that's-not-quite-a-ghost. A kind of trembling of the air. A ripple. A swirling collection of molecules. Like a hologram or a faint 3-D photograph. Only a flicker.

Even his smell has started to fade, and the dripping sound is so faint that I can barely hear it.

But the sense of sadness hasn't gone away. In fact, it's stronger.

Like last night, he's looking out of the window (even though I've closed the curtains) with his back to me. Looking at something only he can see. Maybe he's looking at something that happened hundreds of years ago, before this cottage was even built, before this marsh was reclaimed from the sea.

But, of course, I'm a bit of an expert at this sort of thing now, so I say – as calmly as my pounding heart will let me – "Hello Sam. I'm glad you came back."

And just like he did last night, he slowly turns his head towards me. (And just like last night, I have to fight off this urge to run out of the room as fast as possible.)

Even his smile is beginning to disappear. A few days ago, he was flashing these enormous grins at me and Rachel. Tonight, that seems to be beyond him. He just seems immensely tired. But whatever's driving him must be strong because, in spite of everything, a weary, sad, lonely, tiny smile appears on his poor shadowy face.

I force myself to look into his eyes, and what I see is a million years of misery. Space. Nothing. The end of the universe. The sadness of exploding stars and colliding planets. I don't know. I don't know how to put it in words.

But I do know that I never want to see it again.

There's nothing I can say that will make any difference, but there's still one thing left to try.

Very quietly, I get out of bed and put on my jeans.

And then as quietly as I can, I sit next to Sam on the bed. Believe me, trying not to frighten someone when you're terrified yourself is not easy.

For a bit we sit there. And then, very slowly – taking care not to startle him – I start to lift my right arm.

Very slowly, very carefully, I try to put my arm round his shoulders. For a moment there is just a suggestion that I'm touching someone, a faint resistance to my arm, the idea of a shoulder rather than a shoulder itself.

And then he's gone. That's it. I'm alone again, in my jeans at the end of the bed with my right arm around absolutely nothing.

I can hardly believe what's happened. One minute I'm doing my best to hug a ghost, the next minute he's disappeared. Gone. Cleared out. It's like he was never here. I feel almost angry. I never asked him to come here in the first place and now he's gone without a word.

Everything feels so normal it's weird.

I get undressed again and back into bed. Well, what else can I do? I can't exactly go clubbing. And I certainly don't want to wake Dina up. I can hear her snoring quietly in her room.

I don't expect to go back to sleep, or at least not for hours.

But it seems to take about two minutes. And now it's morning and the mist has gone but the sky is the colour of slate and it's raining hard.

The swallows aren't flying this morning, they must be hiding up somewhere. But in that case, who will feed the chick in the nest?

At least it is still in the nest when I pay my before-breakfast call.

I tell Dina that I'm going to the nature reserve this morning. She asks if I want a lift because of the rain, but I say I'm happy to take the bike. I guess she thinks I'm going to see Gerry because she asks me to give him her love.

It's been raining so hard that there are huge puddles on the road. My bike doesn't have a rear mudguard, so a thin streak of cold water is being sprayed up the middle of my back. But the rain does seem to have cleared the air and to have washed away some of the flies. I hope they've all drowned – painfully if possible. I hope their nasty little lives flashed before their eyes as they went down for the third time. I hope that their last memory was of biting my face and I hope they regretted it.

The water is dripping off the trees in great streams. And after about three minutes, I'm soaked. But I don't care. In fact I'm quite enjoying it and at least I'm doing something.

There are no cars in the car park at the reserve, which I guess isn't very surprising. It's not exactly the ideal day for twitching or for pointing cameras at butterflies. The rain is pouring off the roof of the visitor centre, which makes the large wooden dragonfly look as though it's swimming downstream. Maybe it'll suddenly be snapped up by an even larger wooden trout.

Concentrate.

It occurs to me as I open the door to the visitor centre that I must look a bit of a sight – soaking wet and squelchy.

Moon is sitting in the same place as before – in fact it looks as though she might have been sitting there all her life. It's hard to think of anything urgent enough to get her out of that seat. Maybe she doesn't even go home at night. Maybe they just cover her with a blanket and then uncover her in the morning.

She doesn't seem to do curiosity and the fact that I'm soaked to the skin is nothing to her. People come through the door, some are wet and some are dry. That's just the way things are.

It's also clear that she hasn't got the faintest memory of ever having seen me before.

"Hi," I say.

"Hi," she replies. Perfectly friendly; completely indifferent. If she's surprised that someone has come to explore the nature reserve in the pissing rain, then she's certainly not showing it.

"Hi. I'm Nick. I came here about ten days ago to meet Gerry. I'm staying with my Aunt Dina, Gerry's girlfriend."

Messages can take some time to get from the Earth to Moon and there's a bit of a pause.

"I spoke to you then. You said how hot it was."

"Did I?" She seems surprised. It's like she thinks she said something wise or amusing and is glad to be reminded of it.

She looks at me for a moment, thinking this over.

Then she says, "Do you want me to call Gerry?" But I notice that she makes no move towards the walkie-talkie.

"No thanks. It's you I wanted to talk to. I wanted to ask you something."

"Did you?" No curiosity. No impatience.

"Yes, I wanted to talk to you about the first time I came. Do you remember that while I was out with Gerry, a boy came and asked you where I was?"

It's already clear that she has no idea what I'm talking about. But then, I don't suppose she can remember what she had for breakfast this morning either.

"He was a bit smelly and had no shoes on. You said that he'd been here about half an hour before but that you didn't know where he'd gone."

It's obvious there's no one at home behind those pale blue eyes.

"Sorry," she says, "I don't remember. We get such a lot of people in here."

The very thought of all these people seems to make her tired. And just looking at her makes me tired. It's like her voice is covered in cobwebs.

At this point, most other people would say something like, "What do you need? Is something wrong? Is everything all right?"

But not Moon. She just says, "Are you sure you don't want me to call Gerry?" But she still doesn't make a move towards the walkie-talkie.

"No, it's OK, I don't want to disturb him."

"Oh, all right then." She sits there looking at me. I'm sure she could sit there for days. Not expecting anything.

I have to force myself not to yawn. You need to keep mentally pinching yourself when talking to Moon, otherwise you might fall asleep at her feet and never wake up.

"He was about ten years old. Really dirty. Terrible haircut."

"No, sorry I don't remember him... er, sorry, what did you say your name was?"

"Nick."

"No, sorry, Nick, I don't remember him."

And that's it. There's no more to come.

I guess I've got two choices. I could either stand here looking at Moon for the next hundred years or I could leave. I decide to leave.

"OK, well, thanks. I'd better go."

"Oh, that's all right." What does she mean that's all right? She hasn't done anything. She hasn't helped. She's been the opposite of help. She's like the negative of helpful. She's been about as useful as... as... as something that is completely useless. But it's hard to get angry with her – she exhausts me. And it's not her fault. On planet Moon, when someone says, "thank you", she says, "that's all right." That's just the way things are. It doesn't mean anything. No need to take offence. Might as well blame the grass for growing or the birds for singing.

"Bye."

"Bye, Rick," she says.

I'm sure she's forgotten me before I've even shut the door behind me. If someone were to come up to her now and say, "Has a boy called Nick just been here?" she'd say something like, "I'm not sure. I can't really remember. There might have been a boy here. Or maybe that was yesterday. I don't think he said what his name was."

When you're Moon these are not the kind of question you can be expected to deal with. When you're Moon, it's enough just to be Moon.

I take a couple of huge breaths to wake myself up. And then I want to laugh. I really like Moon even if she doesn't know that I exist. She has no idea how hilarious she is.

I'm still smiling when I head across the mown picnic area towards my bike.

A Land-Rover with the dragonfly logo on its doors draws up and Gerry jumps out. He's wearing the leather hat.

"Hello young master," he says touching the brim of his hat, "to what do we owe this singular honour?"

He's being sarcastic but his eyes are smiling.

"Were you looking for me? Is everything all right?"

"No, I wanted to talk to Moon." I'm doing my best not to look at the hat.

"Really?" he seems amazed. "What about?"

"I wanted to ask her about the other week when I was here and whether she remembered a boy who was looking for me."

"And what did she say?" Gerry looks like he's about to crack up laughing.

"She said that she didn't remember him and I don't think she remembered me."

"That's odd," says Gerry, trying to look serious, "she's usually as bright as a button. Nothing much gets past her."

We're both laughing.

"So who was this kid?"

"It was Sam. You know, the boy who says he lives in Church Lane."

"Yeh, I remember. But why did you want to talk to Moon about him? What gave you the right to put such a strain on what passes for her brain?"

How can I answer this? I can't say, "Because, like me, Moon can see dead people. She may be as crazy as a sack of snakes but she's the only adult I know of who's seen Sam."

So, I say, "I've been looking for Sam for a few days and can't find him anywhere. I thought he might have come here again and I was going to ask Moon if she'd seen him. Maybe I'd be able to track him down."

"You'd have done just as well asking that," he says pointing to the wooden dragonfly surfing on the roof. "What does this Sam look like? I'll keep an eye out for him."

I know there's no point in this and that Gerry could keep 20 eyes out for him but he'd still never see him. But I can't say this. "He's about ten years old, very pale and very thin. Terrible haircut. No shoes. Smells."

"Well he should be easy enough to spot. If I see him, I'll tell him you're looking for him."

Never in a million years.

"Thanks," I say. What else can I say?

"As you've probably noticed, it's pretty quiet around here today. But you're welcome to hang around if you like,"

"No thanks, I told Dina I'd get back for lunch."

"No point in asking what's on the menu?"

"No. Probably not."

"OK, well see you. Give Dina my love. Tell her I'll call her."

It's still raining hard as I cycle back to the cottage, but for some reason talking to Moon has cheered me up. I'm feeling better than I have for days. But I still haven't found anyone I can talk to about Sam.

I have a shower and then, because the ashes from last night's fire are still warm in the grate, I lie full length on the floor in front of it. I can hear Dina's fingers on the PC's keyboard in the office. Harry ambles over. Sniffs the side of my head. And then, having made up his mind, lies full length on top of me. His nose on my shoulders, his back feet reaching down to about my knees. And he never even asked. His fur smells of mud and rain and he's fast asleep and twitching in a couple of minutes.

This isn't the easiest position to think in, but I do my best. I can't talk to Dina about Sam because I know that she wouldn't be able to believe me. She's a scientist and thinks there's a logical explanation for everything. I've tried talking to Rachel about it, but I just seem to have frightened and upset her. And I don't think she wants to hear any more about it. I've tried talking to Moon about him, and that got me precisely nowhere. No one else has seen Sam. But it seems to me that even though they haven't seen him, a couple of people I've spoken to have been really upset by what's been going on. I'm sure it's because he can feel something that Gerry's been so horrible, but I can't imagine telling him about Sam. The other person, of course, is Charley Maddox. I can't really imagine talking about Sam to him either. But I guess I'm going to have to try.

At least, if I can ever get out from under Harry, I'm going to have to try.

It's still raining when I cycle back into Revenant village after lunch, although not as hard as it was this morning. The air definitely feels fresher, even though I'm still getting a stripe of cold muddy water up the middle of my back.

Brenda is behind the counter slicing ham when I get to the shop and she tells me Charley will be "thrilled" to see me.

He's sitting in the purple summer house, with a bright green blanket over his legs.

"Hello, Nick. Thanks for coming to see me. I'm freezing my arse off ('scuse my French), which is why I've got this stupid blanket on. When you get to my age, you feel the cold. It's about the only thing you do feel. My circulation's shot. I think the last time my heart managed to pump blood all the way to my toes was about 1976."

He asks about Dina and Rachel and then he tells me a long story about the article he's writing for next week's *Gazette*. It's about an area of heathland between Norfolk and Suffolk, which has inland sand-dunes. Apparently, in about 1570 these dunes suddenly became active and started moving north east burying farms and other buildings. By 1660, they were blocking parts of the River Ouse five miles away. Charley says that this proves that you can't trust the ground beneath your feet around here. But he also says that he thinks that message will be lost on his readers – "all six of them."

I do my best to concentrate on what he's saying, but since I was visited by Sam it's not been easy focusing on anything else.

As he talks, I can catch glimpses of the Charley I first met – especially when he's being rude about his readers, none of whom, he claims, has any of their own teeth. But he still seems tired and fed up and confused.

Eventually, I can't put it off any longer. So I jump in with both feet.

"Charley, do you believe in ghosts?"

He's been slumped down in his chair, but now he struggles to sit up straighter. This is not something that happens fast.

"I'm so old now that there's hardly anything I don't believe in. But why are you asking?"

Now that I've started, I might as well finish: "Because I think I've seen one. No, cancel that; because I know I've seen one. I expect you think that's stupid or mad."

I don't know what reaction I'm expecting, but for a moment Charley does and says nothing. He's thinking.

"OK, first of all I don't think it's stupid or mad. If you tell me you've seen a ghost then I believe that's what you think. Do I believe in ghosts? Well, I don't know. Why not? I can't think of any reason why they don't have as much right to exist as anyone else. Have I ever seen one myself? No. Would I like to? Yes. Tell me about it."

So I tell him the whole story, from the time I first saw Sam in the playground to his disappearance in my bedroom last night. I tell him about going to the broad with Rachel and hearing that splashing and crashing, and how I think that Sam's presence has been making odd things happen – the flies and the slugs and the weather and the acrobatic bees and the broken birds' nests and all that.

"So it wasn't an earthquake, then?"

"I don't think so."

"Barbara Pardew will be disappointed."

"Charley, do you believe me?"

"Yes, I think I do. I told you when I first met you that this is a pretty weird place, at a funny angle to normal. All kinds of things happen here that you can't imagine happening anywhere else. I know that when I first moved here, a lot of the old people (they were probably about 20 years younger than I am now) used to tell ghost stories to each other and anyone else who'd listen. Stories about ghostly wagons without a driver, marching Roman legions or the crunch of footsteps in the night when no one was there. I remember one old girl in particular (she seemed incredibly ancient but I expect she was young enough to be my daughter) who used to sit in the Ferret (although it wasn't called that then) and tell anyone who'd buy her a pint about the times she saw a ghost in the churchyard when she was a young woman. She was called something like Old Aggie or Old Hettie (I can't remember) – she was a bit mad and a lot smelly. I don't know what was wrong with her exactly, they'd probably find a pill for it these days. Anyway, she used to say that she'd seen a ghost in the churchyard on a few occasions. Even claimed to have had a conversation with him. The interesting thing is that she said that he stopped appearing around the time of the First World War. She said that the last time she saw him was one evening when she'd been tidying up her mother's grave. She turned round and there was the boy in a blue shirt staring at her, but when she spoke to him he just disappeared. Turned away and was gone. She never saw him again although she seems to have spent more time than was good for her hanging around the churchyard waiting for him. Come to think of it, I wonder if he had anything to with your Sam."

First it's "my" swallows, now it's "my" Sam. But you can't own a ghost any more than you can own a wild bird.

"What else did she say about this ghost? Did she say he was wet? Was he crying? Did he smell?" Maybe there is still something I can find out about Sam. Certainly, if that was Sam then I do at least know that he must have been dead for a long time. At least 90 or 100 years.

"Not as far as I remember, but it was a long time ago and too many people had bought her too many pints. But it was definitely a blue shirt. I remember that. What's Sam's like?"

How frustrating is that?

"It's hard to tell what colour it is. It doesn't really seem it have a colour. Maybe it was blue once."

I can't say any more because Brenda turns up with a tray of tea and pink ham sandwiches.

"What are you two conspiring about?" she asks.

Before Charley can answer, I say, "Charley was telling me about the piece he's writing for the *Gazette*."

"Poor you," she says, "you have my sympathy. Maybe the food will help to keep you awake. Oh, and by the way, Dina's just rung to say she's going to drive in to pick you up Nick and to pay her respects to the old crumbly here."

Charley smiles and with that she goes back to the shop.

"It take it that this is our little secret. That you don't want me to talk to that silly baggage about it."

I explain about how difficult I've found it to talk to anyone else about it and how great it is to have someone who's ready to listen.

"You do realise, don't you," says Charley slowly, "that may only be because we're as daft as each other. But maybe you're right. At least for the time being, we'll keep it to ourselves."

"The thing is, that I don't know why Sam's appeared to me. It's like he wants something, but I don't know what."

"Well," says Charley, "what do ghosts normally want? Think of all the books you've read and films you've seen. Sometimes they're people who've died violent deaths and want revenge. Sometimes they want to explain something to the living. Where the treasure was buried, where there's a secret panel or something like that. Sometimes they want to warn us about something. Sometimes they just want to be a pain in the arse and give the living a hard time. You know the kind of thing: young couple move into huge old house which they bought cheaply. They've only been there five minutes when the furniture starts moving of its own accord, strange noises start coming from the cellar, and then mysterious writing appears on the wall in what might be blood."

"But Sam's not like that. He's not a story-book ghost. He's not even frightening. Well, he is, but only because he's a ghost, not because of anything he does. It's just that the idea of him being a ghost is frightening. I'm sure he doesn't mean me any harm."

"No, I was never very convinced by that rattling chains and heads under arms stuff myself. I think maybe ghosts are just the traces of people who had powerful personalities. Or maybe the opposite. Maybe they're just people who can't bear to be forgotten. Whose lives were not fulfilled. Who never had the time to make any difference to anybody. Who want something from the living. If you don't know who this boy was or how he died, then it's pretty hard to work out why he's back."

I know that Charley is only thinking aloud. But this seems right. The word for Sam is "needy" and maybe what he needs isn't much more than a smile or a sign of friendship. Maybe he just wants to tell me that there was a point to his life. That it meant something. That he didn't just disappear forever. But Charley's also right about not knowing who he is. And I can't think of any way of finding out.

That's pretty much all we have time for, because Dina's arrived with a large bottle of "the few bits and pieces that we need."

Charley's eyes light up in the old way, although I'm not sure whether the sight of Dina or the sight of the bottle has made the greatest impression on him.

Dina teases him about the church fete article – tells him that she thinks it was definitely one of his best – and he seems happy to sit there and take it.

In a remarkably short time, the bottle is empty and Dina's saying that it's time for us to go.

But in the pick-up on the way home she says, "I thought Charley seemed better than the last time we saw him. But he's obviously still not right. Did you notice, he didn't even attempt to pinch my bum when I kissed him goodbye?"

I say nothing. I really don't need conversations like this.

As soon as we get back to the cottage, I check the shed. It's nearly dark in here but when I climb the steps I can see that the nest is empty. I search the floor and shine the torch into every corner but the chick isn't there. I really hope that this is a good sign.

... ...
... He is near me...
... but I am still... ...
... alone... ...
... ... The angel puts his hand out to me
... ...
...but his eyes say... ...
... something else.
... ...
I am so cold and the darkness is growing
... but I don't...
... want to... go.
I want to see the sky... and hear the waves
... and feel the wind
... and the rain
... and the sand...
... ...
and hear the reeds...
... as they move... in the breeze...
... ...
... I don't...
want to...
...
...

Unfinished business

This is in danger of turning into the curious incident of the ghost who didn't show up in the night time.

I've been kind of expecting him for the last two nights, but nothing – nothing since the time I tried to put my arm round him.

The last two nights I've had to force myself to go to bed convinced I wouldn't get any sleep. Convinced a ghost would be joining me and taking up part of the bed. But both nights I've fallen asleep almost immediately and slept through without interruption.

I've no idea what this means although the second time Sam appeared I got the feeling that he was only just able to make it. Maybe ghosts run out of energy. Maybe appearing like that takes a lot out of them. Maybe it's not the kind of thing that they can do every night. Maybe they need to recover their strength. On the other hand, maybe he's been somewhere else, waking someone else up.

But I don't really think so.

Am I glad Sam hasn't come to call again? Well, yes, of course I am. Coming face to face with a ghost every night of the week doesn't exactly make for a quiet life.

Do I think he'll be turning up tonight? I'm not sure why, but I don't. It seems to me, for some reason, that I may have seen the last of Sam. But I don't want to count on that for the moment.

The problem is that there is still this sense of unfinished business between us. I'm sure what Charley said was right. Sam appeared because he wanted something. Maybe that's why, if it was him, he appeared to the lady in the churchyard all those years ago. The problem is how can I give him what he needs if I don't know what it is?

261

John Melmoth

And Sam's not the only one to have gone missing, so has the chick and so have the rest of the swallows. When I came back the other night and found the nest empty, I hoped that the chick was with its parents. I hoped that the following morning I would see them all flying round the garden. But since then, I haven't had a glimpse of any of them.

I want to know that the chick is safe but Dina says that's the thing about animals and birds. Because their lives are so different from ours and so hidden, you can't expect everything to always be tied up neatly. I think she's warning me that I may never know how this particular story ends. That I may have to settle for just hoping that everything's all right.

And come to think of it, it may be the same with Sam. If I never see him again – and I'm more and more convinced that I won't – then I'm never going to know the end of that story either. After all, there's nowhere I can go to report a missing ghost. Once again, I may have to settle for hoping that everything's OK and that poor Sam can somehow get what he wants.

It's not as if I haven't tried looking for all of them – the birds and Sam.

After checking the shed about thirty times, I took Harry out on to the marsh yesterday afternoon to look for swallows. And of course there were loads of them, skimming over the tops of the reeds hawking for insects and occasionally dipping into one of the ditches for a drink. Trouble is that when there are so many of them they all look the same and even if the shed ones had been there I don't think I'd would have been able to identify them.

And then, before supper, I cycled down to St Mary's. If it was Sam who appeared to the old lady all those years ago, then maybe there was some clue about him in the churchyard. I spent about half an hour looking around but didn't find anything. There are

262

hundreds of gravestones there, some of them quite old and hard to read. But I couldn't find any with the name Wellsby.

Just like there were too many swallows on the marsh, so there are too many graves in the churchyard, too many dead people. And it seems to me, in spite of what all those films and books say, that a graveyard is not necessarily the best place to look for a ghost. As far as I'm concerned, you're more likely to find one in a school playground, on a country road, at a nature reserve or, for all I know, at a supermarket check-out. And if Sam can be a ghost, then I guess anyone can – teachers, politicians, the lady next door, the person sitting next to you on the bus.

The other thing that happened yesterday was that Dina and I suddenly became very popular and got loads of phone calls.

Rachel called me to say that today would be the last day of her holiday. I already knew that but it was still a bit of a shock. Dina had suggested that we could have a barbecue at the beach, so I invited Rachel and she said she'd love to come. We spoke for about ten minutes but never mentioned Sam once.

Gerry rang Dina, for the first time in ages. She took the call in the office and shut the door. They talked for hours. They were like a pair of bloody teenagers. I could imagine them saying to each other, "You hang up first." "No, you hang up." "No you." And so on. (Not that any teenagers I know would be so uncool.) Afterwards, Dina seemed really pleased.

I got a call from Billy, the mighty shimm hunter. He and his parents are back the UK. He really loved Africa and wanted to talk to Jack about it. But Jack just wanted to talk about Emily. As Billy said, he was happy to talk about Emily, but only for about one second. So he told me about it and only just remembered to ask if I was having a good time. I said that I was.

And then, quite late on, Dad called. I can hardly believe it. Dad for the second time in a row. He didn't have very much to say, just

263

yakked on about how the script was going. He asked me how "the missus" was and I told him she was leaving tomorrow. So he said, *"Take my advice Nick, don't let her go. Tell her you love her. Tell her you'll try to be a better husband. Tell her to think of the children growing up without her. Tell her that marriage is something to be worked at not just walked out on at the first sign of trouble."* He told me that he and Mum had seen Robert De Niro in a restaurant and I only just managed to stop myself from telling him that I'd seen a ghost of someone who's been dead since at least the First World War. I told him that we were going to have a beach barbecue today and he asked what was on the menu. I said that it might be lamb kebabs. He said that Mum sent her love and I sent mine back.

It was a great conversation.

Dina was so chuffed with everything that she declared yesterday evening an official two-beer evening. There seem to have been a few of those recently, not that I'm complaining, even though two tiny beers only make one little one. She must be cutting down, because I swear she didn't get through more than a bottle of red wine.

Rachel arrived about four with her dad in the car. It was the first time I'd met him and he seemed nice enough, although he did keep laughing at nothing in particular. Dina came out to say hello and Rachel's dad (Peter) started admiring everything. He said that the cottage was lovely (although I noticed that Dina didn't offer to show him around the garden) and that Harry was very handsome and that the marsh looked great and the view was fantastic. I almost expected him to congratulate Dina on the wonderful sky or the gracefulness of the trees. Dina said that we'd bring Rachel back in the pick-up afterwards. By now, Peter was running out of things to admire or laugh about and so he left.

The weather was a bit gloomy but it wasn't raining, so Dina suggested that we went and sat in the garden while she got a few more things ready for the barbecue.

Harry sat between us on the bench, with me fondling his left ear and Rachel his right. He looked pretty pleased with himself.

Rachel and I talked about her holiday and how she was sad to be leaving but glad that she'd soon be seeing her friends. What we didn't talk about was Sam. It seemed really weird not to mention him, but we didn't. As we sat there, Sam was as much between us as Harry. Like the ghost of a ghost.

It was warm out in the garden but still no sign of any swallows.

After about ten minutes Dina called us and as we walked back through the garden we could hear a motorbike coming down the track to the cottage.

Rachel's face went tight and she was right. It was Gerry. Dina came running out of the kitchen, lifted the visor of his crash helmet and kissed him. "Gerry's coming to the beach with us," she said, "I hope's that's OK."

I said that it was great but I noticed that Rachel didn't say anything. I guess if she'd known that Gerry was going to be coming she wouldn't have accepted the invitation in the first place.

What with Dina and Gerry and Harry in the cab, there was no room for me and Rachel so we sat in the back of the pickup with all the barbecue things, rugs, coolboxes and so on. It was great bouncing along in the back, but we had to hold onto the truck's sides in order to prevent ourselves being bounced overboard.

The flies are definitely better since all that rain the other day and we didn't see any swarms of bees. There were loads of swallows, though, flying just a couple of feet above the road. They got out of the pick-up's way without any problem and as we looked back we could see them regrouping above the road. Seeing them, made me ache to know what had happened to that last swallow chick.

Walking over the sand dunes with all that beach stuff was hard work. Our feet kept sinking back the way we had come and we had to take twice as many steps as usual to move forwards.

265

Dina had packed a windbreak but we didn't need it – there wasn't a breath of wind. Even though it was nearly evening, Dina took off her dungarees and dived into the sea straight away. Gerry, who was taking no notice of either me or Rachel, slipped out of his clothes and dived in after her. He's also a really strong swimmer and they set off as if they were racing to the horizon.

Rachel turned to me and said, "Did you know that idiot was coming when you asked me?"

"No, I promise I didn't."

"Well OK, but just don't try to persuade me he's a good bloke."

Knowing that Gerry was with Dina made me feel less anxious about how far from the shore they were. And having Rachel with me made waiting for them to come back much easier.

Here we were again, one of my pretend families, with everyone looking out for everyone else.

I'd got my trunks on under my clothes and Rachel had her costume on. In the pale light, her body looked browner and slimmer than ever – not that I was looking, of course. (There's a real difference between being slim and honey coloured like Rachel, and deep brown and skinny like Dina and Gerry. I know which I prefer.)

Rachel and I did our usual thing of splashing around in the shallows with Harry, who seemed to like the waves but hated it if his head went under water.

By now, Dina and Gerry were two little dots in the distance, but as I looked at them they both waved and I waved back.

When we came out of the sea the air was cool so everyone got dressed again and put on pullovers and jackets, although the sand still felt warm to my bare feet.

Gerry seemed in a really good mood. He chatted to me and Rachel while he lit the barbecue – Dina was lying in full length on one of the rugs with a fag in her mouth, deep in a book – but you could tell he wasn't very interested in either of us. He kept looking over at her.

The moment I'd been worrying about arrived: Gerry opened one of the coolboxes and asked who wanted a drink. Dina said she'd have a beer; Rachel and I asked for cokes. And here's the amazing thing: Gerry had one as well. He actually turned down the chance of a beer. He didn't say anything, didn't make a big deal of it. He just opened a can and took a swig, although he looked almost as surprised as Sam had done when he tasted it. Then he lit a roll-up and wandered down to the water's edge. Harry, who'd been lying next to Dina immediately got up and followed him.

To no one's amazement, it was lamb kebabs and lamb burgers, although they tasted better on the beach than they ever did back at the cottage. Dina had also packed salads and crisps and nuts, but no puddings. She really hasn't got a clue about puddings. (Not that Rachel's cake was any better.)

There was a bottle of white wine in the cool box and when Dina fished it out you could see perspiration running down its sides. She'd also packed some plastic glasses. I could tell something was going on. There was something about the way she did it that made it seem like a test or a challenge.

She poured herself a large glass and half a glass for me. Rachel didn't want any and Gerry said he'd stick with coke. We all avoided looking at him.

As we sat there stuffing ourselves, the sun must have started to set because the sky was turning scarlet inland and the blazing clouds were reflected in the sea which was now as still and grey as steel.

Even though I was a bit tense about Rachel and Gerry and Dina and Gerry – why do I always feel that I'm responsible for everyone else? – it was one of the best moments of my life.

267

The light was beginning to fade, so Gerry lit a beach flare. As I looked at the others, the light of the flare made everyone's face seem soft, and warm and friendly.

We all looked up when we heard a ripple a few yards off shore and there was another seal goggling at us. I think I could get used to this. But like the other one, it seemed to get bored quite quickly, took a final sad, glassy-eyed look at us and disappeared without a sound and hardly a ripple.

Gerry and Dina said they were going to have a stroll on the beach. They both had their trousers rolled up and walked with the sea up to their ankles. They'd only gone about ten yards before they put their arms around each other. Hideous, but better than what it had been like in the pub the last couple of times.

Rachel and I sit in silence for a while and then, to my amazement, she reaches over and holds my hand.

As we sit looking out to sea, she says that she wishes she wasn't going back tomorrow and that she's really going to miss me and Dina and Harry. She even admits that Gerry hasn't been too much of a tosser so far (even though she's expecting him to slip back into tosser mode at any moment). She says that she'd really like to meet up when we get back to London. She's much better at saying this sort of stuff than I am, but I manage to agree that it would be nice. Which isn't going to win me any conversational awards but is at least what I really feel.

And then she says, "Oh, and by the way, what was all that stuff the other night about Sam being a ghost?"

I've been expecting this. There's really only one answer that I can give. "Yeh, sorry about that. It was meant to be a joke, but it didn't work. And I kept it going much longer than I should have done. You were right, there wasn't anything funny about it."

"But why did you think of doing it in the first place?"

"I don't know. I suppose it was to scare you. Sorry. It was stupid of me."

"Well that's for sure. It certainly worked. That evening at the broad you almost had me believing in ghosts. What idiots we must have looked – running away from a fisherman or some poor innocent swan."

"Yes."

"And, by the way, what's happened with Sam? Did you find out where he lives? He's weird and hard to be around but I do worry about him. I don't like going home without knowing what's happened to him."

Me too, but I don't say that.

"No, I haven't seen him since that time I met him on the road to Stalton – he really did almost get me run over. I'll keep looking for him and if I see him again before I go to Gran's I'll let you know."

But I'm pretty sure that I won't and that I won't.

Suddenly she says, "Quick they're coming back. Give us a hug."

So I do. I'm always well behaved and do what I'm told.

Dina and Gerry seem happy and Rachel even makes room for Gerry on the rug she's sitting on. He's nice to her, but anyone can see that he's not really interested.

The four of us sit (five if you count Harry who is trying to get onto Gerry's lap) staring out at the sea, which is almost black.

The scarlet has faded from the sky and the first stars are beginning to appear.

There's a small ripple out at sea which, at first, I think must be another seal, but then I see the fin cutting through the water. It must be a shark.

"Look," whispers Gerry, "it's a dolphin."

And then we see another fin and then another. There are three of them.

The fins continue to glide past and there's just enough light to see their shadowy bodies through the water. They swim slowly and peacefully past us, heading down the coast. We are all holding our breath.

"That was wonderful," breathes Rachel. "Amazing to see one let alone three." She asks Gerry, "Do they have a rhyme for dolphins. You know, like they do with magpies – 'one for sorrow, two for joy'."

"Oh yes," says Gerry. "One is great. Two is greater. And three is fan-bleedin'-tastic."

... ...

...

Remembering is... the best way

... to...

... ... to...

... keep going....

...

...Remembering makes me...

... ... what I am... ...

... ...

... But it is...

... ... so hard... ... everything...

... moves... ... and merges.

... ... Remember...

... ...

... Remember...

... ...

...Yes... I remember...

.... I remember the light on the water

... ...

... ... dancing... ...

...Yes

... ... I remember... ...

clouds like ships...

... the stars...

... ... burning in the night sky.

427

I know who Sam was and how he died.

And I found out because, although I can sleep like a baby when there's a ghost in the room, I can't seem to sleep at all when there isn't the slightest chance of one. Which, come to think of it, might be a bit of a problem if it goes on for the rest of my life.

After the barbecue, we dropped Rachel off at her cottage – her dad came to the door and started admiring the pick-up and laughing at something that clearly struck him as very funny. Then we headed back to Dina's where Gerry collected his leathers and helmet, kissed Dina goodbye, shook hands with me and took off on his motorbike.

Dina wasn't upset. In fact, she seemed as happy as I'd ever seen her.

After a shower to get rid of the salt, I went to bed. I was knackered. But maybe I was too tired because I spent the next couple of hours wrestling with the sheets, with everything whirling round in my head. It must have been 3.00am before I finally managed to nod off. I woke up at the normal time feeling like I'd been for a ten mile cross-country run during the night.

All day my eyes felt scratchy and I was almost falling over with tiredness.

It was the same again the next night and I spent most of yesterday mooching around the garden, too tired to do anything.

What those two nights taught me is that there's no point in *trying* to get to sleep. It doesn't work like that; the harder you try the less likely it is to happen.

So last night, I made sure that if I wasn't going to be able to sleep, then at least I'd have something to do.

I took *A Year at Revenant Broad* to bed with me. There's a picture in it that I really like – a swallow feeding a chick on the wing – even though it reminds me how much I miss the swallows from the shed.

After about an hour of turning cartwheels in the bed and mummifying myself in the sheets, I gave up and switched the light on. The greasy, red cover of the notebook reflected the bedside light. I turned to the picture of the swallows.

Old Reg might have been keen to attract birds for posh people to blow to bits, but he sure knew his stuff when he came to drawing them.

In the picture, the parent swallow is transferring food to the gaping beak of the chick in mid air. In the background are two more swallows in flight and below them cattle are grazing at the side of a ditch. The birds look so elegant – Reg has captured how effortless flight is for them.

He's obviously spent more time on this picture than on most of the others. It's a whole scene rather than just a sketch and he's coloured it. Even after a hundred years, the birds' heads are midnight blue, their foreheads and throats scarlet, their breasts a creamy orange. The parent bird has a long forked tail; the chick's is much stubbier.

I know I have to be careful about thinking of animals in human terms, but there's something about the way the parent is holding its body that suggests care and concern. It seems to me to be a picture about tenderness. Who would have thought old Reg had it in him?

I wish I knew what had happened to my swallows. There, even I'm saying "my" now.

All through the cold early spring of 1896, Reg is recording the birds that he saw and the birds that the rich people shot. Opposite the picture of the guy sitting up in the boat with a gun to his shoulder is an account of a day's shooting on 28 February 1896:

> *Mallard: 40*
> *Pochard: 37*
> *Snipe: 8*
> *Coot: 427*
> *Teal: 10*

The hairs on my neck started to prickle. 427 coots in a single day. 427, the magic number that's been bothering me for ages. That's why it sounded familiar when Sam said that 427 coots had been killed. I don't remember reading this page before, but I must have done. Or maybe I just glimpsed it without really knowing it, and carried in around in my head, so that when Sam mentioned it, I knew that I'd seen it or heard it before.

So, maybe Sam was telling the truth. Maybe he really was on that coot shoot. He just forgot to mention that it was nearly 120 years ago.

Having found that, I knew I had to read through the whole book carefully to see if there were any other clues to who Sam was.

In fact, it only took about five minutes. A couple of pages later, the entry for 3 March reads:

"This has been an awful day. We had been out on the water for less than an hour when the son of one of the beaters from the village, in attempting to retrieve a downed snipe, climbed out of the punt and onto the ice. Tragically, the ice couldn't bear his weight and he fell through. By the time anyone could get to him — only a matter of a few minutes — he had succumbed to the icy cold and his body was pulled lifeless from the water. On hearing the news, Lord O

immediately abandoned the day's shooting and instructed
me to send one of the men to the boy's house in the village
to see what help they needed. I sent Slater. How terrible it
must be for them to lose a child in this way. Everyone I have
spoken to confirms that he was a game and respectful lad.
How close we always are to tragedy."

And that's it.

The diary stops for a couple of days and then picks up on 6
March as though nothing had happened. Apparently, there were
loads of redshank and snipe on the marsh that day. And there's an
ink sketch of a little owl sitting on a branch but not another word
about the drowning.

I read through the whole book and there isn't another mention.
The weather continued to be bitterly cold for the next couple of
weeks and the ice on the broad reached record thickness. But it
was as if, when the break in the ice closed over the hole he had
made, everyone had forgotten about the boy who had fallen in.

I don't suppose it was really like this, but that's what it feels
like when the only information I've got is this diary.

Children must have died of illnesses, in farm accidents or
drowned much more often than they do now. I don't suppose
people ever got used to it, but they had to get on with it. They
had no choice.

Reg doesn't say what the boy's name was and I guess he may
not have known. But I know it's Sam. It has to be. It couldn't be
anyone else.

Besides it explains nearly everything. Why Sam's clothes are
wet. Why he looks so thin and undernourished – his family must
have been poor. Why he's so small for his age. Why his clothes are
so terrible. Why he is terrified of the water. The things he said
about shoots on the broad, his eel lures, his hunting for rabbits.

275

But more than that, I think it explains why he comes back. His life was only just beginning, his death was so sudden and unexpected. What did he think about in those couple of minutes after he fell through the ice and before the cold killed him? Did he know he was dying or was he waiting – quite calmly, maybe – for them to pull him out when he lost consciousness. I remember seeing something on TV that said how quickly people can die in cold water in the winter.

All those things would make him want to come back. To remind people that he didn't cease to exist the moment the ice closed over. To remind them of the life he never had.

Maybe he's a ghost because he refused to accept the stupid accident that happened to him. Maybe he's a ghost because he didn't want the world to go on as though he had never been born.

In some ways I now feel much closer to Sam than before. I know when he was born and when he died. I think I know where he went to school and where he lived. But there's still a lot that I don't know. I don't know what he thought and felt. I don't know what it would have been like to be his friend. I don't know what his favourite things were. I don't know what he dreamed about at night. I don't know what he wanted to be when he grew up.

There were tears in my eyes when I put down the book and turned out the light. It was 3.30am, practically time to get up again.

Anyway, finding out who Sam was seems to have sorted out my insomnia. The pillow felt cooler than it had for days and I was asleep in a few minutes.

I woke to the sound of Dina singing and the smell of cigarette smoke. It was very bright and warm in the room.

When I opened the curtains, the sky was pale blue, Harry was spark out on the deckchair and the trees were shining in the low sunlight. As I turned away, I caught a movement out of the corner of my eye.

And there, on the washing line that was hung from the corner of the shed to a tree about 30 feet away were six swallows. Just sitting there, chattering to each other. Their wings and tails twitching occasionally as they adjusted their positions to keep their balance. Their feathers blazing blue and scarlet and cream.

Now, of course, I've no way of being sure that these were my swallows. It could have been a coincidence. They could have come from anywhere. But I've decided that they were mine, even though I don't really mean "mine."

It was like they'd come back to have another look at the place where the chicks were hatched. Another look at the garden that had provided them with mud and moss for their nest and with food. The garden that had been their world up to now.

I know it's stupid, but I also felt like they'd come back to say goodbye to me. It was like they were letting me know that they were OK.

As I stood there looking out of the window, this great wave of happiness washed through me that I know I'm going to remember for the rest of my life. If I make it to 90, I'll still remember how happy I felt this morning.

I'm sure if anyone had been looking, they'd have seen this stupid, crumpled look on my face – no lines, just curves. They'd have seen the stupid, crumpled face of a huge softy unable to keep his face straight just because a few little birds were sitting on a washing line. Not doing anything – just sitting on a line.

I ran downstairs to tell Dina but when we looked through the kitchen window, they were gone. It was almost like I'd imagined them, but I knew that I hadn't.

She said that she was really glad that all my chicks seem to have survived.

I know she was trying to be supportive and it's great that she was pleased. But what I felt – still feel – was so much more than that.

277

I feel that I've passed some kind of test. I feel that if the chicks hadn't made it, it would have been because in some way I had failed them.

But passing this test isn't about the things I did to help them survive – sticking newspaper on the roof or blocking the shed door to keep out predators. It's about *wanting* them to survive. Wanting it so much that it hurt, so much that at times I couldn't think about anything else. And they have. And so I guess I've passed the test.

Dina and I had lunch in the garden. It was warm, but although there weren't any clouds in the sky, the sun is no longer as hot as it was a couple of weeks ago. I certainly didn't need the black umbrella.

For the first time, I realised that the summer is definitely winding down, coming to an end.

Maybe it was because she felt it too that Dina suggested we went to the beach in the afternoon. I said that would be great but that I had to go into the village first to get "a few bits and pieces that I need."

She smiled.

In fact, the only thing I needed in the village was to see Charley.

The ride into the village was better than it's been for ages. There were hardly any flies and no suicidal slugs. The sunlight flickered on the road's surface and I saw loads of pheasants barking and rattling in the fields. There were several groups of swallows gathered on the telephone wires, looking as though they were gossiping about something. And who knows, maybe mine were among them. (What did swallows do before there were telephones?)

As I got near the village, I saw that the combine harvester was at work in the field in front of the church. In a single afternoon, all those acres of wheat that had taken the whole summer to ripen were being swept down and turned into gigantic Swiss rolls.

278

Charley was in the summerhouse (where else would he be?) but still didn't seem like the man I'd met for the first time only a few weeks ago.

"Hi Nick, sorry about the long face but I'm having one of those days. One of the many bloody awful things about getting old is that you can't sleep at night. In fact, I'm so old now that I consider myself fortunate if I get more than two or three hours. The rest of the time I have to lie next to that old walrus Brenda, while she dreams and twitches for hours. It's not the snoring that I mind so much as the breathing. The breathing drives me nuts. Just the regular, shallow breathing of healthy, well adjusted middle-aged woman. It's bleedin' unbearable at times."

I didn't say anything. It was taking all my energy not to think of Charley and Brenda lying in bed in the middle of the night. His brittle old bones just inches away from her warm, perfumey plumpness... No, I'm *not* going to think about it.

"And if that wasn't bad enough, it seems that the less you sleep, the more you dream. Ten, 15, 20 dreams a night. It's exhausting. And the rubbish I dream... you have no idea. Nobody does. Rubbish about my childhood, about when I was working, about novels that I ought to have written but didn't. Rubbish about Brenda wearing the skin of a lion and cycling along the beach on a penny-farthing bicycle. I sometimes think I ought to be locked up. Just last night, I dreamed about Richard Leslie – sodding Richard Leslie. Now you haven't got the faintest idea who he was have you? He was my best friend when I was a kid. His family lived next door to mine about a thousand years ago and, as he was a year older than me, I couldn't ever remember a time when I didn't know him. He was just always there. We used to walk to school together and play cricket in the garden and talk about sex in the shed. He joined the RAF during the Second World War and was shot down and killed over Albania of all ghastly bloody places. He was 22. Anyway, none

279

of that has anything to do with anything. The point is that last night I dreamed that I called at his front door for him, just as I used to all those years ago. Almost immediately he opened the door and smiled. He was as old as I am, but neither of us seemed to mind. There was a woman with him, but I couldn't see her properly because her face was always in the shadow. But it didn't matter, because I was sure that I didn't know her. Anyway... and I promise I'm not going gaga, or no more than I already am, I just want you to hear this – anyway, Richard said that his family were selling the house and that he was helping to clear out the junk they'd accumulated over the years. In the dream, I realised that he must have been living there all my life and that I didn't know it. I realised that I could have visited him many times over the years, but I'd thought he was dead. He told me to hang on, and that he'd bring some of the junk out into the garden. Well, you know what dreams are like, this seemed like a good idea. Anyway, he brought out this large, old-fashioned photograph album – I remember it very clearly, it was covered in expensive looking cream leather and had red Gothic lettering on the front. The three of us, Richard, me and the shadow woman, sat on the grass in the sunshine and opened the album. It was filled with hundreds of black and white photographs with tiny translucent mounts in each corner. The photographs were of women in hats and men with moustaches, children in school uniforms, riding ponies, playing games, families at the beach, families picnicking. To begin with, I said things like 'I remember him,' and 'Do you remember that outing?' but I knew that I was lying. The truth is that I didn't have the faintest idea who any of the silly bastards ('scuse my French) were or what they were doing. In the end, I couldn't bear it any longer, so I told Richard that I hadn't got a clue who anyone was and he said that he didn't either and had decided to throw the album away. Then he closed the album and handed it to the woman with no name and no face. And that was it.

Nothing else happened. I woke up next to old Brenda who was puffing and gurgling like a grampus and lay there full of anger and sadness until it was time to get up. But I haven't been able to get over it. The day was buggered before I even got up. I knew I was going to be haunted by memories of old Richard just like Sam's been haunting you. I suppose people might say that you're lucky to have only one ghost in your life. I've got bloody hundreds in mine. In fact, that's about all I have got. It just made me terribly sad, and I'm too old to be feeling sad. It's such a God awful waste of time. Still, I suppose I should be grateful to be feeling anything at all at my age. Most of everybody I ever knew, old Richard included, is pushing up daisies as we speak, in his case under an Albanian sun. Now I suppose, to be strictly accurate, I should say 'as *I* speak', because you haven't yet had a chance to get a word in edgewise."

At last Charley stopped talking but I didn't know how to respond. I think I'd imagined that as soon as I arrived we'd talk about Sam. I think I'd thought that if there was a ghost to talk about, then nothing else could be as important. I think I'd thought that ghosts always go first and that everything and everyone else gets moved down the queue.

What I hadn't realised was that life goes on even when you've got a ghost for company. Things were happening to Charley that made him happy or sad and he wanted to tell me about them. Knowing about Sam didn't change any of that. I knew that I should feel honoured that he'd chosen to tell me. But I didn't really. Because the truth is that I didn't want to hear all this stuff about old dead friends. I wanted to tell him about Sam. I wanted him to want to talk about Sam. I wanted Sam to be the centre of attention.

I think Charley must have realised this because he then said, "But what can I do for you, Nick? You didn't come all this way to listen to these senile witterings."

In a strange way I felt that I was being told off. I knew that

Charley would never do that, but there was something about the way he said "senile witterings" that made me feel guilty. I felt he was disappointed in me.

"Yes. No. Sorry. I just wanted to tell you that I've found out who Sam was. I've identified him. I found it in this book. Here, look."

Charley did his best, but I could tell he wasn't as interested as I wanted him to be. It was obvious that his thoughts were more with this old friend of his who'd been dead for seventy years and who, as far as I know, has never come back as a ghost, than with Sam who had been dead nearly twice as long and who, at least until a couple of days ago, had been wandering around the village in bare feet and appearing in my bedroom in the middle of the night.

Looking back, I can hardly believe it. It was like I was trying to stage a competition between two ghosts, to see which of us had the better one. (Not that I'm sure what I mean by "better.") A kind of Oxford and Cambridge ghost race.

"Does knowing who he was make you feel better about him?" Charley asked.

"I think it does. I think it's good to have things explained. It's good to know that he wasn't lying to me about where he lived and all that. It's good that things are clearer."

"But are they? It's like we were saying the other day. If ghosts want something from us, then I don't suppose it's that we should know every detail of their lives. I think ghosts may want us to feel and do something, not just reconstitute their histories. If you think that's what ghosts are about aren't you a bit like one of those twitchers that Gerry gets up at the reserve. For them, it seems that it's more important to see something than to understand it. More important to tick the box than *feel* anything."

Now I know I'm being told off – or as close as the man with the kindest eyes I've ever seen would ever get to telling me off.

And he's right. I have been thinking about me rather than Sam. Thinking about how pleased I was to have solved the puzzle of Sam, like I'm some kind of ghost-buster. Forgetting all about the fact that Sam might want something from me and wouldn't stop wanting it just because I'd been able to confirm that his name was what he said it was.

I stayed a while and Charley and I looked through the book together. He liked the drawings he said, but couldn't really get inside the head of people who wanted to record precisely how many redshanks they'd seen in a four-hour period. He supposed that there was some point in it but it seemed a bit like a "painting by numbers" approach to nature. And he said that he was confident that he would have hated Lord O's guts, and the guts of all his London friends, and why didn't they all sod off back where they came from.

In fact, getting angry and unreasonable and rude about Lord O and his mates seemed to cheer Charley up, so that by the time I left he was more like his normal self than he's been for ages. "Don't forget to give my love to Dina," he said, screwing his face up into this hideous leer.

All the way back to the cottage I kept thinking about what Charley had said. I'd thought that the swallows were the test I'd had to pass, but Charley seemed to think that Sam was the real test, and he seemed to be suggesting that I'd failed it.

When I told Dina that I'd seen Charley and that he sent his love, she said, "Dirty old bugger, I know what he'd really like to send."

But I knew better than to ask her what that might be. What's the matter with these people? They're far too old to be thinking and talking like this.

By the time we got to the beach, the sun was already low in the sky and the air was nearly as grey as the sea. But the sand was still warm.

As we were spreading the towels on the sand, Dina dropped her bombshell. "How about coming out for a swim with me today, Nick?"

I started to panic immediately. "I can't. I'm not a strong swimmer like you. I don't like being away from the shore."

"I didn't mean come out all the way with me, just a bit of the way. You never know, you might like it. And you'll be quite safe. I'll be there with you."

I really didn't want to do this, but I couldn't think of any way of getting out of it. "OK, but if I don't like it, you've got to let me come back."

"Of course I will."

So, we stripped off and walked into the water. Dina was holding my hand, which made me feel a bit self-conscious even though there was no one else on the beach.

As soon as the water was above our knees, she let go of my hand and dived into the face of a little wave. She disappeared without a splash and her head bobbed up a couple of yards further out to sea.

"Come on," she yelled at enormous volume. There was nothing else for it, I sort of flopped forward into the waves, making sure that my head didn't go completely under. And swam out towards her.

In a swimming pool, I'm an OK swimmer. Not the world's strongest but not bad. I feel comfortable there, with the ladders you can use to climb out, the lifeguards posing in their shorts and all the people eating ice cream and crisps and drinking pale blue drinks at the café at the side of the pool.

But I don't feel comfortable in the sea. Everything is so uncertain and threatening. I don't like it that I can't see the bottom. I hate the currents that feel as though they are going to push you along the shore in a direction you don't want to go. I hate salt water in my eyes. I hate thinking about what might be in the water with me. For all I know, there's a vicious jellyfish or a huge crab or a hungry seal inches away from my uncovered legs.

Anyway, I swam a few strokes with Dina but when we stopped I couldn't find the bottom with my feet. My heart was pounding and I was trying not to panic. "I don't like this," I said.

"Come on, you're fine," said Dina, "just five more strokes and no more, I promise." She looked absolutely comfortable – as relaxed as she is when she's sitting in the back garden.

So, in spite of being afraid, I swam five more strokes which, to be honest didn't take me more than a few feet further out to sea.

Then we stopped and trod water, moving up and down as the waves passed round us on their way towards the shore. The sky over our heads was silver and gold.

"Look back at the shore," yelled Dina.

I know we'd only come a few yards but it seemed a long way away. I could see Harry running on the beach – needless to say, he wasn't taking any notice of us. The dunes were golden in the evening light; the breakwaters black.

I know that when she comes out here, Dina feels free and happy. Detached from the land. On her own. Lighter than air.

But what I mostly felt was that I wanted to get back to the shore and feel the sand under my feet.

So, trying not to seem in too much of a hurry, I said, "I think I'll go back now and wait for you. Don't go too far."

Of course, the waves were helping so much that I only had to swim a few strokes before I was back to dry land and safety.

Harry came and sniffed my legs while I wrapped myself in my towel and stood with the water up to my ankles watching Dina swim away from us. But she always means what she says, and every so often, she stopped and turned and waved. I waved back and even picked up poor Harry and made him wave to her. He didn't complain or say anything, but I could tell he didn't think too much of this treatment. So, when I put him back down again, he moved down the beach a bit.

As I watched Dina roll over onto her back and drift along out towards the horizon, I was glad I'd gone a bit further out than ever before. I'm not saying I'd got over my fears or anything like it. I'm not saying I particularly enjoyed it. But I was glad that I'd done it.

Then we came home to the cottage and, to celebrate, Dina let me have two bottles of beer.

She's making supper at the moment and I'm sitting in the garden with a blanket wrapped round me and Harry on my lap. We're watching the full moon rising over the marsh.

And we're thinking, at least I am, about everything that has happened today.

Dad doesn't seem to believe that there's anything to do in the countryside. He thinks and maybe even hopes that I'm bored.

But the truth is that I've never in my life had so much to think about.

... ...

...

cold... ... ...

... Mother's hands...

... ...

the angel with hair the colour of flames...

... ...

... Arthur's eyes...

... ... shining...

... ...

... ... I'm flying... ...

Africa... ... ...

... ...

Its beak... ... ... in his...pock... et...

... ...

... zizz... ... ...

... sea... wreck... ...

... wrack

... ... like mad...

... madmen

... gu ... gulls like... leaves

...

never... get... any ...closer

...

... the sound... ... ...

of... ...

... the wind

...

...

... ... cold...

...

Well done

Yesterday Charley said that I probably wouldn't want to spend too much of my holiday listening to him rabbiting on.

I should have told him that he was wrong. I should have said how much I enjoyed listening to him. But I didn't.

Anyway, I've spent most of today – the last day of my holiday – in a cemetery. I'm not quite sure what Dina makes of that.

I was eating breakfast in the garden when my phone rang. I didn't recognise the number and the very last person I expected it to be was Charley. I suppose I didn't think of Charley ever using the phone. He seems too old.

"Hi Nick, I've got some news for you about Sam."

"Good morning, Charley. How are you?"

"Never mind all that. Listen, when you left yesterday I had an idea, and that doesn't happen very often these days. I rang the editor of the Gazette. I'd had a bit of a row with him the other day, all about that piece I wrote and that he wouldn't use about how weird everything had got all of a sudden. I felt that he owed me a favour – and, to be honest, I felt that I ought to apologise to him. You probably won't believe this, but I think I may have used one or two rude words to him on the phone. Brenda says it would take me two lifetimes to work off what I owe the swear box. Anyway, that's all rubbish, why am I not getting to the point? The point is that I told Mick that I was interested in this kid called Sam Wellsby who'd drowned on the broad in 1896. I said I wanted more information for something I was writing and I asked him if he could have a quick trawl through the archives to see if the story had been covered at the time. He promised to have a look if he got a moment. I guess he must have been feeling a bit guilty about the other evening as well because he called be back late yesterday evening to say

that he'd found a piece in the Revenant District Advertiser which was taken over by a larger paper and renamed The East Norfolk Gazette in the 1920s. He emailed the piece over to me and I'll send it on to you if you can let me have Dina's email address."

So not only does Charley know about phones, he seems to know about computers and emails as well, even though I've only seen him using that old typewriter in his summerhouse.

"OK, I'm sending it over now. I'll speak to you later."

Dina was working in the office so I had to ask if it was OK to receive an email from Charley.

Although she's usually very good at not asking awkward questions, this was a bit too much even for her.

"What are you and old Charley cooking up?" she asked.

Having come this far, I didn't think I could start to tell her about Sam now so I said that Charley has been talking to me about an article he was writing and that he was sending some background stuff over.

I know that Dina won't ever check what the email was about.

The message from Charley said, *"Hi Nick. Article attached. If you're looking for the truth about Sam, maybe you'll find it in St Mary's churchyard. Charley."*

I printed off the attachment and took it into the garden to have good look.

It was a cutting from an old newspaper, underneath which someone – Charley or his friend Mick, I guess – had written "6/3/1896."

BROADLAND TRAGEDY

The funeral took place today of SamuelWellsby (12), oldest son of Mr George Wellsby and his wife Martha of Church Lane, Revenant. Samuel was tragically killed in a boating accident when acting as a beater for a coot shoot sponsored by Lord Osley on his Revenant estate.

Several of the mourners commented on Samuel's respectful demeanour, general good humour and enthusiasm for shooting. His accident, however, has led Mr Montague Slater of the Revenant Parish Council to propose a motion that children under 14 should not in future be allowed to beat for the guns on the broad in winter.

The funeral service, which took place in St Mary's Church, Revenant, was conducted by the Reverend Miles Hooton, who chose a reading from the Book of Ecclesiastes.

The mourners included Mr and Mrs Wellsby and their three surviving children, Nigel (10), Sarah(7) and Arthur (5); Mr and Mrs Theodore Brown and Mr Henry and Miss Amelia Judd, also of Church Lane; Miss Bernadette Stephens (school teacher); and Garth Slater and Nathaniel Hooper (estate workers).

Lord Osley sent a wreath of white lilies and a card of condolence signed by a number of his house guests.

This card can currently be seen near the font in St Mary's Church.

I rang Charley straight back, but Brenda answered. She said she'd get him but that it might take a minute or two. In fact, it felt like it took ten but eventually he was on. "Hi, Nick."

"Charley, thanks for the cutting. I'm glad some people went to the funeral and that your mate Lord Osley sent a wreath. But what did you mean about the truth about Sam being in the churchyard?"

"I mean that we now know where he was buried."

"Yes, but I've looked all round the churchyard and couldn't find any sign of him."

"Maybe it's worth another look. At least we know he's got to be there somewhere. I'd offer to come and help but if I ask that mad old missus of mine to drive me, she's going to want to know why, and if I tried to walk it, you'd be a middle aged man by the time I got there. I'm afraid you're on your own, mate. Let me know how it goes."

"OK. Thanks."

So, I told Dina I'd be back for lunch and set off on the bike for the village. Although I've only been here a few weeks, the road into the village seems as familiar as the road I've lived on with Mum and Dad for years. The sun was shining but the coolness in the air proved that summer really is coming to an end. The pheasants in the fields didn't seem to care about that – they're just having a good time in the sunshine.

When you cycle down Church Lane from the village, the lane itself just sort of fades away into the fields once you get past the houses. The church is on your left.

There are gravestones all round the church, and a wooden gate with a huge iron catch. The graveyard is surrounded by an old stone wall about waist high. On the far side of the wall furthest from the village, there's a field, which is used for parking. It probably gets quite busy on Christmas Eve but today there are only two cars.

St Mary's church itself is in the far left-hand corner as you come in through the gate. It has a porch of black and white flints – there's wire netting across the wooden porch gates to keep the swallows out – and an enormous square tower. Dina says that lots of the churches around here are much bigger than they need to be and that even if everyone living in the area went to church at the same time, they would still be three quarters empty. A union flag is hanging limply from the white pole on the top of the tower.

Behind the church is a stand of enormous, dark trees, some of which are nearly as tall as the tower. And in every tree there seem to be dozens of birds – crows or rooks or jackdaws or something

– which are making this incredibly loud cackling. I can't decide whether the noise is funny or spooky.

The graveyard isn't exactly neat – most of the grass isn't cut and some of the headstones are at funny angles – but it's nothing like the graveyard of the ruined church by the sea. It's obvious that people do come here and that some of the graves are looked after. There are a couple of metal benches with the grass cut around them and a long stone bench that runs right down one wall of the church porch. There are a couple of waste bins – one as you come in through the gate and one by the porch – there's a sign saying "no dogs" and there's even a Cornetto wrapper (strawberry) sparkling in the grass and an empty Lucozade Sport bottle by one of the benches.

The problem was that there are hundreds of headstones. It's impossible to believe that each one stands for a life that was really important and unique to the person living it, but I guess it must be true.

How the hell was I expected to find Sam? And what did I mean by expected? Who was expecting it?

I decided that the only way I had any chance of finding his grave was to carry out a methodical search. I'd look at all the graves in a small area of the field and then move on to the next and work my way right round the church.

Some of the headstones I could read quite easily when I was standing on the path; others I had to climb almost on top of. Many of the headstones were so old and eroded or covered in moss that I had to trace the names with my fingers. All those Elizabeths and Stanleys and Augustas and Edwards and Roberts and Judiths. All those "1835 (aged 52)"s and "1870"s and "1911"s. All those "loving husband"s, "loyal friend"s, "darling son"s and "darling daughter"s. All those people who had had lives but had "fallen asleep" or "passed over" or "gone to a better place" or who were "waiting until we are called."

One of the odd things I quickly discovered about graveyards is that hardly any of the people who are buried there seem to have just "died" and got it over with.

By now it was pretty hot in the sun, I was starting to sweat and having no luck at all. The crows or rooks or whatever they were seemed to be laughing at me harder than ever.

In one corner are the most recent graves. Here, the headstones are white. A few of them have inset photographs and dates from the 1980s and 1990s. There are a lot of plastic flowers in pots, although their colours seem to have faded in the sun and wind and rain. There's also a kind of metal cage full of grass cuttings with several bunches of dead flowers thrown in on top.

There was obviously no chance of finding Sam here.

After about an hour, I'd worked my way right round the church and was back where I'd started. I was pretty sure that I'd checked every single headstone but hadn't found anything. I also felt pretty depressed – all those dead people.

I decided to have a final walk round the church and then give it all up as a bad job. I'd done my best, but in spite of what Charley said, there didn't seem to be anything to find.

And then I saw it. Right behind the church, where the woods came down to the dry stone wall, there was patch of graveyard that didn't seem to have been touched for years. It was a narrow strip, maybe six feet wide, of nettles and brambles. Maybe Sam was in there.

I had to lie face down and poke my way into the brambles with a stick. Almost immediately, I found a headstone. It was leaning over at a crazy angle and I had to push my head right into the brambles, scratching my face in the process, to read it. The disappointment was like a slap in the face: this stone marked the place where someone called Catherine Baker had been "laid to rest" in 1904.

But I reckoned that where there was one hidden headstone there might be others. So, I moved along a few feet, lay down again and pushed back the nettles and brambles with the stick. And there it was, hidden in all that tangle of undergrowth: a headstone with ivy wrapped round it, which said: *"In loving memory of our son Samuel, drowned on Revenant Broad, 3 March 1896. A child of light."* There were a couple of other names on the stone, which I recognised from the funeral report – Sam's father, George Wellsby, who died in 1916 aged 62, and his brother Arthur who didn't die until 18 July 1950, aged 59.

My first thought was why wasn't his mother buried here as well?

Lying there in the grass with my head in the brambles, I felt like I'd come to the end of a very long journey. I felt exhausted and sad, like I'd walked a thousand miles, but also excited. There was a buzzing in my ears, and I had pins and needles in my arms and legs. I was close to tears but I'd found him.

And then a voice said, "Are you all right?" I thought I was going to have a heart attack and if I hadn't been caught up in the brambles, I think I'd have leapt about ten feet into the air.

I looked over my shoulder and there was a young bloke, about the same age as Gerry I guess, wearing a grey cardigan over a dog collar. He was one of the few people I've seen around here who isn't thin and brown. In fact, he's pale and plump with reddish hair and freckles. I guessed he must be the vicar.

For some reason, I felt really guilty lying there and the only thing I could think of to say was "sorry."

"I don't think there's anything to be sorry about, unless you know something that I don't. It's just that I saw you lying here and wanted to make sure everything was OK. I'm Tim, Tim Downey, I'm the vicar for my sins." This seemed to strike him as pretty amusing, even though I bet he'd said it hundreds of times before.

I got to my feet and introduced myself. I felt I had to say

something about what I was doing. "I've been researching the life of a boy called Sam, who drowned on the broad over a hundred years ago." I tried to make it sound like a history project, something I had to do, nothing special. "Charley, Mr Maddox, found an article about Sam's funeral in the local paper, which said he'd been buried here. I wanted to find his grave."

"And did you?"

"Yes, I've just found it. It's in this tangle of stuff here."

"Do you mind if I have a look?" And with this, the Rev Tim Downey lay down (downey) full length on the grass and stuck his head into the hedge of brambles.

He emerged a minute or two later with his hair all messed up and said, "How very sad. Was this Sam a family connection? An ancestor of yours?"

"No, he's just someone I found out about and got interested in."

"Right, well… well done. I'll tell you what, we have team of volunteers who help keep the graveyard under control, cut the grass, pick up the rubbish, that sort of thing. Perhaps I could ask them if they get a moment to see if this area can be cleared and tidied up a bit. I don't like seeing any of the churchyard in this overgrown state."

"I could do it."

"Sorry?"

"I could do it. You know, tidy up the area around Sam's grave, cut down the brambles and so on."

"Of course. That would be very kind of you."

"The thing is, it would have to be this afternoon. I'm going back to London tomorrow. Would that be all right?"

"Well, if you're sure…"

"Yes, I'm sure."

I think Dina was a bit disappointed when I said I couldn't go to the beach in the afternoon. I think maybe she'd planned it as a last day treat. I asked if I could borrow some tools and take them into the village. I said that I was going to "help" with a "clearance project" in St Mary's churchyard. I didn't say anything about Sam and I made it sound like there might be other people there as well, that I'd be part of a team. I think she was a bit surprised but she's really good at not interfering. She just said that she'd see me later.

The shed seemed empty without the swallows and I put the logs that I'd placed across the door back in the woodpile. Then I collected the rake and a spade and loaded them into the basket of the bike, upright, leaning on my shoulder. They wobbled and rattled as I cycled, but stayed in the basket.

On the way back to the village, I stopped and bought six 50 pence bunches of flowers. The colours didn't really go together – some of them were bronze, some pink and some purple, but I didn't think Sam would mind.

I wheeled the bike across the churchyard and set to work chopping the brambles with the spade and pulling them out with the rake. Of course, I hadn't thought to bring any gloves and within about two minutes my hands and arms were covered with scratches. When I'd collected an armful of brambles, I dumped them in the metal cage on top of the grass cuttings.

After a few minutes I was sweating buckets, but had got rid of the worst of the brambles and you could clearly see Sam's headstone.

I'd sat down for a five-minute rest when this elderly lady in a flowery frock came over to talk to me. It was Mrs Owen who had taken such a long time to open her purse to pay for her baby food.

She said hello and looked at me as if she couldn't understand what I was doing. It was obvious she didn't recognise me.

"Are you doing work experience?"

"Sort of." It seemed the easiest thing to say.

She looked even more puzzled.

"Jolly good. Well done."

"Thank you." Why is everyone telling me that I've done well?

"I come here to tidy up my husband's grave. He's been dead for 30 years."

I resisted the temptation to say, "Jolly good. Well done," and we chatted for a few minutes more, before she wandered off, looking even more puzzled than she had at the beginning.

Then I pulled the worst of the weeds out of the plot by the headstone – I guessed it hadn't been touched since Arthur was buried in 1950 – and used the spade to dig over the earth to make it look as smart as possible. I didn't have any vases for the flowers, so I just lay them along the edge of the grave.

It wasn't the neatest job you've ever seen, but I think it was a pretty big improvement. I was hoping the vicar would remember to ask the volunteers to clear this area, because it was obvious that if someone didn't, the brambles would be back in no time.

I thought of clearing the area around Catherine Baker's headstone as well, but I was too knackered. I felt a bit bad about that, but I can't take responsibility for everyone who ever died.

I'd realised as I hacked away at the brambles and scratched myself all over that the truth about Sam, if there is a "truth" about anybody, is that he'd been forgotten. That was the truth that I'd been trying to put right.

As I was getting ready to leave, I checked that there was no one else around, and then I said out loud, "There you are, Sam, I hope you like it. See you later, maybe." I don't know, first I'd lectured baby swallows and now I was talking to thin air and turned earth.

As I was wheeling the bike out of the churchyard, my phone rang. I thought it must be Dina but it was Rachel.

"Hi, Nick, how are things? I'm really missing Norfolk and you and Dina. What are you up to?"

I couldn't think of any way of not answering this. "I'm just leaving St Mary's churchyard. I've been helping to clear it up."

Again, I tried to make it seem like there were other people here not just a single nutter, with his rake and his spade.

There was a bit of a pause. "That's nice," she said in a voice that suggested that she didn't have any clear idea of how it could be.

Still, it is nice chatting to her as I cycle back to the cottage. I've got one hand on the handlebars, the rake and spade balancing on my shoulders, and the other is holding my phone to my ear. I'm wondering how many laws I'm breaking. Luckily, there aren't all that many police traps between the village and Dina's, so no one sees me.

I need a shower and to put some cream on the worst of the scratches.

Over supper – chicken, I can't believe it, real chicken, the kind that has feathers and a beak, not a fluffy coat and a docked tail, the kind that goes "cluck" and not "baa" – I give Dina the official version of what happened this afternoon. I say that I spent the time cutting brambles and digging over a grave. It's obvious that she thinks this is a pretty weird of way of passing the time, but she doesn't say so. She asks me who else was there. And I say, the vicar and Mrs Owen and try to suggest that I could have mentioned other names but can't be bothered.

Gran rings and tells me that she's really looking forward to seeing me tomorrow. I tell her "me too" but I don't want to think about it. I love Gran and enjoy staying with her, but that doesn't seem to have anything to do with the way I feel about Dina and being here. I absolutely, positively, definitely don't intend to think about it.

Dina asks if I want to go to the pub for a drink with Gerry and, of course, I say yes. Anyway, I think it was what's known as a rhetorical question. Certainly it doesn't recognise the possibility of a negative reply.

"As it's your last night," (I wish people wouldn't keep saying that), "Maybe we should make a bit of an effort, knock 'em dead in the Ferret."

I go up to my room and put on a clean T-shirt – (On the front it says, "*I am not a geek*" and on the back it says, "*I'm a level twelve Paladin*") – and brush my hair.

Dina looks amazing. She's wearing some kind of hippy dress in green silk and she's got the right sort of make-up on the right bits of her face – eye liner round the eyes, lip-stick in the general area of her lips. She's brushed her hair until it shines. She's even wearing a silver bracelet around her wrist. (The effect is a little spoiled by the fact that she's wearing a checked work shirt on top of everything, but I think she looks great.)

"Come on then, young Nick," she booms, "I'm all set for a night of carousing and debauchery."

... ...

...

...

I... ... ...

... ...

... *I*

...

... ... *I* ember

... ...

... ... *ber*

... ...

... ...

... *rem*... *rem*...

...

...

rem

... ...

... ...

... *ha*

... ...

... ... *happy*

... ...

... ...

...

... ...

Orion's Belt

Now that's a noise I haven't heard for a while.

I don't want to say what it is, but it's being made by Dina and Gerry next door. And it's been going on for hours.

I've got no chance of getting to sleep, what with them creaking and muttering and lighting fags, and the moon making the room nearly as bright as in the day.

I sit by the window for a while, watching the trees rustling in the garden and the silvery marsh where nothing is happening. I'm really going to miss this. It's very hard to think of it being here tomorrow and the days after that and me not being here.

It's like I've come full circle since my first night in the cottage. The moonlight was blinding then and I couldn't sleep and the pair next door were at it even more loudly than they are now. If there was an award for doing what they're doing as loudly as possible, they'd be in with a pretty good chance of a gold medal. It's like that joke about skeletons and biscuit tins.

I have to admit that I feel a bit differently about it tonight, though. If someone held a gun to my head, I'd have to say that I'm pleased for Dina. It's obvious that Gerry makes her happy, at least most of the time. I'm happy for Gerry as well because, in spite of what Rachel says, he's a good bloke. And he's lucky to have Dina. No, I'll rephrase that, he's lucky to be with Dina. No, that's no good either.

As far as I know, nothing's been said about why things were so bad between them for a while. And I haven't really got a clue. If I didn't know it before, one thing this holiday has taught me is how mysterious everyone else's lives and feelings are.

But I do have this theory that it had something to do with Sam. I think part of Gerry knew that a haunting was going on and that it upset him and made him behave in ways that he wouldn't normally. Maybe that's true, maybe it isn't. Certainly, Sam didn't seem to have any effect on Dina – she clearly hasn't got a clue about what's been going on.

I think they made me so angry that first time because I was angry anyway. Angry with Mum and Dad for not taking me with them, but even more angry with myself for not making myself so lovable that they wouldn't have been able to bear to go without me. I don't feel so angry about that anymore. In fact, if they had taken me, I would have missed all this – everything that's happened in the last month.

So, all in all, I'm feeling better about myself than I was when I arrived, and better about those two next door.

I still think it's disgusting though. And it can't be good for them at their age. They'd be much better off with a hobby, like making jam or patchwork quilts or decorative woodwork or something.

Of course, Dina didn't say anything about there being a party for me at the Ferret, but that was what it was, more or less.

I knew something was up as soon as we arrived. The loonies were in their usual place and making their usual racket, but they looked different. Like they'd all washed their hair and faces, put on their best clothes, polished their earrings and studs. Not that their best would be anyone else's best, but in their own way they were dazzling. Clean home-knitted sweaters in hideous colours, clean kaftans, clean Motorhead T-shirts, clean braided dreadlocks.

They still weren't in any danger of winning any fashion awards, but they'd made the effort because it was my last night.

They all turned towards us as we came through the door and shouted hello and made space for us at the table.

Gerry was there, with a large glass of coke in front of him. He was stone-cold sober, but he still had everyone's attention. I've noticed this about him – he's one of those people who everyone listens to. He's got the gift of the gab and can hold the attention of a room full of people without even trying.

I suppose it's what's called charm, although I guess Rachel would deny it. But it's a very different sort of charm from what Dad has. Whereas he's all laid back and quiet and airy, Gerry is larger than life and loud and overwhelming. And always just a bit unpredictable and dangerous.

Anyway, whatever it is, it works on Harry, who squirmed and whined and made a beeline for Gerry's feet, immediately wiping all thoughts of Dina or me from his mind.

Gerry got up and kissed Dina and then before I knew it was coming, put his arms round me and gave me a hug. It was so embarrassing and I went really red and everyone laughed and cheered.

"For God's sake leave the boy alone," said Dina, which made things even worse, because everyone laughed even louder and shouted "Yeh, leave him alone," and wolf-whistled.

As usual, Gerry was telling a story. I wonder if he has a book of these and decides which one to use on any particular night. He certainly doesn't seem to be in any danger of running out.

Anyway, tonight's story was about Papua New Guinea, which fortunately he doesn't claim to have ever been to.

He reckons that the natives of Papua used to hunt birds of paradise, and in particular, the Greater Bird of Paradise, so that they could trade their skins with the early explorers.

The thing was that these explorers rarely went inland, preferring to stay on the coast which meant that the islanders didn't have a chance to get to know much about them. They had to double guess what these "early twitchers" wanted. For some reason, they used to cut off the birds' feet and present the skins without them.

Given what Gerry described as "bloody tourists' uncanny knack for getting hold of the wrong end of the stick," rumours started to circulate that these birds had never had feet in the first place. People started to believe that they were like little angels and had come direct from Paradise and remained in the air all their lives.

And when, in 1758, the famous botanist Linnaeus had to come up with a scientific name for the Greater Bird of Paradise, he decided on *Paradisaea apoda*. "Apoda" being Latin for "footless."

"Can you believe it?" yells Gerry, "bloody idiots. Still, it all goes to show that you should never judge by appearances, for which most of the people around this table, me included, should be profoundly grateful."

Like all Gerry's stories, I have no idea whether this one is true or not. And nor does anyone else. (Come to think of it, maybe that's the best thing about Gerry's stories.)

"It can't be true," said one loony (orange jumper, dangly beard). "As if you'd know," said another (black velvet dress, necklace of silver bats, tongue and lip studs), "when did you last read Linnaeus?" "How could they cut off the legs, so that no one would know that they'd ever had them?" said a third (bright green boiler suit, braids).

Gerry made no attempt to answer any of these questions. Just sat there looking smug and extremely pleased with himself. "Of course it's true," he said. "It's too good not to be."

Dina looked as though she had her own views about whether it was true or not, but all she said was, "Gerry, I can't bear to see you sitting there with that coke any longer. For God's sake, let me buy you a pint."

Gerry put on this little girly voice and said, "Well all right, if you really must."

In fact, he then drank three, one after the other. And looked even more pleased with himself.

The room seemed to be getting hotter and smokier and noisier by the minute. Everyone was having a good time, drinking and shouting and smoking their terrible fags.

Gerry tapped me on the shoulder and said, "There's someone I'd like you to meet."

He led me to a table in the corner of the bar, slightly away from the others. And there, wearing some kind of purple frock and sitting with a glass of wine in front of her with a fag in her hand, was Moon.

Gerry was nearly cracking up as he said, "Moon, I'd like you to meet Nick, he's staying with Dina."

Moon turned her soft blue eyes towards me. Not a glimmer of recognition. Just as Gerry had known there wouldn't be. Knowing that he was standing beside me nearly doubled up laughing wasn't exactly making things any easier.

"Hello," said Moon, "nice to meet you." And then she sort of stopped. Just stopped speaking and sat looking at me.

I had to mentally shake myself awake before I could reply – I was in serious danger of going under before the conversation even got started.

"Hi," I said.

For a moment, I thought that was going to be it, and then she kind of pulled herself together and said, "Oh, and this is my boyfriend, Ian."

I was amazed. Where had she got the energy to find herself a boyfriend? What did they talk about? Was she able to remember from one day to the next who he was? Did they arrange to meet? Or maybe they just happened to run into each other from time to time.

Mr Moon looked about the same age as me (although Gerry told me afterwards that he was 25) and about as dippy as Moon. I guess that figures. He was thin and brown with hair nearly down to his waist. He had Moon's blue eyes and this brilliant, empty smile. And when he smiled at me I felt a bit pleased and a bit terrified. He said hi in the same slow, vague way as Moon and then turned his attention back to rolling a fag.

But by now, Moon was into her stride.

"How long have you been staying with Dina?"

"Just over a month."

"A month, and in all that time Gerry never once brought you to the nature reserve. What's the matter with him?"

I didn't really know what to say and at this point Gerry headed back to our table, without ever making eye contact with me or Moon.

That left me trying to make conversation with the two of them. Talk about nailing jelly to the wall. I got this feeling that both of them were trying to remember how to communicate with humanoids, but weren't quite able to come up with anything.

After a few minutes about how nice Norfolk was and how good the weather had been, I said I had to get back to Dina and that it had been nice to meet them.

"Nice to meet you too, Mick," said Moon. Young Mr Moon just sort of waved apologetically.

Gerry, hardly able to control himself, said, "How did that go? I could see that you were deep in conversation and I didn't like to interrupt."

"I really like them both," I said, "especially Moon. It's not often you meet someone who shows so much interest in you. Ian's a lucky guy."

Gerry sniggered – that's the only word for it – and looked more pleased with himself than ever.

Then everyone had a few more drinks and a few more fags and shouted a bit more. And the room got a bit hotter and a bit smokier (although, a few minutes earlier that had seemed impossible). And my head started to spin.

I was just starting to worry that it was getting towards karaoke time and that Dina and Gerry might be tempted to do one of their duets, when I noticed a kind of kerfuffle at the door and in walked Brenda and Charley.

There was a sudden silence, like in cowboy movies when a stranger goes into the saloon.

In the silence Charley, who was using a stick, walked very slowly towards the bar not looking at anyone.

Before he got there, however, all the loonies stood up and started cheering and clapping, hooting and whistling. There were some other people in the bar and maybe they thought it was some strange local custom or that Charley was someone really important, because they stood up and clapped too.

Charley seemed to find it very funny, and shouted to the room in general, "Sit down you silly bastards, 'scuse my French Nick. Have you never seen a man buy his lovely wife a drink before? You make me feel like the Queen Mother. Come to think of it, though, if anyone would like to buy me a drink, there's still plenty of time to get to the bar before I do. Don't be shy."

Four loonies leapt up immediately and scampered over to the bar.

Gerry cleared a space at the head of our table and brought two chairs over for Brenda and Charley. And Charley was right, they were treated like visiting royalty, with everyone buying drinks for them and hanging on Charley's every word. It seemed like no one could do too much for them.

It took me ages to get to talk to him.

"We're going to miss you, Nick," he said.

I couldn't imagine why this should be the case and I couldn't think of anything to say, so I said, "Me too." I hope he knew what I meant.

Then Charley and Brenda talked to Dina for ages about some new people who were moving into the village and who, for some reason, Charley had decided that he didn't like. "But you've never even met them," said Brenda. "No, but I've seen their car," said Charley, as though that proved it.

When I next got to talk to Charley, I said, "I've been thinking about that dream you were telling me about. You know, about your old friend Richard. I think the dream was about the life that he never had. You didn't know who the people in the photograph album were or anything about the parties and picnics because they never happened. I think the dream was about the parallel life you might have lived if Richard hadn't been shot down in the war. It was about what a good friend he might have continued to be."

"Nice of you to think about it. I felt a bit guilty after you left the other day, binding on like that about a dream. I guess you're right. It's not that Richard was the great love of my life or anything like that. I've managed to lead an averagely inadequate life without him. It's just that he was a really nice guy and I miss him from time to time. When I think of him, I think about the life he didn't have and the friendship we didn't have. But, good bloke though he certainly was, I would be very grateful if he stayed away from my dreams. There's precious little room in our pit of a bed – what with Brenda expanding in the way she is (Yes darling, just telling Nick about the joys of marriage) – without all these people from my past trying to get in with us. I guess you know what I mean."

I said that I thought I knew what he meant.

And then Charley said that he'd brought me a present. He handed me a paper bag under the table. Inside was an old hard-backed book. It was a novel called *Between the Water and the Sky* and on the back was a picture of Charley, looking pretty much as he does now, only with short dark hair. But even then, he'd had that look in his eyes which said, "Actually, I don't give a shit." Inside he's written, "To Nick, from the silly old bastard in the summerhouse."

"Charley, thanks. This is fantastic."

"I don't know about that. It's only a book that no one wanted to read. It took two years of my life about fifty years ago. There's a pretty good sex scene on page 154, though. I remember I enjoyed writing that."

I was really honoured but even at the moment he gave it to me I thought, "I don't suppose Dad's going to be very pleased when he sees this." Still, tough.

After about an hour, Brenda said to Charley, "That's quite enough excitement for one night, young man. It's up the stairs to Bedfordshire for you."

Charley said his goodbyes (I saw his hand slip under the table when he kissed Dina – Brenda winked at me.) And then he and Brenda walked slowly towards the door. And just as they had done when he arrived, the loonies stood up and cheered and hooted him all the way.

When he reached the door, Charley slowly turned round, smiled and gave the whole room the finger. And then he was gone.

Neither of us had mentioned Sam's name. But I guess that was because it didn't seem necessary.

After Charley and Brenda had gone, a few more pints were drunk, a few more fags were lit and the temperature in the Ferret rose another notch or two (there wasn't room for any more smoke). But things were definitely beginning to wind down.

Eventually Dina said it was time for us to go and when Gerry asked if he could come as well, she said yes.

All the loonies said goodbye to me and hoped I'd had a good holiday and that they would see me again. And I said I hoped so too. And I meant it. I was hoping that Moon might say something like "Goodbye, Dick," but she and Ian seemed to be focused on something else and I don't think they noticed us leaving.

The air outside was cold and clear and the stars were brilliant.

And Gerry, who had only had about six pints, was finally able to point out Orion's Belt – three pretty ordinary-looking stars minding their own business down a bit and left a bit of the moon.

The four of us jammed into the pick-up's cab, but it was too cold to have the window down.

Gerry drove back really slowly. The headlights picked out the road ahead and I could imagine rather than see the trees practically touching overhead.

The lights on the dashboard were just bright enough to create a reflection in the cab's windows. As I looked out at the hedges, I could faintly see myself in the window looking back at me.

And just for an instant – and maybe I imagined this – my reflected face looked a bit like Sam's. And then the moment was gone and I was back in the window.

When we got back to the cottage, Dina produced a bottle of champagne, poured three glasses and proposed a toast, "To us." We all drank to us.

Then she said to Gerry that she wanted to have a word in private with me, and that perhaps he'd like to make himself scarce for a bit. He wandered into the office and started looking through the bookshelves.

I was starting to feel a bit nervous.

Then Dina said that maybe we should go into the garden. So, we wrapped ourselves in blankets and took a towel out to lay on the bench which was soaked with dew. As we sat there under the stars, we could feel the cold creeping in from the marsh and hear the rustling of the leaves and the reeds in the breeze.

"There's nothing to look so worried about," Dina said in a whisper that must have carried most of the way back to the Ferret. "I just wanted to say that I've really enjoyed having you here. You've been great and fitted in so well. I wasn't sure how it was going to work when you first arrived. I didn't know that I could share my life with someone day to day. But it's been great. And now bugger off to bed because I need to spend some time with Gerry."

"And I just wanted to say that it's been the best holiday of my life. Thank you."

I get the feeling that Dina's not very good at being thanked.

But before she went in, she added, "I won't be here at half-term, I'm off on a field trip to Mauritius. But I will be here at Christmas, and I want you to promise me that you'll come and spend some time here then. It can be pretty cold, but provided you like your own company and sitting in front of log fires, it's possible to have a good time. There won't be any chicks to worry about. And there might even be snow."

"I'd love to," I said. "And maybe you could promise me something in return."

"OK, what is it?"

"Do you think that, just for me, you might possibly give some thought to cutting down on the cigarettes?"

Acknowledgements

The beautiful photograph on the front cover is by Mike Pope at www.kuwaitbirding.blogspot.com

The brilliant cover design is by Gordon Butler: www.gordonbutler.me

And thanks to Dean Fetzer for the superb design and layout of this print version: www.gunboss.com